The Prince and The Butterfly

NATALINA REIS

INTERNATIONAL BEST SELLING AUTHOR

Contents

To all women.

There's a warrior inside you.

Prologue

There once was a butterfly, wings as blue as the night sky
The beautiful creature, very much alive,
had wings but could not fly.
She was locked inside a jar
on an evil old warlock's sleazy bar.
The butterfly dreamed of flying the skies
and the yearning in her heart was so strong, so alive,
that one day the butterfly did indeed take flight.
Free she might be, body and soul,
but in her heart the seed of hate did grow.
Her one and only mission,
her old captor to find and to him deliver
the same fate he once had pushed on the butterfly.
One day, she hoped to find her captor
and send him straight to a dark hereafter.

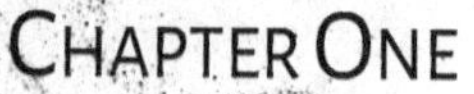

CHAPTER ONE

The Stranger

Hú Dié

THE PUNCH DIDN'T QUITE hit the target as I'd hoped. My bloodied hand missed the prominent nose and barely grazed his high cheekbone. "Damn, asshole," I growled under my breath, spinning around to face the goat-faced man again. "Stay still for a second."

He didn't, of course, and his aim was better than mine as he propelled his fist into my face. I swear my skull exploded. I would have cursed, but my lips weren't working, the metallic taste of blood slipping past them and into my mouth. Was my nose bleeding, or had I bitten my tongue?

"You never learn, Hú Dié," the beast of a man croaked with what might have been a chuckle. "Why do you insist on messing with those who are far stronger than you?"

I bent over with my hands on my knees, trying to catch my breath while struggling for some kind of control over the pain that radiated through my head like the silk of a poisonous spider's web. I wouldn't let him see me squirm, so I turned my head and smirked at him—at least, I hope I did. The pain obliterated all other sensations.

"Stupid *shānyáng*," I spat out along with a stream of bright red blood. Probably not the smartest thing to call this wall of muscle a goat, but I was out of clever retorts as pain overwhelmed my senses. "You don't need strength to win over idiots like you. Just brains."

His lips contorted into a sneer, and he lifted his hand again, pulling it as far as he could behind him. Oh, this was going to hurt! I flinched automatically and hated myself for it. He was right about one thing: I never learned. It was almost as if I had the need to see how far my body could go, how much it could take, with no respect for my own life.

I braced myself for the blow, but it never came.

"What the fuck are you doing, *lǎo tiě*?" I heard the goat-man say, and I risked a peek. Someone had my foe's wrist in a viselike hold and didn't look as if he was going to let it go. "Let me go. This wimpy butterfly asked for it."

"I'd be ashamed of hitting such a small creature." The stranger's warm, deep voice echoed in the cul-de-sac where we had chosen to come to blows. "What are you getting out of this, *gē*?"

How civilized of him to address the noxious hunk of brainless muscle as a friend. Who was this guy? I couldn't see him from my position—half crouched and with a curtain of bloody sweat running over my eyes.

"I'm not your bro," the goat-man snapped back. "Let go of my hand, or I'll kick your ass."

Much to my surprise—and possibly the *shānyáng*'s—the man dropped the hand and said, "I'd like to see you try."

"Wait!" I yelled out. Well, it was more of a squeak, really. "I appreciate you trying to help me, but this is my fight, not yours."

The stranger stepped from behind Goat Face and bowed to me.

Wait! What? He's actually bowing to me? What is wrong with him?

"*Xiǎo gūniáng*, you're obviously pretty hurt, so no worries, I will handle this for you."

Little girl? Who does he think he's talking to? His sister?

I had never been a girl. I was born a grown-ass woman. And I could totally take care of myself.

I wanted to protest, but truth be told, I was quickly slipping into unconsciousness. He must have hit me harder than I thought, because as soon as I tried to straighten up, my head swam as if I had drunk twenty bottles of apple *jiǔ* on an empty stomach. I went down hard but didn't completely pass out. I managed to roll onto my side so my face was not against the sharp edges of the stones that covered the street and threw a glance at the two men who were now entwined in what—if I didn't know better—looked like a loving embrace. I might have smiled at the thought, but darkness came shortly after.

I only hoped that Goat Face got what he deserved even if it wasn't me delivering the goods.

"So, what exactly did the goat-man do to you?"

I had barely opened my eyes, still woozy from whatever had exploded inside my skull, and I wasn't ready for twenty questions. But the stranger—presumably the same one who had come to my rescue in the street—didn't seem to care. We weren't out in the street anymore. As my eyes adjusted to the soft light of the room, I could see fine pieces of furniture scattered throughout the large open space and the man who sat on the edge of my bed, leisurely stirring a cup of tea.

Wait! My bed? This was not my home. Where the hell was I? And how did I get here? Also—after a quick look under the covers—where were my clothes?

"Don't worry," the stranger crooned, a lazy smile spreading over his well-shaped lips. "I didn't undress you. One of my maids did it. Your clothes are being burned as we speak."

"Burned?" The sudden movement as I sat upright made me see stars, and it wasn't a pretty sight. "Why would you burn my clothes?" It wasn't as if I had that many, and the tunic and pants were in perfectly decent condition—well, decent-ish.

"They stank and were soaked with blood," he said, still not raising his gaze from the teacup. "Not to mention, there were so many tears and holes in them that I'm surprised you haven't frozen to death yet."

"I have better clothes at home," I protested defensively. "I only wear those for...." For what? Brawling? That sounded preposterous even to my own ears. Besides the question was he—whoever he might be—had no right to mess with my stuff, even if it was shit.

"Stop fretting," he said, taking a dainty sip from the cup. He had fine hands with long, elegant fingers belying the bravado I had witnessed earlier. "You had a nasty blow to the head and need rest. I sent out for some bird's nest soup to help you heal."

"Bird's nest?" He had to be joking. Only the rich could afford such a soup. But the longer I studied my surroundings, the more I realized that everything in this room spelled out wealth, from the beautiful, minimalist furniture to the silky and satiny furnishings on the bed and the elegant art hanging on the walls. Was that a Lu Han painting by the window?

As if I had summoned her, a maid walked in on silent feet, carrying a wooden tray. She was young, younger than me, with a lovely round face and heart-shaped lips. Her simple but pretty pink-and-green dress clung to her legs as she approached the bed, eyes kept low and mouth shut.

"Ah, here it is," the stranger exclaimed, putting his teacup down on a small side table and looking at the young woman. "Thank you, Yushu. You can give me the bowl and spoon."

Never raising her eyes, the girl set the tray down on the table and handed the steaming bowl of soup to her master. I watched in disbelief as the man began to stir and blow on the soup. I never had a mother, but I guess this was what one would do.

"Are you planning on feeding me the soup?" I asked, half amused but mostly offended that he thought I needed him to feed me.

He finally looked up at me, and I thought I had been hit right on the face again. His eyes took my breath away. Caramel brown with upturned outer edges and crowned by almost-straight, dark eyebrows, they shone with intelligence and cunning even as he cocked his head in apparent surprise.

"Of course not," he exclaimed. "I'm just cooling it down for you like a good host should do. I wouldn't dare be so intimate with a strange female."

Was he saying I was a stranger to him or calling me odd? The man was hard to read. I chose the former. I was hungry, and I couldn't remember the last time I had had such a treat. I wasn't about to ruin the opportunity. I could let him know what I really thought of him after I ate.

He handed me the bowl and sat, studying me while I devoured the hot delicacy. I watched him from underneath my lashes. He was handsome, almost pretty, with perfect cheekbones, immaculate ivory skin, full lips, and long black silken hair he wore loose over his shoulders.

Without a sound, he took the empty bowl from my hands when I was done, and I couldn't hold my curiosity in any longer. "Who the hell are you?" I asked, forgetting my manners—not that I had many of those. "And why did you bring me here?"

"Would you believe me if I told you I'm just doing what I think it's right?"

I shook my head.

He pouted. "That's hurtful." He paused for a second, lost the pout, and said, "But you're right, I brought you here for another reason."

There was not such a thing as a true altruist. Everybody wanted something in return for their good deeds, I had learned that the hard way a long time ago.

"So, what is it?" I asked, licking my lips where a drop of the delicious soup still remained. "If it's sex, forget about it. I'd sooner poke my eyes out than be intimate with a stranger."

He had the nerve to chuckle softly. "Sex with you?"

How was that idea so funny?

"No, no, you misunderstand me. You're not my type, anyway."

What did he mean by that? Was he rudely calling me hideous?

"No, nothing like that, I assure you."

All right, no reason to keep emphasizing the issue.

He paused for a minute, picked up his teacup again, and took a sip before speaking. "I need someone with your gifts."

Gifts? What was he talking about? "Sorry, but you must have confused me with someone else," I said. "What are you talking about?"

"I need someone who can fly into tiny spaces virtually undetected."

If I hadn't been lying in bed, I would have fallen on the floor. How did he know about my special talent? We had just met in that alley, and I certainly hadn't used my so-called gifts to escape—which in retrospect was a pretty dumb choice.

I opened my mouth a couple times, stunned, but no words came out.

He put the teacup down and said, "Yes, I know about your gifts. After all, you are a butterfly fairy, aren't you?"

Well, cover me in honey and drop me in a feather bed! How in heavens' name did he know I was a butterfly?

CHAPTER TWO

The Proposal

SHÉN MÌ

B LACK, BLUE, AND A sickly shade of ocher obscured her features, but even from behind that mask of bruises and wounds, the natural beauty of the butterfly fairy came through. I wondered what could have pushed a normally gentle breed of fairy to become this belligerent and embroiled in so many fights. I had been following her activity for weeks now, after having accidentally stumbled upon one of her seemingly never-ending brawls with creatures bigger and stronger than her. As much as I hated to admit it, Hú Dié was interesting. A bit too interesting for her own good, it seemed.

"Who the hell are you?" she asked, fire in her brown eyes.

"My name is Cheng Shén Mì, but you can call me Shén Mì," I told her, setting my teacup down. Even in her white nightclothes, she looked wild and fierce, as if she could—and would—jump on me at any time. Butterflies were physically weak by nature, but this fairy was anything but. "What you really want to ask me, though, is how do I know you're a butterfly fairy, *duì ma*?"

She crossed her arms over her chest and stuck her chin defiantly out. "Yes. How do you know?"

I almost chuckled at her expression. "I just know," I said, more than willing to piss her off. "I have called Dr. Ming to tend to your wounds. She should be here any minute."

"I don't need a doctor," she protested, pulling the sheets aside. "I can take care of myself."

Before she could slide off the bed, I sat on the edge and pushed her back onto the pillows. "You're not going anywhere right now," I said. "After Dr. Ming takes care of you, we'll have a little chat. I have a business proposal for you that you might be interested in."

With a glare that was positively as sharp as a blade, she stated, "I am not interested in any business with you."

I clucked my tongue. "Now, little butterfly, don't get your undies all in a twist. You haven't heard my proposal yet. And besides, are you really planning on living your very long life being punched and kicked by creatures who are not worthy of your attention?"

I could have sworn I saw a hint of hesitation in her eyes, but it was gone before I could be sure. She opened her mouth, but a new voice interrupted whatever she was about to say.

"Is this our patient, Mì Mì?"

Dr. Ming was a taller-than-average woman, as elegant as she was efficient. She had been our family doctor since I could remember, and even though she didn't look older than me, she was in fact my senior by a few decades, an immortal who was as fiercely independent as her crane true form.

Our patient snorted. "Mì Mì? Really? Could you be any cheesier? Your nickname is *secret*?"

I could have been offended, but I chose to bite back. "Coming from someone whose name literally means butterfly, that is very hurtful," I said with a mock frown as I flattened my hand over my heart.

To her credit she did not react to my barb. Instead, she turned her attention to Dr. Ming, who had set up her bag on the table and was busy going through it. "A crane immortal, eh? I haven't seen one of your kind in a long time."

Dr. Ming smiled but never took her eyes from her bag. "Yes, we are a dying species, I guess. Even immortals eventually die out," she commented as if speaking about the weather. "But how did you know I was a crane?"

Again, a cloud of hesitation, maybe even fear, crossed her gaze. "I used to know one and got used to his mannerisms." Whatever had crossed her mind cleared quickly as she added, "You know, every immortal has a tell of sorts. You just have to know what it is and pay attention."

The doctor, satisfied with what she had retrieved from inside her bag, turned her gaze to the woman on the bed. "Do you butterflies also have a tell?"

For once, Hú Dié looked stunned. She did not expect the doctor to recognize her as another immortal, much less identify her true form.

"How do I know?" the doctor replied as if she had been asked an actual question. "I'm a doctor. I make it my business to—just like yourself—recognize what's beneath the outer mask." She approached the bed and studied Hú Dié for a moment. "Wow, do you even have a face under that mess?"

"Where are your bedside manners, doctor?" Hú Dié asked without missing a beat. "Can you at least pretend I still look pretty?"

Dr. Ming chuckled and then clucked her tongue. "Girl, I'm sure there is beauty underneath all that bruising, but for now you look like a very old potato. Scoot back so I can examine you closer." She turned to me, one single eyebrow raised. "Are you really going to stand there while I undress this female?"

Stung into action, I practically jumped to my feet, bowed briefly, and retreated out of the room, hoping I hadn't lost my hard-practiced semblance of aloofness and calm in the process.

I waited outside the room, pacing back and forth on the running veranda while mulling over what I knew about the battered butterfly inside. I knew her past was buried in mystery. It was as if she didn't exist until a couple of years ago when she became a sort of local celebrity for her penchant to pick fights with creatures much larger than herself. What other people saw as misguided bravery, I saw for what it was: foolishness. Hú Dié took any excuse, no matter how feeble, to start a fight. Sometimes she intervened when the weak were being bullied, but more often than not, the person or persons she stepped in to help did not need her assistance at all. The butterfly had some kind of death wish, which in the case of an immortal was a high order. She'd have to take quite a gargantuan number of beatings to actually die. In the meantime, she chose to live in perpetual pain and anger.

Why was that?

I had no idea, but I fully intended to find out.

"She'll live." Dr. Ming's diagnosis seemed lacking.

"Can you be a little more specific? I did not expect her to die or anything," I said. I had been waiting outside the room for so long, my legs were itching to go somewhere else.

Dr. Ming sighed. "She'll be fine," she said, cocking her head to the side. "It doesn't look like this was the first time she's gotten herself completely black and blue. I stitched a gash she had on her chest—a dagger cut, by the looks of it—and restored most of her *qi*. Her full power will return once she rests for a few days and cultivates."

I found it hard to imagine someone like Hú Dié would have the patience to meditate long enough to enhance her immortal *qi*. "I'll try my best to convince her to stay put for a while," I promised, almost certain it would be close to impossible to do so. "Did she share her story with you?" I asked, unable to squelch my curiosity.

The doctor raised her eyebrows in that motherly way she always used on me when she thought I was out of line. "Even if she did—and she didn't—I would never betray doctor-patient confidentiality. You know that." She brushed something invisible from her bodice. "Ask her yourself if you really want to know. And be careful. She might be only a butterfly, but inside her burns the fire of a dragon. I wouldn't put it past her to sneak in your room at night and bury a knife in your chest."

I didn't doubt it, either, but I was used to dealing with difficult and dangerous creatures. I could handle her.

"What exactly do you want with her?" Dr. Ming asked as she walked with me to the front gate. "It's not like you to take females into your home."

Leave it to the doctor to bring heat to my neck and cheeks. "Nothing like that, doctor," I hurried to clarify. "I am thinking of hiring her to work for me. She has a particular set of skills I could really use."

The woman snorted. "Skills? Like getting herself into trouble and not have enough strength to fend it off?"

I flipped open the latch on the gate. "She looks weak, but she has obviously worked herself up to an impressive level of strength. And she can move and go places almost invisibly, not to mention that people are more than happy to see a butterfly, so they don't bother getting suspicious about their presence."

Dr. Ming nodded. "I see," she said, throwing one last glance toward the house at the end of the rock path. "Well, good luck taming that one. Call me if you need me, Mì Mì."

I thanked her and then watched as she walked slowly and elegantly down the street in the direction of town, a dozen or so *li* away from where I had built my house. This secluded corner of the bamboo forest was ideal for keeping nosy or overcurious eyes and ears off my business. The semi-isolation was also beneficial to keep my true identity a secret. I wore many masks that I picked depending on my audience. Here in this small town, I was the odd but elegant nobleman who bestowed the poor with much needed charity.

When I returned to Hú Dié's bedside, she looked almost human. The doctor had erased most of the bruising from her face, and there was no more swelling to distort her features, which were—I hated to admit it—very pretty. That said, her mouth was still twisted into an angry grimace.

"Are you going to hold me here against my will?" she asked as soon as she saw me walking through the open door.

I smiled inwardly. Even if I wanted to, I couldn't hold a butterfly unless I used immortal rope, and that would cost me quite a bit of my *qi*, which was not something I was willing to do unless I absolutely had to.

"I think you will be pleased with my proposal," I said, avoiding her question.

She leaned over slightly, waiting.

I pulled my fan from a pocket and snapped it open. "Would you like some tea?"

"Stop the frou frou crap," she barked out, waving a hand in my direction. "Just tell me what your fucking proposal is so I can turn you down and be on my way."

I feigned outrage. "Watch your language, young lady," I said, taking my gentle image a step further. "You are not in the streets anymore. Here at my house, we mind our manners."

She groaned and crossed her arms, impatience clear in her body language. "You might have been born with a silver spoon in your mouth, but I wasn't," she said, an almost imperceptible shadow clouding her eyes. "I speak as I see it. So tell me, what exactly are you going to propose? And I hope to the gods it's not marriage because that's a flat-out big, giant no."

I squelched the impulse to laugh out loud. Marrying her? Gods no. "I run a special organization, and I could use your butterfly skills and gifts."

She squinted, twisting her nose. "Special how? Does it involve skimpy clothes and lots of *jiǔ*?"

"No, no." I stifled another chuckle. What did she think? That I was trying to hire her for some kind of high-end brothel? "It's a delicate matter, and you must promise me this information won't leave this room."

Hú Dié wiped her mouth with the palm of her hand. "For fuck's sake, man, just tell me already. Who am I going to tell, anyway? I have no family, no friends.... Do you actually think I will tell the bullies I often encounter or the beggars in the street?"

I closed the fan and sat down on a chair near the bed. "I run a network of spies."

That made her stop talking and moving. For a moment it was as if she was frozen, not managing even a blink.

"I need someone like you who can infiltrate sensitive places without being noticed."

"Sensitive?" she managed to ask, her voice betraying her surprise. "What does that mean? Dangerous? Stupidly perilous?"

"I'm impressed with your vocabulary," I quipped to lighten the mood.

She was not amused.

"Could be dangerous, I'm not going to lie. But you'd be mostly flying into places where secrets are kept and unsavory plots are hatched."

With her lips pursed, she shook her head slowly. "So, potentially deadly."

I couldn't deny it. Not completely. She would be in dangerous situations where she could possibly die if discovered. But she didn't strike me as someone who feared danger. In fact, she seemed as attracted to it as a moth to a flame. Maybe it was the butterfly curiosity in her or that strange death wish she had. Whatever it was made her perfect for this job.

"What do I get in return?" she asked.

"Lodging, food, and a salary of ten *yin* a week plus a stipend for clothing." She wouldn't be rich, but she'd be able to live comfortably on that salary even if I didn't offer her a place to stay and food to fill her belly. Her eyes widened, and I knew I had her. "What do you say? I will give you time to recover and cultivate for a few weeks before going to work. And training, of course."

"And a weapon?" she asked, eyes now as round as the sun.

I nodded. "And any weapons of your choice," I told her. "Do we have a deal?"

She thought for a moment and then offered me her hand. "We have a deal."

Now the question remained: could I really trust her?

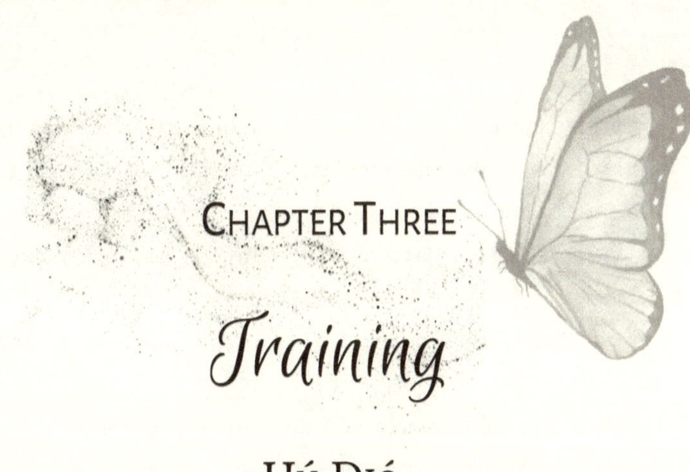

Chapter Three

Training

Hú Dié

"**B**AD FORM. TRY AGAIN."

My arm was burning as I held my bow-drawing posture for what felt like the hundredth time, only to have the idiot I had accepted as my master tell me to do it again because it wasn't up to his standards.

"*Shīfu*! Can I take a rest first? My arms are about to fall off," I complained instead of doing what I wanted to do: clobber him with my metaphorical bow. I congratulated myself for not having added the word idiot to the word master. He *was* paying for my nice lodgings and excellent meals, after all.

Shén Mì waved his white silk fan in my direction. "Stop being such a slacker and get into a proper position. Your forward fist is as limp as an old scallion. You look like a hundred-year-old woman."

I gritted my teeth to avoid snapping at him, but it didn't quite work. "I am almost two hundred," I said, shaking my hand to bring back some blood circulation to it.

"I'm speaking of mortal years, Butterfly," he retorted, looking bored.

How did he seem to have only two expressions? Bored and annoyed.

"Do it again. You need to cultivate to get your *qi* back."

I knew exactly what I wanted to do with my *qi* once it was fully restored. It *so* involved his pretty face.

Sighing in resignation, I stepped forward with my left leg, bent it slightly at the knee, and pulled my bent right arm all the way back while stretching my left fist forward.

"Elbows higher!" Shén Mì yelled out, slapping my left arm with his fan. "Shoulders back."

Ugh. Was it really worth putting up with him for the sake of a comfy bed and satisfying meals? Yes, of course it was. I had had to put up with a lot worse in my life. This was nothing. That didn't mean I liked it or that I wasn't planning on taking my revenge on him eventually. That would have to wait, though. I had another, much more serious and urgent revenge to accomplish.

Shén Mì stood there with his ridiculous fan, barking out orders for hours before allowing me a moment of rest. When he finally let me go, I ran straight out to the kitchen where the cook, a grumpy old mortal man with magic fingers, reigned undisputed and with as much authority as a real king. I called him Lǎo Cōng because he did look like a very old, wrinkled onion. Surprisingly enough he didn't seem to mind, acting as if I had just given him a title of honor instead of an insulting nickname. In the few weeks I had lived there—almost three now—I had come to think of him as an uncle or grandfather. Not that I would know what that felt like, but I could imagine it.

"What do you have for me today, Lǎo Cōng?" I asked, peeking over the counter where he had several large steamers going. I lifted the cover of the one closest to me and stole a bun, almost dropping it as the heat burned my fingers.

The cook hit the back of my hand with his long chopsticks, and I yelped.

"Keep your sticky fingers off the food, girl," he said. After a quick glance around him, he nodded to the side, pointing me toward a covered bowl on the table by the window. "Leftovers."

Taking the hint, I took the cover off the bowl to reveal two delicious-looking drumsticks and a small and pretty osmanthus cake. "Thank you," I yelled as I ran out of the kitchen with the bowl in my hands.

I would eat it in the back garden, which was quiet and full of nooks and crannies where I could hide for a moment of blissful solitude, something this place didn't provide much of. Anywhere you turned there were people: servants, guards, merchants who poured in everyday with baskets of produce, fish or meat, and all sorts of suspicious-looking individuals normally dressed in muted colors to better blend in with the surroundings. It was a strange household, always crawling with activity. The back garden was a haven of peace compared to the rest of the place.

Dead set on getting to the garden before being intercepted by anyone, I ran head-on onto a hard body as I maneuvered my fast-moving self around a bend.

"Watch where you're going, *báichī*!" I exclaimed, pushing the offending body away from me while trying to keep the bowl from spilling over. My hand found rock, or what felt like it.

"Who are you calling an idiot?"

I looked up, and my gaze met a pair of purplish-blue eyes I had never seen before. A cat immortal with a feral smile on his full lips. He stared at my hand still splayed on his chest, and I belatedly pulled it away.

He crossed his arms over his powerful chest and smirked. "What do we have here? A beauty for sure...." He mused for a few seconds before saying, "Shén Mì has been keeping secrets from me. When did he bring you in, pretty one?"

In my book, being called "pretty one" was a worse insult than being called a whore. "Don't call me that or I may address you as kitten."

Much to my dismay, he barked out a loud chuckle, throwing his head back.

I tilted my head back to look at his face. "What's so funny, *kitten*?" My attempt at pissing him off backfired. By the looks of it, he was enjoying it.

"So you know I'm a cat," he said once he stopped laughing. He bent forward to level his eyes with mine. "So what are you? I can tell you're an immortal, but your aura is blurry."

Good. That was how I liked it. I still wasn't sure how Shén Mì had figured it out, since I kept my wards up all the time, a trick—possibly the only useful one—I had learned from my former master.

"No worries. I will soon find out."

"Who are you? What are you doing here?" I asked, finally coming to my senses. No visitors were allowed in this part of the house.

"How rude of me," he said, folding into a deep bow, his hands clasped in front. "Ding Māo, at your service."

I couldn't be sure whether he was mocking me, so I did not return the courtesy of a bow or a name. Instead, I snapped, "I don't care what your name is. I just want to know what the hell you're doing here."

Ding Māo straightened, feigned outrage on his face. "My, how protective of the master of the house," he said. "He knows I'm here. Business, you see?"

"But not in this part of the house," I protested, waving a hand around me and almost dropping my food. "This is a private side."

His lips stretched in a truly feline smile. "Ah yes, I came over the wall," he explained. "Shortcut."

"I was wondering where you were, Ding Māo."

Shén Mì's voice startled me, making tiny goose bumps erupt over the skin of my arms.

"I've been waiting for you up front." My new master stopped next to me, tall and imposing despite his elegant, often foppish style.

"I was just telling him he's not allowed here," I said, suddenly feeling self-conscious about carrying a big bowl of food.

Shén Mì snapped his fan open. "He has a bad habit of bending the rules," he told me, hiding his words behind the fan. He turned to the intruder and smiled in that overly polite way of his that always seemed to hide a threat. "I have another meeting after this," he said. "We should get going."

The man-cat winked at me and followed my master toward the main courtyard. As they walked away, I heard him ask, "So what's with the beauty? When did you start hoarding pretty creatures? I didn't even think you liked females much."

Just as I thought I could finally sit down somewhere and eat my now-cold food, Ding Māo turned halfway around to look at me and wiggled his fingers. If I didn't know better, I would have sworn he licked his lips like a cat who had just swallowed a canary.

"Stay away from him."

The command didn't sit well with me. I had had enough of males telling me what to do and when to do it. I bristled.

"And don't give me that look," Shén Mì added, underlining his words with a swipe of the fan. "Ding Mǎo is a player. A very skilled one. You'll be better off staying away."

Challenge accepted.

"I thought he was very handsome and intriguing," I said, all too happy to have something I could use to irritate my master. Unfortunately for me, he did not seem bothered in the least. "I'm sure he's popular with the ladies." Digging that knife a little deeper never hurt.

"Don't come running to me later with a broken heart," he said dismissively. "Let's go back to business."

Business entailed the usual daily physical torture of hours of *qi gong* without any water or food. "Commune with nature", "Be one with the wind", "Let your inner butterfly rejoice." Bullshit! All I got from these sessions was sore arms and legs and a growling stomach.

But my *qi* was getting replenished, something I would never, ever admit to my master.

Eager to steer him away from the so-called business, I asked, "Are you ever going to tell me more about what you want me to do for you? Or are you just enjoying seeing me exhausted, aggravated, and hungry?"

His face showed zero emotion, his golden eyes neither blinking or narrowing.

Why doesn't he react to things the way normal people do?

"In time," he said, pointing at the spot he had chosen for me to *commune* with nature this morning. "You have to be fully recovered to be of any use to me."

So clinical, so... so exasperating.

"And you will never get there unless you work harder." He did raise his gaze to mine then, but all I saw there was authority.

I hate him.

Sighing, I closed my eyes and began my inhales and exhales, bringing my hands together in front of me and lowering and raising them to the rhythm of my breath. Despite my ever-present reluctance to do anything my master ordered me to, I enjoyed this part of the exercise, as it cleared my mind and my lungs, allowing energy to flow freely inwards, filling me with something that teetered between peace and power.

Later, famished and annoyed, I walked into the kitchen to find Lǎo Cōng fiddling with the oven, red-faced and coughing. Smoke rose from the open oven door in great big puffs, and tried as he may, the old cook couldn't avoid breathing in the fumes.

"What the hell are you doing, Lǎo Cōng?" I asked, rushing to him and crouching by his side. "Are you trying to poison yourself with smoke?"

Cook fanned the air in front of him with one big hand and coughed again. "Damn Li Su can't do anything right."

I wondered what the poor young girl could have possibly done wrong this time. She had been hired to help around the house a week after I came to live here, and she'd been in constant trouble ever since.

"I asked her to bring logs for the fire, and the ditz brought me the wrong kind of wood. It took forever to burn, and now there is more smoke than flames."

"Well, did anyone teach her to choose the right wood for the stove?" I asked, knowing the answer all too well. The cook seemed to think that everybody was born with these things already ingrained in their memories. "The poor girl is very young and needs to be taught, not yelled at."

"Are you going to help me or lecture me on how to deal with my staff?" he asked, sour-faced and covered in ashes.

I sighed. "Move over," I told him, scooting closer to the oven opening. I peeked inside to find out that whatever wood had been burning in there was mostly turned to ashes already, but before Lǎo Cōng had a conniption fit, I waved my hand and put the rest of it out with my magic. "There! Problem solved."

The cook, who had clambered to his feet and stood just a few paces away, opened and closed his mouth like an odd koi. "How did you do this?" he sputtered, blinking furiously. "You fairies are full of surprises. I thought your magic was mostly gone."

I would never admit it, but the master's daily torture was working. My magic was slowly but steadily coming back with each passing day. "This is small magic," I said, dismissing it. "You can pay me with food. I'm starved."

He wiped his stained face with a white cloth, draped it over his shoulder, and opened one of the steamers. "Fresh *bao* buns. Want some?"

Do I ever!

I made my way out of the kitchen, a *bao* stuck between my teeth and another in my hand, and headed to my room, humming a happy song under my breath. I was so focused on the delicious smell and taste of the heavenly buns that I didn't see him until I was practically standing on his toes.

"What are you doing, Butterfly?" The master's sour countenance never disappointed. He crossed his arms over his chest, the long, wide sleeves of his flowing *changshan* flapping like the wings of a vulture. He stared down at the food I was carrying. "You really need to eat less. A good cultivator cares about what goes into their body and knows that moderation is the key."

Every fiber of my body prickled. "The key to what? Starvation? Unhappiness?" I had had too much of both in my life to heed his words. If food was available, I was going to eat and enjoy it. Just to prove my point—or to egg him on—I took a huge bite of the bun that had been hanging precariously from my mouth.

"'Gluttony and self-indulgence do not happiness bring,'" he quoted, and I bet that the old prophet groaned in his tomb. "'Frugality and service to others are the road to true happiness.'"

I tried not to, but I still rolled my eyes. "I'm frugal," I protested despite my determination not to say anything. "You don't see me walking around in fancy clothes or decorating my hair with dozens of pretty, expensive pins, do you? Spare me the philosophical shit." I took a step forward to go around him, but he sidestepped to block me. "What do you want now?" I was aware I sounded like a spoiled child, but I was tired and sore. And hungry, very hungry.

"If you stopped whining long enough for me to explain...." He paused, a note of true emotion in his voice and expression. Or maybe, in my hunger haze, I had imagined it. "I came to invite you to a banquet tonight."

What? Hunger must have cluttered my ears.

"I have a few associates coming tonight, and I think you are almost ready to take part in missions. I'd like to introduce you to the rest of the crew."

This was the first time he had even mentioned my so-called mission—which I still knew close to nothing about—since that first day. It stunned me into silence.

"I'll send appropriate clothing to you room later today," he said, his expression and voice reflecting the usual ennui. "You're small and weak, but we don't want the others to notice that."

What the hell does that mean?

He didn't give me the chance to ask as he swiveled on his heel and dashed away, one arm properly folded behind his waist, the other in front. The man was infuriating. I couldn't read him at all, and that alone pissed me off to no end.

But there's a party to go to tonight.

Which meant good food and abundant wine. Definitely something to look forward to.

CHAPTER FOUR

The Introduction

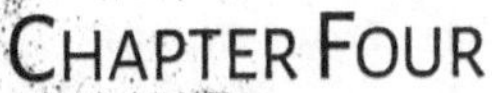

SHÉN MÌ

S HE WAS LATE. OF course she was. Hú Dié excelled in being as annoying as possible. Especially when it came to me. I had watched her being perfectly charming with other members of my household, but as soon as I entered the scene, the side of hers that was all spikes and poisonous darts came out in force.

"The crew is hungry, Shén Mì," Ding Māo whispered by my side. "You'll have a full-on riot if you don't tell the servants to bring in the food soon."

I exhaled deeply and slowly, trying not to get too frustrated. I had a reputation to uphold, and cool and collected under any circumstances were my trademarks. I couldn't let a tiny butterfly ruffle me enough to break my own rules.

"We wait for the butterfly," I said, despite my wish to say the opposite. "After all, this banquet is to introduce her to the others."

Ding Mão chuckled, covering his mouth with a big hand. "This little butterfly of yours is very interesting indeed," he said. He had no idea! "Such a pretty, frail creature with the power to hold more than ten men in stitches."

As if on cue, Hú Dié burst into the banquet hall. Literally. With a show of strength I knew she didn't have, she pushed the heavy doors wide open and stepped into the room, a picture of power and mystery in a tiny package. Every eye turned to her as voices dialed down into silence. She was wearing the clothes I had chosen for her, a crimson *changshan* gathered at the waist by a wide leather belt from which thin straps with silver metal studs and aglets hung. Black fabric edged the bodice part of the outer garment, the only decorative touch to the simple but effective outfit. Her hair was braided tightly behind her neck, and if she was wearing any makeup, it had been artfully applied to be invisible.

She looks stunning.

For a moment, even I lost the power of speech, joining the other men in their imitation of a carp waiting for food. Ding Mão, much to my annoyance, was the first one to snap out of the trance, elbowing me not-so-gently on my side. "Say something," he whispered.

I cleared my throat, hoping she hadn't noticed my momentary slip. "Brothers, let me introduce you to the newest member of our crew," I announced, managing to keep my voice loud and steady. "This is Hú Dié. She is currently in training and ready for her first mission. I expect every one of you to treat her with the same respect you treat everyone else in this crew." She was the only female member as of now. "Please take a seat."

I expected her to sit next to me, being the guest of honor, but true to her personality, she chose to sit next to Ding Mão instead, wearing a smirk on her face. A tiny knot of irritation formed in my throat.

You can't let her get to you.

Easier said than done, I had come to discover. Hú Dié was an expert at doing what others couldn't: getting under my skin.

Hoping my face didn't betray the wave of annoyance exploding inside me, I lifted my fine ceramic cup and said, "To you, brothers."

Everyone drank their wine. A sneaky glance told me that even the butterfly had downed her cup, the pink tip of her tongue running over her full lips.

I refilled my cup and lifted it up again, turning slightly to face my new crew member, a gesture soon followed by the rest of the crew. "To Hú Dié."

After another round of courtesy toasts, a few of my men were already showing signs of tipsiness. I stole another glance toward the butterfly, fully expecting her to be slurring her speech and having trouble keeping her eyes open. I was thoroughly disappointed; the woman was as alert and in control of herself as she was before she drank all the wine. I was so surprised that I lowered my guard, and she caught my eye, an instant mocking smile stretching her lips. I quickly collected myself and turned my attention to the food a servant had put in my bowl, delicious-looking morsels of steamed fish over a bed of snowy rice.

I did my best to ignore my new *brother*, and she did the same, engaging in a long, animated conversation with Ding Māo. Not a single word of what was said reached my ears, drowned by voices that echoed louder in the banquet hall as men became more inebriated.

After the meal was over, dancers were brought in to perform for a few minutes, as it was customary. The dance crew consisted of females my men and I had rescued from lives that weren't worth living. Two of them were also extraordinary singers and guqin virtuosi. They had been given the choice to leave once their lives were back together, but they had opted to stay and be part of my household. Having such a large and diverse staff at my disposal was one of the benefits of being who I was. One of the only perks, in my opinion.

Ding Mǎo suddenly stood up, his black *changshan* tight enough across his chest to enhance his powerful muscles. He was such a showoff. But an excellent spy and warrior.

"Let's have some music," he yelled out, raising his cup over his head. "Hú Dié and I would like to dance."

My head snapped up. What? My jaw dropped, and I must have looked like a frog waiting to swallow a fly. They were going to dance? Together? Having come to know the butterfly, I thought she would refuse, but much to my shock and dismay, she stood up in one fluid movement and followed my brother-in-arms to the floor.

Quick to follow Ding Mǎo's orders, the musicians were already playing a popular dance tune while the couple gathered in front of the raised dais where my table stood. They held hands, looking at each other with smiles on their faces. The prickly creature was actually going to dance in front of all my men?

My most-prized spy bowed elegantly to his dance partner, and then with a graceful flip of his hand, he spun her in front of him, the skirt of her outer dress floating around her like the wings of a phoenix. I was mesmerized by the beauty of her movement, fluid and lovely in its simplicity. It should not have come as a surprise, considering she was after all a butterfly immortal, but it still stunned me. I couldn't take my eyes off her. It was as if everything else in the banquet hall had vanished, dispersed like the morning mist to reveal a single beautiful creature spinning and floating across the marble floors.

I don't know how long she danced. I'm not even sure Ding Mǎo moved at all. It was the applause and exclamations of approval from my men that widened my perception, bringing me back to the here and now. After a confused glance around me, I joined the others in applauding the performance as the couple bowed to me.

"Well done," I said, hoping my voice didn't betray the tremors inside. "Beautiful dance." I grabbed a cup and raised it in front of me. "*Qiánbēi*! Cheers!"

I waited for two servants to dash across the floor, bringing the dancers a couple cups of wine for the toast, and then gulped down the drink. I needed something to help me recover from whatever it was I felt while watching my newest crew member dance.

What the hell is wrong with me?

"So let me get this straight," Hú Dié said for the third time. "You want me to fly into the imperial palace, sneak into the empress's quarters, and listen to whatever she says to one of the concubines?"

I nodded, stifling my impatience and hiding it behind my fan.

"Are you a real spy or just a gossip?"

This butterfly could really push my buttons. I kept my face hidden for a moment longer, afraid my frustration would be too obvious. "I have reason to believe that the empress is plotting something against the throne." This was a lot more information than what I was initially willing to share with her. "Your job as my spy is to follow orders without question. There is a reason behind each and every one of my orders, and gossip is not one of them."

She shrugged. "Whatever you say, *shīfu*," she uttered, not sounding repentant in the least. "What if I'm caught? I mean, we're talking about the empress."

"I told you there would be danger involved, didn't I?" Could we stop with the twenty questions and move on? "The empress is very superstitious. If she does see you, she will take it as a good omen and leave you be." Butterflies were largely believed to be the bearers of good luck, which was one of the reasons Hú Dié was perfect for the job.

"I just don't want to end up in another cage," she mumbled under her breath.

Another cage? Had she been in one before? She'd never mentioned it, but again, she was not the type to share too much personal information—or any at all.

"Keeping a butterfly imprisoned is bad luck," I assured her, more curious than ever about her past. "The empress would never risk pissing off the fates."

Letting out a long and loud exhale, she trained her brown eyes on me. "Anything in particular you want me to pay attention to?"

I shook my head and closed my fan with a snap. "No, just listen carefully and memorize the conversation so you can relate it to me later. Simple."

A tiny smirk kicked up the corner of her lips. "Even if the conversation revolves around the different types of tea and pastries?"

"Yes, even that." My words caused her beautifully shaped eyebrows to rise, and a silly sense of satisfaction filled me. I had surprised her, and for some reason that made me very happy.

CHAPTER FIVE

First Mission

Hú Dié

M Y WINGS TREMBLED, UNACCUSTOMED to flying. It had been a few months since the last time I had transformed into my butterfly shape, and the silk of my blue wings ached like unused muscles on a long run. It made me feel light and free, and for a moment, I pondered why I had waited so long to do it, but the answer came to me promptly; with the amazing feeling of flying came memories, and those were far from welcome. I'd rather abstain from the lovely feeling than bring up those painful memories.

Pushing my thoughts of the past away, I fluttered across the main courtyard and skirted the wraparound porch, sneaking peeks inside each room. I had almost given up when I finally spied the empress half hidden behind a large rock in one of the gardens.

Strange place for an encounter.

For she wasn't alone. Beside her, another woman stood, patiently listening to what her royal companion was saying.

I flapped my wings harder, getting closer so I could hear what was being said. The empress was a beautiful woman in her early forties, identifiable by the yellow dragon on her dress and the elaborate hairdo held in place on the top of her head by a myriad of ornamental pins. The other woman was plainer in dress but a noblewoman as well. Likely one of the fifteen concubines who made up the ever-growing imperial harem. This woman was younger and stood taller despite the vertiginous height of the empress's hair, but she kept her head slightly bowed in deference to the other's higher status.

If at first I had thought the conversation would be nothing but boring, revolving around clothing and tea, I now was certain I had been wrong. No one ducked behind huge boulders to converse about tea and pastries. These two women were hiding something inside the palace where conspiracy ran rampant at any time of day or night. That could only translate into something insidious, and I was all about that as long as it didn't involve my own skin or freedom.

"Prince Wang Li is garnering too much attention and admiration from the emperor," the empress whispered, my oversensitive sense of hearing kicking in. "It must be stopped. The throne must go to my son, not to the child of a concubine of low rank."

Aha! So my master had been right in assuming something was afoot. Interesting....

"What do you want me to do, Xian Yi Hòu?" the other woman whispered back, her head still bowed.

"Find *Wū* Li Jun and tell him I want a reading."

What could a shaman possibly be able to do to help with that situation? But obviously the empress knew something I didn't. The so-called reading was most likely hiding something else.

The concubine bowed deeply. "Right away, Xian Yi Hòu." And she scurried away, her hands clasped together in front of her and chin still tucked into her chest.

I decided to follow her. The empress was not likely to leave the palace grounds while this inconsequential baby-maker could probably sneak out easily.

Flapping my wings, I tailed the young concubine through the inner courtyard, wondering where exactly she was going. She wasn't heading toward the gates but to one of the many single storied buildings of the harem. Afraid my luminescent wings would be noticed entering a dark room, I slipped through a hole in the rice paper screen in one of the windows. I allowed my eyes to adapt to the darkness before moving forward. There was nothing particularly notable about the space. Just a room that might have been one of the concubines' residences but was now a storage room. Furniture, flowerpots, bolts of fabric, and other domestic accoutrements littered the room, creating a maze that even I, in my minute size, was having trouble navigating.

Where is she?

I spotted a movement ahead of me, next to the opposite wall, so I flew in that direction. I arrived just in time to see her ducking through a small door hidden behind a pile of chests. *What a clever little minx.* No one would ever suspect a secret passageway in a storage room. Rushing to follow her, I almost got one of my wings caught in the door as she closed it behind her. I spun in the air and had to take a moment to gather my bearings as my sight swam with the unexpected motion.

The door opened to a narrow corridor that sank suddenly into the ground as a dark staircase appeared. The woman dashed down the steps, obviously well acquainted with it, as she managed not to trip in the dark. At the bottom, she pushed on the wall until another door creaked open, and light inundated the staircase. One advantage of being a butterfly was that my eyes quickly adapted to changes in lighting, so I immediately realized where we were: just outside the outer walls of the royal compound.

The sun had made its descent already, and the world had sunk into dusk, lingering rays of light quickly fading into the horizon as night began its rule. The concubine didn't slow down, taking to the dirt path that meandered down the hill where the palaces were built like a feral cat in pursuit of a meal. I flew after her, not too close but also not far enough that I risked losing her tracks.

At the bottom of the hill, there was a hut nestled into the rock-side and protected from the elements by a stone outcrop. Chances were that if you didn't know it was there, you'd never find it. The woman circled around the house to its front door on the opposite side and knocked. Was this place even inhabited? It looked dilapidated as if abandoned for years, the curtains on the windows torn and frayed, the wood of the door riddled with rot. However, not even a minute later, someone did come to the door, opening it just enough to identify the sneaky concubine.

"It's me, Lu Min," she said.

I couldn't see who was inside the house, but the door opened wider to let her in, and I wasted no time and flew inside with her. The place was dark and smelled of mold, but there was a fire in the hearth.

"Xian Yi Hòu sent me with orders," she continued.

The mystery person turned out to be a man with long, grey hair and dressed like a beggar. He waved at an old chair by the fire, and Lu Min sat down. "What does she want?" The man had a deep but raspy voice, as if he hadn't used it in a long time.

"She wants to see *Wú* Li Jun."

The man cleared his throat.

"Can you arrange a meeting?"

He nodded, his scarred face never changing expression. "I will talk to him tomorrow," he said. "Anything else?"

The concubine looked around her, and I darted behind a teakettle before her eyes landed on me. Satisfied that there were no others around, the woman leaned forward a little and, lowering her voice, said, "She hinted at dealing with Wang Li but didn't specify how or when."

Gods! Were they planning to get rid of the prince? I didn't know him or care to, but it seemed a bit extreme to want to kill him just because the emperor had been paying more attention to him lately. Life in the palace sounded as dangerous and cruel as the life of an imprisoned immortal.

"Noted," the man said with a nod followed by the longest spit I had ever seen. Was this guy a lizard demon? No, he recked of humanity and not the good kind.

The woman stood there for a moment longer, looking a bit awkward and clearly not sure what to do next. The spit-champion finally just gestured to the door with his chin, and the concubine hurried toward it, a look of relief on her face.

I flew out of one of the open windows. It was time to report this strange exchange to my master, and I was really curious to see his reaction. I still couldn't quite understand what his role in this whole mess was, given that he was a fop who seemed more concerned about matching his fan with his clothes than anything else. Why would someone like him be so interested in palace intrigue?

"*Nǐ Hǎo*, beautiful," a now-familiar voice greeted me as I entered what I liked to call the throne room but was really just a reception hall where my master received and entertained his many guests.

Ding Mǎo, handsome as always, was sprawled on a wide wooden chair, his long legs draped over the armrest. "Back so soon? You're either very efficient or have no idea what you're doing."

"Stay out of my business, handsome *báichī*." I scowled at him, just in case he didn't quite interpret my words correctly.

Which he didn't, judging by his reply. "Aww, you think I'm handsome?" he said with a feigned air of gratitude. "I'm flattered, Butterfly."

I grunted in annoyance but didn't spare him another glance, my attention turning exclusively to the pretty man sitting beside him. "*Shīfu*, I have news," I told him. "Maybe you should tell the idiot here to leave." I tilted my head not so discreetly in Ding Mǎo's direction.

If I didn't know better, I would have sworn Shén Mì suppressed a chuckle as he hid his lips behind the white fan. He had a whole collection, it seemed. This one was plain white covered in sparse but elegant black script that read, "Dripping water can penetrate the stone." A quote of some sort. I hadn't had much time in my life for literary endeavors, so I had no idea where the words came from, but I wondered what kind of meaning it had for this man.

"I gather that your mission was successful," Cheng Shén Mì said, snapping the fan closed. He had the most amazingly full lips I had ever seen. They begged to be kissed.

Kissed? Was I losing my mind?

No kissing anyone unless it involved a well-paid brothel worker with a clean bill of health.

I must have frowned, because he asked, "Something stinks? Yushu just replaced the incense in the burners." He sniffed the air, searching for the offending odor, and I almost laughed.

"Just an itch on my nose," I lied, scratching it for good measure. "Yes, but should I speak in front of the idiot?"

This time I was sure he was smiling. So, the pretty man had a sense of humor after all.

"Ding Māo is part of the team. You can speak in front of him."

I related all that I had learned then, as close to the words actually spoken by the two women as I could remember. He didn't seem surprised.

"What I don't understand," I said, "is why she wants to get rid of the prince when he hasn't even been declared the crown prince."

I bit my tongue, pissed at myself for voicing my thoughts. Who cared why? My job was finding and relaying the information, I didn't have to be any more involved. Despite all that, I was curious. You know the old saying curiosity killed the cat? Well, it killed butterflies, too, and I had no death wish.

"If Wang Li dies before being chosen as the crown prince, it makes things easier," the master said.

The fact that he referred to a prominent member of the imperial family by his name, not his title was very interesting. Did he know the prince personally? Was my master someone who rubbed shoulders with the high nobility? If so, why did he live in such a secluded place, away from the palace or even the noble families in town and run a spy organization? There was more to this man than a pretty face and fashionable clothes, it appeared.

"It clears the path for the next in line," Ding Māo added, swinging his legs off the armrest. "Xian Yi wants her son to shine. Right now he's obscured by the brilliancy of Wang Li."

There was no sarcasm in his words, and again, I noticed how he also didn't use the empress's title when referring to her.

"Should we warn your—" He stopped suddenly, and I cocked my head to the side, wondering what he had been ready to say. "Should we warn Wang Li?"

Cheng Shén Mì nodded. "Yes. And ask Xiao Bin to come see me."

Ding Māo unfolded like a giant cat, his hand resting casually on the hilt of his sword. The man was big! As tall as the Gods Tower, and with such wide shoulders, he would never fit through the doors of the humble homes in the city. "*Hǎo*, right away," he said, winking at me before taking off at a trot.

I scratched my head. "Who's Xiao Bin?" I asked and then wished I hadn't. Curiosity would be my downfall one day.

"No one you need to be concerned about," the pretty man said.

Heat flooded my cheeks and neck. I so wanted to strangle him, but he was paying for my comfortable living right now. I could kill him when I didn't need him anymore.

"You did a good job. I will call you when I have another mission for you."

Like an idiot, I stood there waiting. For what, I wasn't sure. I didn't know what to do with myself. Should I go back to my room? Go to the training grounds and practice my martial arts?

My master glanced up at me, seeming surprised I was still here. "What are you waiting for?" he asked. "You're free to go."

"Where?" Gods, I sounded as stupid as I felt. When had I become this dumb and indecisive?

"Wherever you want to," he replied, a glint of amusement in his beautiful golden eyes. "Just don't leave the compound alone. There are bandits in the area."

"Can I go to town?" I asked, hating that I sounded like a young adolescent asking her parents for permission. I was a fucking butterfly. I could just turn and fly wherever I wanted. Why did I suddenly feel I needed validation?

"Take Su Ming with you," he said. "He'll protect you." Su Ming was one of his guards, a man who was short but made of solid muscle. "Tell him I said so."

I hesitated for a moment before turning around and walking away. I had heard the servant girls talking about the market in town, and it had been a while since I had coin to buy anything fun. I would grab Mr. Muscle Man and drag him on a shopping trip.

It's just shopping, woman.

Why did it feel so exciting, then? Had my master slipped some drug in my tea?

Whatever! For once in my life, I was going to just have fun and enjoy it too.

CHAPTER SIX

The Visit

SHÉN MÌ

I T MIGHT HAVE BEEN a reflection from the sun, but I could have sworn her wings were visible even in her human form. But that was impossible, wasn't it? Fairies could only show one of their forms at a time. Even higher-ranking immortals couldn't maintain any part of their two forms simultaneously.

I shook my head and continued to watch Hú Dié as she twirled around in the back garden, unaware I was witness to her almost child-ish glee over a trinket she had bought at the market. She held the wooden bird over her head, watching its mechanical wings flap as she spun like a child's top. Had she never owned toys before? She was at least what amounted to twenty-five mortal years old, probably more, for fairies tended to look a lot younger than their actual years, but she acted like a young girl when no one was looking. Endearing as it was, it was also strange that someone like her, all edges and thorns, could hold such vulnerability and softness inside.

Afraid she would spot me as her twirling brought her closer to where I was hiding behind a tree, I turned around and rushed out of the garden. I often followed her here, her favorite spot in the compound, and studied her. Sometimes Ding Māo joined her, much to her annoyance, but mostly she kept to herself. I told myself I spied on her to make sure she wouldn't betray our mission, but truth be told, I was mostly curious about her past. Despite the fact that it had nothing to do with what I needed her for, I still wondered what made her, a butterfly fairy, be the way she was.

"That butterfly has really caught your eye, hasn't she?" Ding Māo asked after materializing, as he too often did, in front of me, startling me for a moment.

I huffed in annoyance and denial, and he fell in beside me, his long legs keeping up easily with my wide, impatient stride.

"Don't deny it. I have seen the way you look at her. She's a fascinating creature, isn't she?"

"I wouldn't know," I said, knowing all too well I was lying to myself. "I'm only interested in her as an asset to our mission."

He chuckled softly, and I bristled, stopping in my tracks to look him in the eye. Ding Māo was at least a couple inches taller than me, which at times like this rattled me irrationally.

"Why? Are you interested in her? Be my guest. Go for it, but don't be surprised when she chops off your balls while you sleep."

Ding Māo made a big show of being shocked, his hands flying to the sides of his head and his eyes snapping almost shut like clams. "Whoa, Master, calm down," he said, his amused tone of voice belying his body language. "I would never attempt to take what is rightfully yours."

"Hú Dié is not a thing," I protested, not sure where the anger was coming from. "She doesn't belong to me. She works *for* me, and that's a whole other business. She is free to do whatever she wants as long as she does her job. If she is foolish enough to fall for your dubious charms, it's her problem, not mine."

Still chuckling under his breath, he followed me as I resumed my walk. "Wow, what did you eat for breakfast, Your Majesty? You're a little too sensitive today."

"I've told you a million times not to call me that," I snapped at him without pausing my pace. "Call me master, call me Mì Mì—shit, call me idiot if you want, but don't call me that."

"*Hǎo de*! All right," Ding Māo exclaimed. "I was just joking. Sheesh, you're really cranky this morning. Did the cook burn your breakfast or something?"

I rolled my eyes and then chided myself silently for doing something so immature. I had known Ding Māo since our childhood, and being around him always brought those days back when we competed for everything: praise from the adults, grades from our masters, food from the kitchen—you name it, we'd fight for it. He was bigger and stronger than me, so he often won, but as frustrating as that was, he was my sworn brother, and I could never hold a grudge against him for long.

"Let's go to my office and talk," I said, determined to stop the conversation about my mood or anything to do with the butterfly.

It wasn't a long walk to the building where I had my office, a room only a few close associates were allowed inside. I sat cross legged behind the low desk and watched my friend fidget around the space like he always did before finally settling on the cushion across from me.

"I am going out tonight," I told him, grabbing a brush and dipping it into the ink stone. "I got word that Xiao Mó is on the move."

That caught his attention. He leaned forward. "Do you need me along?" he asked, the immature, mischievous man from a few minutes ago gone.

I shook my head. "No, I can handle this one by myself," I said, beginning to write on the white piece of paper before me. "But I need you to deliver a letter to my brother." I didn't have to specify which one. Ding Mǎo knew exactly which one of my two brothers I was talking about. "To his eyes only." Not that I needed to remind him of that, but the words spilled out just the same. I finished writing the missive and looked at him. "Then you can come back and flirt with the butterfly fairy until either your heart bursts or she yanks it from your chest."

He scoffed. "Like she could."

I smiled, remembering how she had fought fiercely against the much bigger, much stronger hoodlum when I first met her. "Be careful of your assumptions," I told him. "You haven't seen her fight. Don't underestimate her."

As much as I cared for my sworn brother, a part of me wished the butterfly would kick his ass. Odd, really, but I couldn't understand why the idea of her beating the crap out of him was so pleasing to me.

I had always thought dressing like this was overly dramatic. That was until I realized it was really the most effective disguise for this kind of mission. The night was dark, the cloud-covered sky as black as coal and refusing to allow any light to slip through. The moon and her sisters were losing the fight. Garbed in black from head to toe, I blended seamlessly with the night.

Unlike most, I didn't need light to move through the bamboo forest to the other side of town. I had done it so many times, I was sure I could do it with my eyes closed. This had been my territory since my early teens when I had broken with tradition and moved away from my family. I couldn't conform to the rules and dogmas of palace life, too constrictive and soul-sucking for someone like me to thrive in. So instead of going along with the flow, I had chosen another path. There had been a bit of an uproar at first. For anyone in my family to move out of the palace was unheard of, but I wasn't important enough to sustain that outrage. Soon, people forgot about it. Soon they forgot about me.

That suited me perfectly.

By the time I got into town, the few souls who might still be roaming the night had fallen asleep with the rest. Restaurants, tearooms, and brothels were closed for the night, and even the beggars had taken shelter somewhere to rest. I walked through the streets on padded feet, avoiding the weak light of the remaining lanterns, staying invisible.

The house I was looking for was in the more affluent side of town, just south of the palace, the houses spreading from the bottom of the hill like ants around a dead animal. I circled quietly to the back and climbed the high wall as I had done a million times in the past before dropping softly on to the grassy ground on the other side. I followed the stone path to the house, hugging the edges where the light didn't quite reach, then going over the small wooden bridge that arched elegantly over the fishpond. Her rooms were impossible to miss, centered in the courtyard like a beacon. Su Lin had never been one for subtlety. "The best strategy is to hide in plain sight," she had always said. It worked for her. I had to be a bit more subtle.

I knocked three times in quick succession before entering the building. The soft light of candles illuminated the interior, a welcome change from the darkness outside. A gentle glow on the opposite side from the doors held my seeking glance—Su Lin's bed, protected by a translucent white silk curtain, stood like a royal throne on an elevated dais. A smile crept over my lips. Ever the drama queen, Su Lin had made it impossible not to sigh in awe of her lodgings and by proxy, its owner.

"Are you coming in, or will you just lurk by the door all night, Mì Mì?"

Her silken voice wafted through the air like an expensive perfume and tugged at my senses. I had a moment to feel sorry for all the other fools who had been caught in her graceful, sensual web.

"Well, are you coming or not?"

"I'm coming, *Mèimei*," I said with a soft chuckle. There was no saying no to my younger sister. Gods knew I'd tried. "You have to stop being so bossy. You'll never find a husband like that."

She snorted as I padded my way across the bamboo floor. "Like I need a husband. I'm perfectly fine without."

It wasn't a boast. My sister was in the rare and enviable position of never needing a man in her life to survive in the male-controlled imperial court. It sometimes paid to be the emperor's favorite and the widow of one of the most powerful and wealthy men in the empire. A man who had been known to break the rules often but whom no one expected to leave all his riches to the beautiful and smart woman he had married.

"You, on the other hand, should think of getting yourself a wife. People are beginning to talk, you know."

I sat next to her on the edge of the bed, stretching my neck to drop a brief kiss on her cheek. "Oh really? And what exactly are they talking about?" I asked, knowing all too well what the gossip was about.

"They say you are more delicate and feminine than a lot of women and that you are most likely a *duan xiu*, a cut-sleeve who only has eyes for pretty men like Ding Māo," she explained unnecessarily.

We had had this same conversation several times, but I put on the appropriate outraged expression she always expected.

"Stop. You know this already, so don't act surprised. I know you do it on purpose as a cover, but it's becoming harder and harder to defend you around others in court. It's rather embarrassing sometimes."

"Would you love me less if I were indeed a *duan xiu*?" I stuck my lower lip out in a pretend pout. "Because I'll marry the first female who walks through that door if that's the case."

Su Lin laughed. "You're awful," she said, cupping my cheek with her palm. "If you weren't my favorite brother, I'd kill you."

"*Mèimei*, I say a prayer of thanks to the gods every day for that." It was only a half lie. I was indeed grateful to the heavens for giving me her as my only sister, but I wasn't much for prayer. "I need you again."

With a sigh, she dropped her hand to her lap. "I knew you wouldn't just come to see me because you miss me."

I laughed. "Well, it *is* the middle of the night, sister. Why would I come to visit you now if it were only a social visit?"

Su Lin's shoulders slumped in feigned resignation. "*Shuō*! Tell me, then," she replied. "I'll make some tea."

While she busied herself pouring hot water from the kettle into the teapot, I went straight to the reason I was visiting my sister in the middle of the night, dressed like a bat. "The empress is plotting against Wang Li. Again."

She threw me a brief glance, arching her perfectly shaped eyebrows.

"She has called *Wū* Li Jun."

She set down the kettle and began pouring the tea into the small cups, her lower lip stuck between her teeth. "Interesting," she muttered. "I wonder what she's planning. The shaman is well-known for his poisons, some of which are said to be undetectable."

I nodded, accepting the teacup she handed to me. "But he's also known for being an expert at creating problems where none exist."

Taking a sip from her tea, my sister hummed her agreement. "So you want me to find out exactly what our evil empress is up to, right?"

The tea was rich, the fragrant steam from the cup teasing my taste buds. "*Duì!* And put a kink in her plans if possible. If not, let me take care of that."

Su Lin threw me a sideway glance. "Why not tell Father about this?" she asked.

The familiar knot in my throat I always got when my father was mentioned made me gulp. "He doesn't want to hear anything I have to say," I said, disguising the croak in my voice with a sip of the tea. "You know that. Coming from me, it might as well be a blast of air. Inconsequential at best."

"He loves you," she countered, her head tilted to one side.

"Like someone loves the drunk *shūshu* at a banquet: fondly but dismissively," I said. "I am nothing but an irritating bug in our father's ear."

My sister made a clucking sound, and I had to laugh. A mother hen she was not. "That's what you get for leaving the nest too early. Or at all," she said.

"Well, *Mèimei*, it's not easy being our father's son, is it?" I said, taking another sip of the hot tea.

She sighed, her shoulders slumping a bit. "I suppose not," she whispered. "Not easy for any of us having the emperor as our father."

Truer words had never been uttered. Having the emperor for a father had been an uphill struggle for me my whole life. Why should it be any different now?

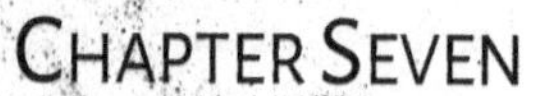
CHAPTER SEVEN

The Cat

Hú Dié

T HE MAN WAS SHIFTY. I had watched him sneak out of the compound under the cover of the night a few times already, dressed all in black like a would-be assassin. He could be one, but his dandy behavior and outlook didn't quite match with the image of a hardcore criminal. I could imagine him as a clerical crook, always on the lookout for a way to cheat people out of their money, but an assassin? No way! It just didn't make sense.

A deep voice yanked me out of my daydreaming. "How pensive, little butterfly."

I groaned at Ding Māo, who, like the cat he was, had the unsavory penchant for showing up at any given moment out of empty air.

"What is that tiny brain of yours up to?"

"Before you comment on the size of my brain, you should check inside your pants," I barked at him, narrowing my eyes to slits.

He let out a very insincere "Ouch" as his hand flew to his chest.

"What the hell are you doing here again? Have you moved in, and I wasn't informed?"

He clucked his tongue a few times. "You so hurt my feelings, Beauty," he said, his words as fake as the expression of outrage on his face. "I am here to see you, of course. One day without setting my tired eyes on your beautiful and graceful self is too horrible to bear."

One more groan escaped my lips. The truth was that, as annoying as he was, I had started looking forward to his visits. It was the one time of the day when I could sharpen my tongue, since the master was a rare sight outside my training sessions. Ding Māo could give as much as he could take, and that alone made the word-sparring so much more enjoyable.

"Quit the bullshit," I told him. "It's starting to smell."

With a chuckle he took a seat next to me on the makeshift bench I was sitting on—a large rock the top of which had been smoothed over the years by the collection of buttocks that had chosen to rest there.

"What were you thinking about just now?" he asked, brushing a bug off his pants.

"Trying to figure out where the master goes at night dressed to kill—literally." Why hide the truth? And maybe he would actually tell me, but I wasn't holding my breath.

"I was wondering when you'd notice his nighttime excursions," he said, a wicked smile on his lips. "I bet he's visiting a lover in town."

Lover? Dressed like that? What kind of lover would require such subterfuge? Was he sharing a bed with some high-ranking official? Even then, illicit sex was not considered much of a crime in the imperial court. In fact, it was almost expected.

"No, that is not it," I said emphatically. "No way."

With a feline glance, he lowered his voice and said, "Jealous, are you?"

Heat rose up my neck and into my cheeks. "What are you talking about?" I protested a bit too enthusiastically. "Why would I be jealous? The master is just a rich dandy who cares more about his appearance than anything else."

Ding Māo clicked his tongue and shook his head. "You shouldn't judge by what things look like," he said, serious for once. "Cheng Shén Mì might surprise you."

I couldn't deny it, considering I had seen him leave the house dressed like the very opposite of the image he projected during the day. He was hiding secrets for sure, and I wouldn't rest until I found out what they were.

"But since you claim not to have any interest in him, I am now free to woo you," he continued, almost knocking me off my feet—metaphorically and literally, for I stumbled backward in shock and tripped over a big rock. He reached out to grab my arm and pull me against him. "Whoa, Butterfly, no need to fall ass over heels for me."

I guffawed and pushed away from him. "Very funny," I said, my voice a bit rough from the surprise. "Like I have any interest in you either."

He pursed his lips and said, "Not yet, but I am nothing if not persistent, and I know I can woo you straight into my heart."

I chuckled, crossing my arms. "Like you can," I said, fully aware I sounded like a fifteen-year-old. "I have a natural immunity to male charm." A gift from years of being mistreated by creatures of the male species. Not that I would ever admit that to him or anyone else. My past was mine to bear and to protect. No one needed to know about my emotional wounds, some of which still hadn't healed completely.

With a shrug, he said, "We'll see."

"What will we see?"

Resplendent in his embroidered silk clothes, Cheng Shén Mì was like a cloud of deep blue wafting silently into our midst. How it was possible that such a pretty boy could emit such danger-and-mystery vibes was beyond me, but I sure could feel them every time he showed up.

"We were talking about you," my feckless partner said, earning a murderous glare from me. "I was telling her you have no interest in her, and since she doesn't in you, either, I will be the one wooing her."

I glared even more fiercely, but the fool didn't read eyes, apparently.

"She almost swooned in bliss."

My master's intense eyes found their way to me, and I swallowed hard, suddenly embarrassed by Ding Māo's choice of words. "Pay him no mind, *shīfu*," I said, stuttering slightly. "He's an idiot."

I had the distinct impression that he was annoyed, but whatever I had seen in his eyes was gone before I could be sure. "What you do in your free time is your business," he said. "No need to explain."

Ding Māo pointed at my master with an open hand. "See? I told you; he doesn't care if I pursue you."

Shén Mì cleared his throat and muttered, "If you're stupid and naive enough to fall for him, then that's your problem."

His voice was so low, I almost thought I'd imagined it. But there was no doubt now; he *was* pissed. Was it because of what we were talking about or had something else happened?

"What did your sister say when you saw her last night?" Ding Māo asked, and an odd sense of relief flowed through me. So he had gone to see his sister, not a lover. But how did that explain his clothing? Maybe he wanted to go incognito.

"She'll take care of it, no problem." The master took a deep breath and looked at me again. "You should soak in the White Lake to strengthen your *qi*."

"White Lake?" I had never heard of it.

"Tell Yushu to show you where it is. Take your bathing clothes," he told me, dismissing me with a wave. "Go now. I need to talk to Ding Mão."

And just like that, I was forgotten. But who cared? I was about to take a dip in a lake, something I hadn't done in a long time. The gods were on my side.

If pleasure were a liquid, this lake was pure bliss. I wasn't sure how it was done, but the water was hot and bubbly, tickling my toes and massaging my sore muscles. I sank all the way up to my chin and closed my eyes, a sigh of pure satisfaction escaping my lips. Besides the feeling of utter delight, there was something else, an inexplicable wave of power that entered through every pore of my body and rushed through my veins to recharge me.

"You look like a dead koi."

Damned if it wasn't Ding Mão, intruding on my personal moment. As much as I wanted to glare at him, I kept my eyes stubbornly shut, not willing to give him the pleasure of seeing me rattled.

"A very beautiful dead fish, but still...," he continued, undeterred by my refusal to acknowledge his presence.

I closed my hands into fists underneath the water and asked, "What the hell are you doing here, Ding Mão? Can't a girl take a bath without an audience?"

"It's not as if you were naked or anything," he said and then wistfully added, "You aren't, right?"

I was wearing bathing clothes. I might be reckless, but I knew better than to get rid of all my clothes anywhere close to a male. It often didn't end well, and I was not too keen on fighting in my birthday suit.

"I'm joining you."

That made me snap my eyes open just in time to see the handsome idiot begin to remove his clothes. "What the fuck do you think you're doing?" I yelled.

He threw his outer garments on top of a rock and stood there dressed only in his long white underpants. For a moment, I forgot my outrage to admire the view. The man was beautiful, with wide shoulders framing a perfectly sculptured chest and biceps that would make any woman swoon. I didn't even want to think about what lay beyond the point where the V between his hips met the waist of his pants.

Without another word, he chuckled softly, removed his boots and socks, and ran to the edge of the lake. "Here I come, Beauty."

His movement broke the spell and I blinked, watching him step into the water and waddle his way to me. Was he utterly insane?

The lake was not very deep, maybe six feet in its deepest area, but its waters somehow managed to submerge the entire six-foot-plus man swimming toward me. I had a moment of panic. I knew how to fight. In fact, I was a damned good fighter, and now that my *qi* was almost completely restored, I was strong beyond my size. But fighting such a large male in the buoyancy of the lake was not something I had any wish to do.

I decided to make a run—swim—for it, but just as I started to move toward the bank, he broke the surface right beside me with a huge splash. His long raven-black hair fell heavily onto his strong shoulders, and I froze for a moment, mesmerized by the drops of water that rolled down his face and hung on to his thick dark eyelashes.

"I forgot how amazing this water is," he said, shaking his head like a wet dog and splattering water on my face. "Glad Mì Mì suggested this."

Should I point out that it was suggested to me, not him? I went with, "Why did you follow me? Don't you have friends you can hang out with?"

"I do. Many," he said with a wink. "None as interesting and beautiful as you, though."

Was I supposed to be flattered? "What do you want?" I asked, carefully dodging his flirtation. "I have nothing for you: no money, no valuables, not even that much power."

"Did I say I wanted something besides your company?" He acted outraged, offended even, and I almost burst out laughing. "I just find you intriguing, that's all. A butterfly fairy with a death wish—what's there not to like?"

I sobered up quickly. "I do not have a death wish," I protested.

"Then why provoke every thug in the kingdom into fighting with you?" For once he seemed genuinely curious.

"Training," I said and then wished I hadn't.

He cocked his head. "Training? For what, exactly? To see how quickly you can turn black and blue?"

I had already said too much. "Just toughening myself up for the future." It was true enough. The tougher I got, the better chances I had to do what I had long ago decided to do.

He squinted as if confused. "You know there are easier and better ways to train, right?"

"Not everyone was born with a silver spoon in their mouths," I snapped back a lot more bitterly than I intended. "I can't afford to pay for the training, and no master would take a feeble butterfly."

"Shén Mì did."

Yes, but how many years had I looked for someone willing to train me, only to find one closed door after another?

"What's eating you, Butterfly, that you need all this training?"

"The stronger I get, the better chances I have of survival," I said, choosing to tell him only a tiny part of the truth.

He seemed to consider this for a while, never taking his eyes from mine. Then he said, "Well, you got lucky when Mì Mì decided to take you as his apprentice. You couldn't have landed a better master."

I wasn't sure I was in total agreement, but Shén Mì's training had been excellent so far, despite his foppish ways, so I didn't argue.

"And you got me as well," he added with a grin, opening his arms wide. "How lucky for you, right?"

I bit my lip, torn between amusement and annoyance. "I understand cats can't swim very well," I said with a smirk.

His eyebrows curved high. "Says who? I can beat you any day."

"Care to make a bet?" I was an excellent swimmer, a side benefit of a less than positive past. "Ten *yìn*?"

"Do you even have that much money?"

"No, but you can request a different prize from me," I said.

"A date," he said without any hesitation. "You lose, you go on a date with me."

I choked on my own spit. "W-what? A date?" What was this fool up to?

"Yes, a simple date in town with me, that's all." He grinned, crossing his arms over his wet chest. "Deal?"

I thought for a moment. There was no way he could win. He was a cat immortal, and cats were not known for their swimming skills. And even if he did win, a date didn't sound so bad as long as there were no other things involved. "No kissing or any sexual stuff, right? Just a date."

He nodded and stretched out a hand toward me. I took it and shook it after a final moment of hesitation. "It's a deal," I said, not feeling as confident as I had a moment ago.

He let go of my hand and took off swimming before I could react. *Cheater!*

I took a long breath and rushed after him. I knew I would win this as long as I could catch up.

I *had* to catch up! Suddenly the idea of going on a date with him filled me with an itchy anxiety that I couldn't tell if it was fear or excitement. I wasn't sure I wanted to find out.

CHAPTER EIGHT

Confusion

SHÉN MÌ

I SLAPPED THE TOP of the wooden table so hard, my hand tingled with a mixture of pain and numbness. Why couldn't I focus? A mountain of documents awaited my attention, but I couldn't keep my mind on the job at hand. The parchment I had unrolled and weighed down almost an hour ago had yet to be properly read and signed. My thoughts were stuck on one thing and one thing only: Hú Dié was going on a date with Ding Māo.

"What do you care?" I muttered to myself, rubbing my eyes.

Why did the idea of those two together on a date bother me so much? It wasn't as if I had a hold on either of them—or had any plans for a romantic relationship. Māo Māo had been my friend and partner in crime since childhood, and I was well acquainted with his charm. He had always been a favorite of the town beauties, a familiar and frequent visitor to the brothels. Hú Dié was only an asset, a useful tool for my mission. What did I care whom she dated? As long as it didn't interfere with her work, I couldn't care less who she went out with.

"Then why does it bother me so much?" I said out loud with another painful slap on the table.

"Damn! What kind of bug crawled up your pants, *gē*?" Ding Māo exclaimed from the open door of my study. He was leaning against the door frame, his arms crossed over his chest, an amused grin on his face. "It's a rare thing to see you this pissed off."

A quiet grunt escaped my lips, and I stared at the paper spread in front of me. At this speed I would still be going through the documents the next week. "Nothing," I lied. "Just not feeling good today."

"Should I call Dr. Ming?" my friend asked, suppressed laughter in his voice.

I shook my head, avoiding his gaze. He knew me too well, and I certainly didn't want him to realize the source of my irritation. "What do you want?" The question was coated in an irrational anger, and I immediately wished I could retract it.

My friend raised his hands. "Whoa, *gē*! Whatever I did, I apologize," he said, the smirk on his lips belying his tone. He crossed the room and sat across from me, leaning over the dark tabletop. "Does it really bother you that much that I am taking the butterfly fairy into town for some fun?"

Fuck! He can read me like a book.

"Why would I care?" I lied, knowing all too well I couldn't fool him. "Just don't mess up with her. I need her for this mission."

He chuckled softly and leaned back a little, his long legs crossed in front of him. "Right! Don't worry, I have no intention of ruining anything," he said, unconvincingly. "But a little love never hurt anyone, right?"

Despite myself, I looked up at him, glaring. "She's not one of your courtesans," I barked out.

He tilted his head to one side, a tiny smile lifting the corner of his mouth. "But she is a beauty and of age," he argued.

I knew he was egging me on, yet I couldn't help myself; I had to confront him about it.

"Are you jealous? Do you want her yourself? Because you know what my motto is."

Xiōngdì before girls, he always said. The problem was that until now, none of the women he had romanced held any interest for me.

Wait! What am I thinking?

I had no interest at all in the butterfly fairy other than as a professional investment. She was beautiful and interesting, but I had better things to do than fall for anyone.

"I am not interested in her," I said, hoping to the gods I wasn't lying. "She's my spy, and I don't want you to get her distracted, that's all. You can do whatever you want."

Ding Mǎo threw me a skeptical look but didn't say anything else about it. "What's our next step, then?" he asked, back to business.

"We wait for my sister's message," I said, sniffing at the cold tea I had forgotten to drink. "Then we plan our next step. Did you talk to Wang Li?"

He nodded. "And I asked Xiao Bin to come and see you too," he said. "I'm surprised he hasn't come yet."

Now that he mentioned it, it was odd than my palace spy hadn't reported to me yet. Had something happened? "Maybe we need to check on him, just in case he's been discovered."

It looked as if I was going on another undercover excursion that night.

Ding Māo sat up, brushed imaginary dust from his clothes and turned to leave. Without as much as a peek back at me, he declared, "And by the way, *gē*, I have no intentions of taking your precious fairy on a date. I wouldn't do that to you."

Before I could react, he left.

Fuck! Is my irrational jealousy that obvious?

I must have lost my mind!

Not sure why I would take such a high risk and for what it looked like no good reason whatsoever. Maybe I had been poisoned and whatever I ingested had muddled my brain so much, I thought bringing Hú Dié along on a mission was a great idea.

"These clothes are itchy," she mumbled beside me as we crouched behind a bush, waiting for the guards to move on. "You couldn't find any better fabric for it?"

I sighed, lowering my gaze to the ground and praying for patience. "You're a tough one, aren't you? Live with it." She had been bemoaning the scratchiness of our black disguises since we left the house. "Just shut up before we give ourselves away."

She went silent for a moment, and I foolishly thought she was following my orders. "Besides, forest green would be a much better camouflage color, especially if we are going to be hiding behind greenery like scared chickens."

Foolish. I had never been known for foolish behavior but here I was now.

"What the hell are we even doing here anyway? You never told me."

I lost it! Turning toward her, I pulled down the black scarf that covered my nose and mouth and glared. "For the love of all the gods and all the heavens, be quiet for a moment," I whispered-yelled, my patience stretched to the limit. "Did you talk this much when you went to spy on the empress?"

My glare had very little effect on her. "No, but then again, I had no one to talk to that night."

I tightened my jaw until it hurt.

"No one can hear me anyway. I'm using my butterfly voice," she added, a smile dancing in her eyes.

"I can hear it, can't I?" I barked back. "If I can, so can other people."

She snorted. "Obviously you don't know as much about butterfly fairies as you think you do," she said with an eye-roll. "We can modulate our voices to be heard only by whom we choose. To others it sounds like a low buzz, sort of like the noise a mosquito makes."

Heat climbed up my neck and invaded my cheeks. Grateful it was dark enough that she couldn't see the redness on my face, I replaced the scarf and mumbled, "Idiot!" I was talking to myself. Why did this fairy make me so muddle brained that I even forgot that detail about butterfly immortals?

"Finally something we can agree on," she snapped back.

I had also forgotten how sharp their hearing was.

For the sake of the mission, I let it go while seething inside.

The guards, after what felt like an eternity, began to disperse in pairs, heading to their duty stations around the compound and leaving only two to guard the gate. It was our chance now.

I turned to my irritating sidekick. "Fly to that tree over there," I told her, waving in the general direction of a large plum tree that grew on the far side of the gate. "Drop these and then fly back to join me."

I handed her a tiny sachet full of what looked like seeds. They were anything but.

Hú Dié's eyes shone with mistrust. "What are those?"

I grunted. "Stop asking so many questions and just do it." When she didn't move, I said, "Go!"

In the weeks she had been at my house, I had yet to see her transform. Despite my many years in the business and having dealt with immortals of all kinds, I was still mesmerized by her process. After a huff, she grabbed the sachet, and then her whole being began to shimmer as if catching on fire. When the cloud of glittering bubbles dissipated, the human had vanished and a large blue butterfly hovered in its stead, no evidence left of her clothes or the secret sachet I'd given her.

Even as a butterfly, Hú Dié's disapproval of me came through loud and clear.

She fluttered her luminous wings for a few seconds before flying up and across the width of the massive gate. She disappeared into the darkness for a moment, only to reappear under the soft light of the gate's lanterns. As she landed on one of the top branches of the tree, I prepared myself for action.

All I saw was a flicker of light as she conjured the tiny pouch I had given her and dropped the seeds. A burst of soundless mist rose as the beads—not seeds—hit the ground. There was a moment of surprise when the guards jerked out of that semislumber the boredom of keeping watch always incited. What followed was exactly what I was expecting: one went down before the other, dropping to the dirt road like a heavy sack of turnips with a muffled thump.

It was done!

I left the shelter of the bushes and headed to the gate, checking the scarf over my face. The guards would sleep for at least an hour and wake up with a major headache, but they'd be alive, if a little confused by what happened. A flutter of wings tickled my right ear as Hú Dié flew down from her perch on the tree. If I didn't know better, I would have sworn she hissed at me as she flitted by.

Dashing across the courtyard, I kept my hand on the pommel of my sword. Xiao Bin was not the type to disregard orders, which could mean only one thing: trouble. His rooms were on the far end of the courtyard, a modest compound in the foothill of the palace. He had always had a flair for blending in, a true chameleon who was perfect for spy work. From this far away, I could see lights in the windows.

I didn't knock.

Hugging the side of the building, I went around to the back and climbed in through the usual unlocked window, not sure whether the butterfly had followed. Inside, it was hot and stuffy, as several fires were lit in freestanding fireplaces around the room. Sweat beaded on my forehead as I tiptoed toward the curtained bed against the wall. Nothing in this room screamed royalty or even wealth. Despite its generous size, the space was sparsely decorated with elegant but humble furnishings as well as several shelves packed with books and manuscripts.

Hú Dié chose that moment to change into her human form, almost giving me a heart attack. True to her reckless personality, and much to my exasperation, she leaned over the bed to stare at whoever lay there. I was still too far away to stop her, and all I managed was a grunt.

"Who is this man?" she asked, not bothering to lower her voice. "He looks dead."

My heart skipped a beat, and I picked up my speed. Xiao Bin was dead? It couldn't be.

Just as I reached the bed, anxious to check on my operative's state of health, a loud sneeze preceded what could only be compared to a volcanic explosion—one that sent snot flying rather than lava. I barely had time to step back to avoid the unsanitary shower coming from Xiao Bin's nose and mouth.

The butterfly, who in a sudden burst of caution had retreated from her perch over the bed, muttered, "Well, fuck! He's not dead after all."

CHAPTER NINE

Surprises

Hú Dié

I F ANYONE HAD TOLD me, I wouldn't have believed it.

My master, the dandy who doubled as a mysterious and cranky spy, and who I had never once seen caring for anyone or anything other than his own clothes and precious fans, was tenderly ministering to the very sick man on the bed. As soon as the disgusting nose explosion had cleared enough for it to be safe to approach the bed, Shén Mì sat on the edge, slipped an arm behind the man's back, and proceeded to wipe his face with a silky cloth he conjured from out of one of his sleeves.

"Why didn't you send word that you were this sick?" he asked, touching two fingers to the ailing man's forehead. "You're running a fever."

Is this his lover?

"You shouldn't be here, *gē*," the sick man said in between fits of coughing. "You'll get sick too."

"You're my brother, Bin'er. How could I not come to help you?"

Wait! Brother as in brother-in-arms, friend, or actual we-shared-the-same-womb brothers?

"You're an idiot," the man said with what might have been a chuckle or another hack. "If you get sick, who's going to take care of our mission?"

Shén Mì stood up and crossed the space to a tall stand where a basin full of water rested. He dropped one of the cloths piled next to it into the water and then wrung it tightly before coming back to the bed.

"I have a powerful immune system, you know that," he protested, running the wet cloth over the other man's face. "And I have magic to protect me."

Interesting.

The sick man lifted his head from the pillow and threw a glance at me. "Who's the beauty?" he asked.

As if only just remembering I was there, Master looked at me for a moment. "Yes, that's Hú Dié, my newest spy," he said. "She's a butterfly immortal."

The man's eyes rounded. "And the first female you've hired," he said with a smile. "Well met, Hú Dié. I'm Xiao Bin, this idiot's adopted brother. Stay away from me if you don't want to get sick."

I shook my head. "I don't get sick."

It was the simple truth. I had never been sick a day in my life. Not even when I had been confined to that wretched cage, kept away from the sun, the fresh air, and everything else that kept any fairy alive and well. I had a strong constitution, an old hag once told me.

As if to prove it, I took a few steps closer. "So, you're not his lover, then." It wasn't as much a question as a statement of fact.

Xiao Bin burst out laughing, which in turn caused him to have a long cough attack. Master held his shoulders and rubbed his back with one hand in an oddly gentle way. Gentleness was not something I would have accused my benefactor of.

"Lovers?" the man finally said once he could catch his breath. "I don't know what you heard, but my brother very much likes females."

Shén Mì glared at his brother. "Enough talk about me," he said. "Let's talk business. What have you heard?"

I was still confused about so many things. If this was a family member, why go through the whole ruse with the guards? Why not just knock at the door? And even though this house was not flashy, it was obviously the home of a nobleman, which meant my master was higher in society's hierarchy than I had thought.

"I've been stuck to this bed for the past week," Xiao Bin said, his breathing shallow and ragged. "The last I heard, mommy dearest was meeting with the Great Shaman yesterday." The words dripped sarcasm. "To plan Wang Li's demise, I bet."

My head was reeling. Why was he calling the empress "mommy dearest," and how did he know about the meeting with the shaman?

"Ding Māo has warned him," Shén Mì said, "but I was hoping you'd have a chat with the shaman."

Xiao Bin coughed again. "Oh, I did," he managed to say. "He will be providing me with the antidote before he poisons our brother."

At that, I stepped forward and raised my hand to stop them. "I need a clarification," I said, enunciating the words so they wouldn't be misunderstood. "Are you calling the crown prince your brother as in a close male friend or like you share the same blood?"

Master opened his mouth to answer, but I pressed two fingers against his lips to shut him up. "Don't talk! Let your sick brother here answer me. You never seem to tell me the whole truth."

The sick man bounced a glance between the two of us, clearly considering what to say next. "Brother as in we share the same father," he finally said with a little apologetic shrug in Shén Mì's direction.

I was quiet for a while, digesting the information and making sure I had heard it correctly. Then I spoke. "You're telling me that you are both imperial princes?"

My master lowered his eyes, and I took that for a yes. Holy fuck! I was working for one of the emperor's sons. You'd think he would have mentioned that small detail.

"But technically Wang Li is not the crown prince," Xiao Bin interjected. "Privately, the emperor might have chosen Wang Li as his heir, but he has yet to formally pick one."

I glared at my master. "So *you* could be named crown prince." If it sounded like an accusation, that was because it was.

Shén Mì had the nerve to laugh. "My father would never pick me," he said, throwing a glance at his brother as if asking for support. "I'm the black sheep of the family."

Xiao Bin rushed to confirm it, nodding with enthusiasm. "He really is," he coughed out. "Ever since he decided to live outside the palace and having gained the reputation for being a—" He stopped himself, but I knew exactly what he was about to say.

"A cut-sleeve?" I finished it for him. "Why would that matter?" Homosexuality was not much of a taboo in the kingdom.

Master cocked his head and lifted a single eyebrow. "You're kidding me, right?" he exclaimed. "Heirs. An emperor needs heirs."

I wrinkled my nose and matched the movement of his head. "But Xiao Bin just told me you like women. Why not just tell your father the truth?"

Was it my imagination, or was his face turning crimson red? His head looked like a candied hawthorn berry sticking up from his shoulders. "I feed the doubt about my sexual preferences to keep me out of the political web. No one worries about a prince who is a dandy and a *duan xiu*."

I had to give it to him—that was a smart move. It kept him out of the running for the crown and thus under the line of sight of those who would do anything to climb to the top. Not to mention, he could move around freely without raising suspicions. My respect for my master went up a few notches.

"If you mention this conversation to anyone at all, I will pull out your wings and pin them to my study wall."

And then it went back down again.

The million questions buzzing around inside my head like irritating bugs were making me dizzy. As we walked back home hidden under the darkness of the night, I had to bite my tongue a few times so I wouldn't ask them.

We were almost back to the house when my curiosity got the best of me, and words slipped out. "So this whole I-only-care-about-clothes-and-beautiful-fans routine is all a cover?"

Shén Mì had been quiet the whole way here, a mere shadow beside me—a very solid, warm shadow. As if I needed something else to confuse me about my master, his presence next to me radiated heat. It made me itchy and restless, yearning for something I couldn't quite identify.

He threw me a glance without slowing his pace. "Yes." It was more of a grunt than a word.

So this is how he wanted to play it. Why was it so hard to get anything out of him other than barked orders?

"Can you for once just be honest?" I asked. It wasn't as if he had been lying to me, but he also hadn't been forthcoming with the truth. Why had he hidden the fact that he was royalty? A freaking imperial prince, for gods' sake! You'd think that would be something he would have mentioned.

"I don't like talking about myself," he answered as we crossed from city streets into the rural road that would take us home.

I crossed my arms. "Fine! I will just ask Ding Mão, then," I said. "He'll tell me."

There was no ruse behind my words, but somehow they managed to do what all my questions hadn't: Master stopped abruptly and stared at me for a moment before saying, "All right, I will tell you."

Interesting that the mention of his friend was the catalyst for his change of mind. I filed the information away for the future.

"I left the palace as a teen," he started, resuming his walk down the road. "It was unheard of for an imperial prince to do so, but I wanted my freedom. I also wanted to protect my oldest brother, who was by far the most capable of all my siblings and in line for the crown. Ding Mão was telling me about one of his many travels to a faraway kingdom that was in trouble because their only heir to the crown was *duan xiu* and refused to impregnate his wife."

I had a vague memory of that. My time inside the cage didn't have many silver linings, but I did hear a lot of stories I would have otherwise missed.

"The kingdom descended into chaos as many noble families began plotting to take over the throne," he continued. "Eventually the emperor had no choice but to name one of his own siblings as the crown prince to bring it all to a stop. That way he confined the political plotting to only one family instead of the whole court." He turned his face to me. "So I thought that if I pretended to lean toward other males, I would be left alone and free to protect my brother."

I scratched my head. "But both your sister and Xiao Bin live outside of the palace as well," I said. "Why do you have to sneak into their homes when they are your own family?"

The gates of our compound appeared in the distance as we went around a bend. Shén Mì said, "They moved out after I did, and I don't visit them openly because we all are keeping up the illusion that we are not on good terms. That way we can all work together without much suspicion."

My respect for my master went up again a bit.

"As the only girl in the family, isn't Su Lin expected to marry someone important for the empire?"

He chuckled. "She did. Su Lin has my father wrapped around her little finger, but she did marry an important man of the court," he explained. "It was a marriage for love, though. My father would do a lot of questionable things for the sake of the empire and the people, but he would never use his only daughter as a political pawn. Life is unpredictable, and my brother-in-law died unexpectantly a few years ago, leaving everything he owned to my sister. Including all his connections as a man who was loyal to the emperor but unwilling to live by society's rules."

There was such love in his tone, I had to once again adjust my opinion of his character. This dandy—however fake—was a lot more complex and multilayered than I had at first thought.

"Wait! How do you know Su Lin is my sister?" he exclaimed suddenly, his eyebrows rising into perfect dark arches. "In fact, how do you know about her at all?"

I lowered my gaze, sure that my answer would anger him. "Ding Māo told me about her," I breathed, hoping he wouldn't hear it.

Shén Mì said nothing. But I could feel heat seething under the surface, the anger percolating inside him like lava in a volcano.

"In his defense, I wrung the information out of him," I interjected, feeling a little guilty about it.

"Ding Māo needs to have his feline mouth sewed shut," he grumbled, signaling the guards to open the gates.

The two men didn't ask any questions, rushing to open the massive doors and let us in. If they wondered where we were coming from dressed like assassins, they didn't ask, each uttering a low *wǎn'ān* as we passed.

"Good night," my master called back, striding down the lit path toward the main house. As we approached his room, he stopped and stared at me. "Are you planning on sleeping with me?" he asked.

I blinked.

What does he mean?

The master waited a few seconds and then he pointed at his door and said, "*My* room?"

Holy shit! I followed him all the way to his bedroom.

A fire erupted inside me, running wild up to my cheeks but not remaining there. A pool of molten rock seemed to have settled low in my belly, something that made me blush even more fiercely.

"No, of course not," I stammered like an idiot. "I was just walking you back, *shīfu*."

When he didn't say anything, I pivoted on the balls of my feet and almost sprinted across the courtyard toward the safe haven of my bedroom, but as I went up the two steps, I paused and changed my mind.

I won't be able to sleep now.

I decided to head to the baths and dunk myself in cold water instead.

There was a wildfire inside me that needed to be extinguished.

CHAPTER TEN

Crisis

SHÉN MÌ

I LEFT THE ROOM almost as soon as I walked in. As late as it was, I didn't want to bother any of the servants to prepare me a bath, so I'd just use the natural pool. I couldn't wait for the morning, the need for a shockingly cold bath too compelling to deter me from the middle-of-the-night excursion. I didn't know why I always felt so out of sorts—hot and unsettled—every time I was around the butterfly fairy. What was it about her that left me so—no, I wouldn't dwell on it even if there were areas of my body that refused to behave when in her presence.

She's a beautiful woman. There's no harm in reacting to her this way.

Except I couldn't accept that truth. I had been alone by choice for many a year, and never in all that time had I felt as alive as when I was with her. Hú Dié was my employee, one of my spies, and it was ridiculous to have any other more personal feelings toward her.

The moon was almost full, bathing the small pond with its light, the water a dark mirror reflecting the starry skies. Years ago, when I'd first decided to move out of the palace, I wanted a secluded place in the country as far as possible from the city but close enough to reach it quickly if needed. I had searched high and low for months, but every house I found was either too decrepit or too grand, nothing in between. Until I found this place and this pond. It was love at first sight. The house itself, not too big, not too small, was hidden in a bamboo forest and protected by mountains on two sides, perfect for my needs. The two natural pools in the back of the house—one hot, the other cold—nestled at the bottom of two hills and hidden from prying eyes by a line of fruit trees was just what I needed for those moments when every muscle in my body was as tense and achy as tonight.

I discarded my clothes along the rock path, neglecting to pick them up, only one thing on my mind: the cold, soothing waters of my pond. By the time I reached the edge of the water, I was wearing only my skin. As I waded into the pool, I threw a glance at my arms, my ivory skin glistening under the light of the moon. At times like this, I was reminded of who I really was.

A prince of the high court.

One who was disgraced by choice and working for his brother and imperial father under the mask of a man who cared nothing about politics or power but everything about the shallower side of life. There were times when it irked me to be thought of as a superficial, vain creature who collected valuable silk fans and was rumored to favor certain male courtesans. Then I reminded myself of why I did all I did, and the feeling was gone. It didn't matter what others thought. I knew the what and the why, and that was all it mattered.

There was much that others didn't know about me, and that served me perfectly. My deepest secrets were my best weapon, one I might have to use someday, but that could lie underneath the guise of self-indulgence and vanity for now.

A shiver ran up my spine as the icy cold water lapped at my ankles, my calves, and my hips before I took a deep breath to dive in the liquid night. Even with my eyes open, there was nothing to see under the water, just pure darkness. I stayed below the surface for a while, enjoying the pressure on my eardrums and the fluid caress of the waters against my skin. In that silence, all my problems disappeared and only peace remained.

When my lungs began to burn, I kicked off from the bottom of the pond and propelled myself upwards, breaking the surface only seconds later. Despite the chilly temperature of the night, I felt warm and renewed.

"What are you doing in my bath?"

The female voice snatched me from my reverie. Startled, I turned around to face none other than the butterfly. "*Your* bath?"

"I'm here, am I not?" she asked, pointing at herself. A very naked self, I noticed with a gulp. "I was here first, so get out."

Try as I might to focus on my irritation about having someone intrude on my privacy, I couldn't quite shake the idea that a beautiful woman was in my pond, naked and glittering under the moonlight.

What is wrong with me?

"Well?" the butterfly demanded, her arms crossed just underneath the surface of the water. "Are you leaving or what?"

The heat pooling low in my body finally made its way to my brain, and I snapped back, "This is my house. My pond. *You* get out."

I regretted it mere seconds later when the infuriating fairy huffed, turned her back on me, and waded her way to the shallow side of the pond. Not a stitch on!

"Cover yourself, woman," I yelled out, unable to take my eyes off her smooth skin, her graceful backside tapering down to a waist that begged to be held right before it flared into soft, rounded mounds of flesh and bone.

That was yet another mistake.

Piqued by my words, she turned around to face me, and I froze. This grown, jaded man couldn't move if his life depended on it.

Hú Dié was a work of art.

Her body reflected nothing of her prickly personality. She was all softness and gentle curves. As full of beauty as she was lacking in modesty. She stood there under the moonlight, a perfect vision I couldn't take my eyes from.

"If you don't want to see, just close your fucking eyes," she barked out, eyes shooting fire. "You're complaining, but you haven't looked away once. You must like what you're seeing."

She was right. I did like what I saw. A little too much for comfort as the pressure and heat in my lower body increased with every second. I wouldn't be leaving the pond any time soon. Not with her there, witnessing my obvious arousal.

Forcing myself to look away, I focused on the gentle ripple of the waters around me. "Sorry, didn't mean to gawk," I told her, embarrassment mingling with lust. "You took me by surprise. I wasn't expecting anyone to be here this time of night."

My apology must have mollified her because for a moment, there was only silence. Then I heard the subtle sound of movement, the lapping of water against the bank, and then the telltale splash of someone jumping out of the pool.

"I'll leave now," she said, the rustling of cloth telling me she was getting dressed. "But not because you told me to."

Despite my irritation and frustration, my lips curved into a smile. When and why had she become so competitive about everything?

This time I was willing to let her win. Gods knew she had won over my senses. What I was beginning to fear the most was her winning over my heart.

The word came before the rooster's morning call. Still dazed from a restless night's sleep, I dragged myself out of bed to open the doors to a panic-stricken Ding Mão, which in itself was cause for alarm. My childhood friend and best spy never allowed himself to display any emotions he deemed a sign of weakness.

"What the hell happened?" I asked, slipping my arms through the sleeves of my overcoat. I sat on the edge of the bed, reaching for a glass of water.

He followed me across the room from the door after closing it behind him. "Your brother has fallen ill," he said even before sitting down on the chair he had pulled closer to me.

My heart skipped a beat.

"It looks like what we feared: poison. He needs the antidote now."

The way his face had gone pale and strained left me with the certainty that my brother was very sick indeed. I had just talked to Xiao Bin and doubted if he had the time to get a hold of the antidote since then.

I jumped to my feet and peeled off my nightclothes as fast as I could before I began putting on the black disguise I had just taken off a few hours before. The clothes needed a wash, but I didn't care. My brother's life was at stake.

"Xiao Bin was going to acquire the antidote," I explained as I layered the black clothing over my body. "Not sure he was able to do it yet."

"You'll never make it on time."

The voice came from the door that had been closed just a few seconds before. Hú Dié stood in the frame, her long black hair spilling over her shoulders, still tousled by sleep, and wearing a simple white shift.

Ding Mão and I froze for a moment, staring at her in surprise.

"By the time you distract the guards, your brother could be dead."

She was right. It would take me at least a half hour to run to his house, then another half hour or more until I'd be able to distract the guards and go in. But I had to try.

"What are you doing here?" Ding Mão asked, running his fingers through his unusually messy hair. "It's not even five yet."

"I don't sleep much," she said, stepping into the room. "My butterfly hearing couldn't miss you."

I didn't have time to waste, so I waved her away. "Go back to bed. We have things to do."

Bracing her hands on her hips, she glowered. "Cheng Shén Mì!" Her tone was that of a mother who had just been disrespected by her children. "You might be my master, but you can't tell me what to do," she growled. "You need my help, so stop being dismissive and let me do it."

It finally dawned on me what she was trying to say. Hú Dié was right; as a butterfly she could be at Xiao Bin's house in mere minutes and go totally undetected by the guards and house staff. Why had I not thought of that? Was my brain still so muddled by visions of her naked body that I couldn't think straight?

"That's a great idea," I said, the words tasting bitter in my tongue. "Are you willing to do it?"

She snorted. "Why else would I be here this time of morning?" she replied, her arms still tightly knotted across her chest. "To bask in your male beauty?"

A mixture of annoyance and embarrassment flooded my face in the form of heat, and I thanked the semidarkness of my room for hiding it.

"All right, go now." She had been there with me before, so she knew who to look for and what to do. "Tell my brother there's no time to waste."

Hú Dié turned around to leave, but Ding Mão stopped her. "Wait, Beauty!"

She half turned to look at him, eyebrows raised.

"Be careful, you hear? Stay far from the guards. Your iridescent wings are a little too noticeable at night."

She smiled, one corner of her lips lifting up in amusement. "Aw, you're worried about me, Mão Mão," she said, her head cocked to the side. "I'm touched."

And she rushed off, leaving a void in my room. In my mind.

I should have been the one telling her to be careful.

Where did that thought come from? What did it matter if she didn't think I cared about her safety? And why did the room feel so empty now?

"You look forlorn." Ding Mão's panicky look had been replaced by an all-knowing smirk. "She just left, and you miss her already?"

I groaned under my breath. "Stop being ridiculous. She's my spy, so of course I'll be worried about her."

He had the nerve to snort. "Right, and I will grow wings and fly." The mirth dancing in his green eyes was more feline than human. "Back to business then; what do we do now?"

In the midst of all these unwelcome feelings, I had almost forgotten about the danger the crown prince was in.

What is wrong with me?

"Go check with our palace spies," I ordered. "And send word to my sister. Tell her to meet me at the usual place tomorrow."

Ding Māo nodded and left on silent feet, his inner cat taking over. Left on my own, I stood in the middle of my room, the full import of what was happening finally hitting me. Now that neither my friend nor the butterfly was here, the silence was oppressive, almost suffocating.

My beloved brother was in mortal danger. Why was I worried about the rebellious butterfly instead?

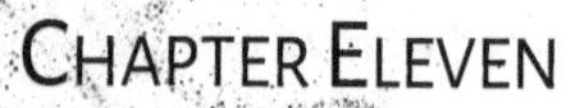

CHAPTER ELEVEN

The Crown Prince

Hú Dié

Xiao Bin did not have the antidote. His man was somewhere between his house and the source for the substance, but he had no way of knowing how close or how far.

"I'll fetch it," I said, the decision coming out of nowhere. Why was I volunteering for something I had not been asked to do? To save a prince I didn't know or cared for? "Where do I go?"

Shén Mì's brother smiled, relief softening his face and relaxing his shoulders. "I'll draw you a map." He grabbed a piece of parchment and unrolled it on the desk. "Mì Mì will be eternally grateful to you."

Master's face popped into my mind, and my lips twitched. Was I happy I could bring him joy? What did I care about how he felt? He was just my master, a provider of much-needed comfort in my life but nothing else. He was arrogant, grumpy, and a sadist who enjoyed torturing me with endless training sessions. So why was I feeling a twinge of satisfaction for doing something that would bring him peace?

"I don't need his gratitude," I lied. To him and myself. "I just don't want to see another tyrant stealing the throne."

Is that an amused little smile on his face?

He quickly drew a map. It was sketchy but clear, the work of someone who was used to doing it often. Once again, I wondered about the three siblings joined together to protect the crown prince, three imperial heirs who did not follow the complicated ways and expectations of the court and had gladly given up on their natural rights as princes to protect their kingdom and their people. As much as I hated to admit it, I admired them. It was refreshing to meet people who danced to the beat of a different drum, an unselfish, non-power-seeking beat. I didn't know such people existed.

"I don't know how my brother, with his sour moods, managed to charm you onto his side of the fight, but I'm grateful he did," Xiao Bin said, his mocking smirk turning into a genuine smile.

I was about to protest when he handed me the finished map carefully rolled into a small cylinder. I shut my mouth and accepted it, slipping the tiny roll inside my sleeve.

"I can't promise anything," I felt the need to say, "but I'll do my best. Where do I bring the antidote?"

"That's the tricky part," he said. "You'll have to bring it straight to the palace. I'll try to be by my brother's side. But not sure they'll let me. Same with my sister. She might not be allowed to be with him." He paused, pensive for a moment.

The possible consequences of trespassing in the imperial palace exploded in my mind, multiplying by thousands. At best I would die if caught. I didn't dare think about the worst. I wouldn't allow anyone to capture and keep me prisoner. I'd sooner kill myself than let it happen again.

"If all else fails, Dr. Ming will be there," Xiao Bin continued. "Just give it to her. Don't trust anyone else."

I nodded, pushing all my fears and doubts into that dark room in my head where I kept everything I preferred not to think about, and without any further goodbyes, I turned into my butterfly form and flew out the open window.

The flight was uneventful. Nobody paid attention to a butterfly, especially at night when even my semiluminescent wings made me more visible than I would like to be. It was what awaited at the end that shocked me.

Haven't I been here before?

The rundown hut, built awkwardly in a crevice on the mountainside, could not be mistaken; this was the same place I had been to when I followed the empress's servant.

I'm getting the antidote from the same person who gave them the poison?

The same grey-haired man opened the door to my now-human form, squinting and wiping sleep from his eyes.

"What do you want?" he barked out with a frown. "It's the middle of the night."

I swallowed the knot in my throat and said, "Prince Xiao Bin requests an antidote." Should I be clearer about what poison I was talking about? How did he know which antidote to give me? The man was a poison expert and a peddler. He must sell dozens of potions every day.

Dismissing my misgivings, he spun on the balls of his feet and went back inside, closing the door behind him.

Is he going to just ignore me?

I waited for a moment while the sound of rustling and dishes clinking and clanking seeped through the flimsy door.

I knocked. "Hey, what's going on?" I yelled, trying to sneak a peek through the wide cracks of the wood.

No answer.

Just as I was about to kick the door in, it opened wide. The man handed me a small crockery pot with no explanation.

I took it from him. "Is this it? For the crown prince, right?" I was still not sure he knew which antidote I was here for.

He groaned. "Of course, you stupid *gūniáng*," he said. "What else could it be?"

Was this bedraggled man a double agent? Or did he just not care as long as he was paid?

I was about to ask him that when he slammed the door in my face. "That was fucking rude," I grumbled under my breath.

There's no time to waste.

The crown prince needed the antidote sooner rather than later. And I wasn't keen on being the one who caused his demise.

I turned back into my butterfly, the antidote in my hand merging seamlessly with my delicate wings, and soared over the ridge, heading to the palace. I would either be a hero or a victim. I was fervently hoping and praying for the former.

I had been to the palace before, but it still surprised me how enormous it was. Ridiculously, unnecessarily huge. What human or immortal could possibly need such a large space to live in? All I ever dreamed of was a room and a kitchen to call my own. A lifetime of captivity does that to one's soul; even a sliver of personal space can make your heart sing.

The palace was spread out over several courtyards, large square or rectangular spaces framed by sumptuous buildings, their red roofs covered with flower-shaped tiles that broke the monotony of the otherwise green-and-white area. From the skies it all looked like a strange, beautiful garden, and yet, I felt no yearning to be inside it. Now that I had been living with one of the imperial heirs and met a couple more, I knew that they were not as free as I'd thought. Those in the palace were kept captive by a deadly political game and its never-ending rules and conventions. I did not envy any of them. They could keep their money and power. I understood now why my master and his two siblings had removed themselves from it—at least as far as they could.

It wasn't hard to identify the crown prince's lodgings. His courtyard was packed with guards and servants who dashed from one building to another, carrying bowls of water, food, and cloth as they all converged into a single building.

I began my descent, my tiny butterfly heart slamming against my chest.

Careful not to go too close to the humans crowding the yard, I circumnavigated the building in search of an entrance. It took two whole rounds to find a back window shutter that was cracked open just enough for me to slip through.

I didn't transform right away. Flying high, close to the boxed ceiling, I surveyed the room for a few moments. Unlike the courtyard, the room was almost empty of people. Two figures lingered by the bed, and it didn't take me long to recognize one of them.

Dr. Ming.

A sigh of relief echoed in my mind. But who was the other person? The man was tall and imposing even with his shoulders slumped and his mature face creased with worry. He wore simple robes and no ornaments on his pinned-up hair, but I recognized the ring he was wearing, a thick green jade circlet that fully encased the lower part of his thumb.

The imperial ring.

Shock made my wings tremble, and I almost dropped to the ground. The emperor was here. If I revealed my human form to him, I could be immediately arrested for trespassing, but on the other hand, I was bringing the one thing that could save his favored son's life. After a moment of hesitation, I spiraled down and shimmered into a human at a respectful distance from the emperor.

"Ah, help has arrived," Dr. Ming exclaimed, her somber face opening into a smile. Ignoring the fact that the emperor seemed to be about to suffer a fainting spell, she stepped next to me and opened her palm. "Where is it? Time is of the essence."

With a stolen glance toward the man who ruled the country, I pulled the small container from my sleeve and handed to her.

"Wh-who's this?" the emperor stuttered, eyes almost bulging out of his skull. "What's she doing here?"

Dr. Ming, graceful as usual, opened the tiny pot, took a sniff, and headed back to the bedside. "This is Hú Dié, your son's savior," she said, fully unaffected by the man's obvious panic. "She works with one of your sons, and she volunteered to go pick up the only antidote that will save Wang Li."

To his credit, the emperor managed to calm himself down quickly, taking a couple deep breaths before setting his incredible golden eyes on me. "In that case, thank you," he said, falling to his knees and bowing deeply. "I will be in your debt forever."

The doctor, who was now sitting next to the sick prince and feeding him whatever was inside the crockery pot, threw a glance at us and chuckled. "Wow, you got our powerful emperor to bow to you," she said, mirth spilling out with her words. "That's quite an accomplishment, child."

I didn't know whether to be flattered or scared, seeing the mighty emperor kowtowing to me the way I should be bowing to *him*. After a moment of hesitation, I rushed forward to coax the man to his feet. "Your Imperial Majesty, please don't." I stumbled on my words, feeling foolish for not knowing what to say.

Dr. Ming chuckled softly again, not bothering to spare us a look.

My attention veered off to the sick prince for the first time. He was extremely pale, lips a sickly blue. He was very different from Shén Mì, though there were enough similarities to identify them as siblings: a straight nose, high cheeks, and thick onyx hair. But where my master's lips were full and perfectly shaped, this prince's were thin and less defined. His dark eyebrows were bushy, unlike Shén Mì's, and a faded scar marred the skin by his right eye.

I was so intently studying the prince, I almost missed the subtle movement of his lips, the flutter of his lashes, and the tiny moan that escaped his mouth.

"He's waking up," I exclaimed, momentarily forgetting the emperor.

"The antidote is doing its work," Dr. Ming said as the emperor sat beside her on the bed, holding his son's hand.

There was tenderness in his touch, in the softness of his golden eyes as he looked at the prince.

And worry!

His lips were stretched thin, and his hands shook as he whispered-called the prince's name. "Wang Li, wake up."

"We must come up with a better plan to protect your son, Your Majesty," the doctor said. "We almost lost him this time."

Surprising even myself, I offered, "Why don't you let everyone think he's dead?"

Both the emperor and the doctor turned to look at me.

"What?" the emperor said. "Are you out of your mind? His relatives and all the greedy members of the court will be killing one another for the chance of being named crown prince or nominating one in his stead."

The doctor raised her hand just as I was starting to regret having said anything. "Let her finish," she said. "I think she might be on to something."

I swallowed the giant knot that had formed in my throat. "If they think he's dead, they won't try to kill him anymore," I explained. "And you can postpone naming a crown prince for as long as you want."

Dr. Ming added, "With the bonus that if your idiot progeny and ministers kill one another off, you'll be left with fewer problems to deal with."

The emperor glowered at the doctor, who just rolled her eyes.

"The prince can hide somewhere safe until you have rooted out all those who would conspire to harm him," I continued, the plan becoming clearer and clearer in my mind.

"Shén Mì would be glad to find a safe haven for his brother," Dr. Ming said.

Is it safe to bring up his outcast son?

Despite my fears, the emperor took the information in and was silent for a moment.

"I know Mì Mì will come up with a brilliant plan. He always does," His Imperial Majesty mused, shocking me. Was he being sarcastic? "But isn't it too risky??"

"Worse than the danger the prince is in right now?" the crane immortal said. "Methinks not."

The emperor thought about it a while longer, his hands over his mouth and eyes never leaving his son's pale face.

I stepped forward. "Can I give him some of my *qi*?" I asked the emperor. "I'm not very powerful, but I've been getting stronger under your son's tutelage." Somehow, I felt I needed to give the outcast prince credit. "I think I'll be all right sharing some with the crown prince."

The emperor glanced at the doctor as if asking for permission. She nodded. When his eyes turned back to me, they were shiny with tears.

"I'd be eternally grateful to you, *gūniáng*," he said, letting go of his son's hand to grasp mine. "Can you?"

To be honest, I wasn't sure I could do it. And if I did, how much could I spare before depleting myself? It was a risk. One I normally wouldn't consider taking, but it felt like the right thing to do.

Wait! When did I start risking my safety for strangers?

Shén Mì's influence was not a good thing if it put me in danger. I couldn't afford to stick my neck out too much. Not until my past was dealt with.

Nevertheless, I nodded and stepped closer to the bed, then kneeled on the edge with my palms starfished over the prince's chest. I took a deep breath, closed my eyes, and focused on channeling all my energy into the connection between our bodies.

A surge of power ran through me from my toes to the roots of my hair before shooting out through my fingers into the man's body. The prince jerked for a second as my *qi* entered his body and then relaxed, a soft shade of pink spreading over his cheeks. I held on to the connection until the man's eyes opened, his deep brown eyes unfocused but full of life.

"It worked!" Dr. Ming exclaimed, touching my shoulder. "Let go now."

I did what I was told, lifting my hands from the prince and taking another deep breath. The room swayed around me when I tried to get to my feet, and I fell to the ground, a boneless mass of human flesh.

The doctor's voice calling my name was the last thing I heard before my world turned pitch-black and silent.

A familiar growling sound woke me up from a dreamless slumber.

He's back already?

Dread filled my stomach. What new torment would he inflict on me today?

Blurred by the dirty glass that encased my cell, the guài *stretched his bulky, hairy arms over his head, letting out another loud growl before leaning over to peek into the amulet.*

"Are you ready to dance for me, beauty?"

His bulbous nose looked even larger so close to the glass. My wings quivered as I squeezed myself against the back of the amulet.

"I need more of your powder," he said, his large hand reaching for the tiny metal lock.

In the time it took to blink, the locket was wide open, freedom staring me in the face, goading me into foolish action.

Foolish because I had tried many times to fly away, but the giant bastard was ridiculously fast for someone his size, and he always managed to catch me before too long. This time was no different. As soon as I flew over his head, he closed a meaty fist around me, almost crushing my wings.

"You never give up, do you?" he said with a laugh. "You're a feisty little thing."

If only I could change into a human, I would be able to bite or kick him, but he had stolen so much of my powder, my energy, that I couldn't do it anymore. The old fox was cautious enough that he wouldn't allow more than a couple days between each harvest so I didn't have time to gather enough qi to turn.

He held my two wings between his index finger and his thumb and shook me. "It's time, little butterfly," he singsang in a mockery of a child's voice. "Show me what you got."

With his free hand, he dragged a widemouthed glass jar over the table so it sat directly below me. Then he started his routine of shaking and squeezing me to forcibly extract my qi. Often if I didn't produce enough to satisfy his greed, he would force me into human form so he could beat me black and blue.

"Not enough, you little bitch," he yelled after a particularly forceful jolt. I knew what was coming next. I closed my eyes, bracing myself for the pinch, the shattering pain that always followed, and the overwhelming sense of helplessness.

My body shuddered, my wings beginning to stretch as my whole self fought against the forced transformation—one that sapped my already depleted store of qi.

Unlike a voluntary metamorphosis, doing it this way was excruciatingly painful, as if someone were yanking my wings from the rest of me. Not having a human voice in butterfly form, my scream started and echoed in my head before escaping my human mouth.

The guài's hand, solid like a rock and ruthless, came down on me in a slap that threw my head backward, my neck cracking with the sudden movement. In my weakened state, I couldn't balance against the assault, and I fell backward and hit my head on the hard floor.

His hand rose again, this time holding a paddle aimed at my body.

"No." The scream escaped my lips as I jerked up to a sitting position, my arms crossed over my head, waiting for the hit.

But it never came.

"You're okay," a familiar voice said. Not the Monster's. "You're safe."

I opened one eye, lowering my arms slowly, then the other, surprised to find my master's face hovering over mine, his hands grasping my shoulders.

"It was a nightmare," he said, pushing me gently down onto the bed. "Just lie down and rest. You need to restore your *qi*."

I did not know what to think. Where was the Monster? Why was Shén Mì here?

Slowly, my memory cleared; flashes of the emperor standing by his son, my hands on the prince's chest, my *qi* flowing like a river from my body to his, and then the darkness.

It was a nightmare, a rogue memory from my past. Nothing else.

I sighed with relief, a sob escaping my lips with a breath. Shén Mì's face was still too close to mine as he bore into my soul with his strange golden eyes.

The eyes of a dragon.

I shook my head, dismissing the fanciful thought and pushing him away from me.

"What happened?" I asked, trying to conceal the heat his glance ignited in me.

Master sat down on the edge of the bed. "After you fainted, Dr. Ming sent for me." Belatedly, I noticed his black clothes. He had snuck into the palace to check on me.

No, it can't be.

He would never risk being caught in the imperial compound just for little old me. Or would he?

"Why did you come here?" I asked.

His brow wrinkled. "Didn't I just tell you?" he snapped. "I came to make sure you're all right."

"But it's dangerous." I wasn't sure why I sounded as if I was complaining. Or was I worried about him instead?

He huffed. "You're my responsibility, aren't you? Why would I abandon you among the enemy?"

Because I'm an outspoken, reckless fairy who's worthless to you.

I pushed the thought aside. For now. "How's your brother?" I asked instead, remembering the color surfacing in the crown prince's cheeks.

"He'll be fine," Shin Mì answered. "Thanks to you."

Relief flooded my whole body, quickly followed by surprise. Why did I care that the prince was alive and well? Something had shifted inside me, and I wasn't too sure I liked it.

"So how are you going to pay me?" I asked to annoy my master. "I mean, I risked my life for the prince, right? I'm not in the charity business."

I couldn't be sure, but I thought he rolled his eyes in a very un-Shén Mì style. He turned his back on me. "Get dressed," he said. "We better get out of here soon, before the palace learns of my brother's demise."

So they took my suggestion seriously.

"A coffin has been brought to Wang Li's room already, and he should be a safe distance from here by now."

I wonder where they will hide him.

But what did I care? I jumped out of bed so quickly, my head swam for a moment.

My master walked to the door, and I followed. "My father has kept the guards away from this side of the palace, but we have to hurry," he said, opening the door and peeking outside. But before he stepped out, he half turned to me and said, "And for the record, I don't believe your I-don't-care attitude anymore. So thank you for saving Wang Li."

My cheeks burned hot. Disdain, I could easily handle. Compliments and kindness? Not so much. "So, how are you going to thank me then?"

He let out an irritated chuckle and turned his back on me. "Well, if you insist on being paid, I might just make you my wife."

And with these stunning words, he ran into the darkness of the night.

CHAPTER TWELVE

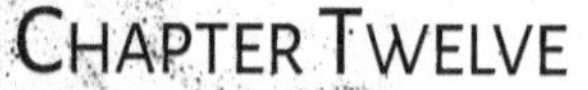

Grateful

SHÉN MÌ

"**Y**OU DID WHAT?" DING Māo's mouth had not closed yet. "You told her you'd marry her?"

I shrugged nonchalantly on the outside while my insides sizzled. "It was a joke."

Was it?

"Good. Because *I* like the butterfly," my friend said, a smirk on his face. "I've never thought of marriage before, but then again, I've never met anyone like Hú Dié before either." He was having fun goading me.

I knew Ding Māo was egging me on, checking for my reaction. Yet, I totally took the bait. "You're not marrying her," I said, a bit louder than I'd planned, my simmering innards flaring up again.

My friend stared at me, a question in his eyes.

"She's my disciple, my protégé."

"And? Does that mean you own her or something?"

"You know how you are with women, Māo Māo," I said, trying not to dwell on the rising anger in my chest. "For you, she would be just a plaything until you were bored. I can't allow that to happen to Hú Dié."

I knew he would ask me why not. And I didn't have an answer. They were both adults and could do whatever they pleased. Who was I to play her protector? Did she even need one?

I deflected. "Let's focus on what's important," I said, shuffling papers on the desk for the sake of keeping my hands busy. "Is everything ready for my brother?"

Ding Māo nodded. "He should be getting here any minute. His lodgings are ready, and I have ordered a few of our men to keep guard."

"Discreetly, right?" I asked. "We don't want any locals or spies to start wondering why the imperial *duan xiu* needs extra guards outside his gates."

My friend nodded again, and my shoulders relaxed just a bit.

"Has the diversion been set in place?" I continued.

A plan had been devised to keep everyone's attention away from my compound to allow Wang Li to enter undetected. After all, news of his death had been grossly manufactured. He was to shelter here until such time as it was safe for his return.

"My men are raising hell in town as we speak," Ding Māo said, balancing one of my brushes on his fingertip. "No one will be paying any attention to us for the next couple hours."

Yushu stopped at the open door and bowed. "Shén *qīnwáng*, the guests have arrived," she announced.

I frowned at her. "How many times do I have to tell you not to call me that?" I chided gently. "Here, I am simply *shīfu*, nothing else." Being constantly reminded of my status grated on me. I knew I could never be just a simple man with no ties to royalty, but damned if I wouldn't pretend while in my own house.

Ding Māo was the first out the door, but I wasn't far behind. Out in the main courtyard, a small procession was slowly and methodically being dismantled as the stablemen unhitched the horse from the small carriage, and my brother's most faithful servant and confidant, Gu Ming, helped my brother step down.

"Welcome to my humble home, *gē*," I said as I approached.

Wang Li smiled, and my heart clenched. He looked haggard—thin and pale with dark circles under his eyes. I had inherited my father's golden eyes, but Wang Li had the ever-changing hazel irises of my late mother. The poison had erased the brightness from his gaze.

I'll make them pay.

"Mì Mì, you're looking elegant as usual," he said, a mere fraction of the usual lightness in his tone. "Nice place you have here, *gē*."

Gu Ming continued to support him, a hand under his elbow and the other protectively on his shoulder.

I hurried to his side, replacing his servant to guide him to his lodgings. "I trust it wasn't a rough ride here," I said, my voice strangled by emotion. My brother was one of the strongest men in the empire. To see him reduced to this weakened state made my heart bleed.

"The smoothest ride ever," he lied with a chuckle. "Did you have your spies soften the dirt road for me?"

Ding Māo, who was uncharacteristically quiet, walked beside us, worry creasing his forehead.

"I did tell Māo Māo to clear your path with his magic," I joked, throwing my friend a smile.

"And where is my savior?" Wang Li asked as we crossed the threshold to his rooms. "I understand a butterfly fairy was the one who brought me the antidote. I want to meet her."

Hú Dié had made herself scarce for the past couple days, almost as if she was avoiding me. I didn't understand why, since I couldn't be more grateful for what she had done. I had sent Yushu to the market to buy her thank-you gifts, but I was yet to find out whether she liked them.

"I'll send for her," I said, nodding toward the girl servant. "Yushu, go fetch her, please."

The young woman wasted no time. With a quick bow, she turned and raced across the courtyard.

Once my brother was settled in his bed, the white linens matching his pallor, we all melted into chairs while Gu Ming poured everyone the tea Yushu had brewed beforehand.

"Don't look so worried, Shén Mì," my brother said. "I feel a lot stronger. I'll be back to my old self in no time."

Gods, I hoped so. He looked so frail, so unlike him.

"But tell me, *gē*, where did you find this gem of a fairy, and how did you convince her to work for you?"

I opened my mouth in vain.

"He didn't *find* me—he tripped over me by accident." Hú Dié stood just inside the room, the light from outside creating an odd halo around her and giving her an otherworldly appearance. "And it wasn't him who convinced me to stay but the promise of a soft bed and good food."

The butterfly fairy looked like an enraged warrior with her arms tightly crossed over her chest and a scowl on her face.

"My savior," my brother exclaimed, sitting straighter on the bed. "I want to thank you for what you did."

She didn't move, her glance bouncing from me to my brother. *Will she ever trust me?*

"Come closer," I urged as gently as my annoyance would allow me. "We won't pluck your wings, I promise."

It was an attempt at a joke, but the sudden wince on her face told me I had hit a nerve. I wondered at her past once again. What had she been through that had made her the way she was, suspicious and angry? Not at all the usual temperance of a butterfly personality.

After a moment of hesitation, she did come forward at my brother's silent request. "I only did what any decent creature would do."

Not true. She had risked her own life to give my brother a boost of much-needed life energy.

"Come and sit here," Wang Li insisted, patting the space next to him.

Surprisingly enough, the butterfly complied, her arms finally relaxing along her sides. Once she sat down on the edge of the bed, my brother reached out for her hands. She gasped but didn't back away.

"You're my hero, Hú Dié, and I will be in your debt for the rest of my life. Ask, and it will be yours."

Hú Dié's eyes opened wider, and a tiny smile twitched the corner of her lips.

My brother looked at me. "I don't know how you got so lucky to have such a spy in your ranks, but I couldn't be happier, *gē*."

Ding Māo chose that time to open his mouth and, to my utter mortification, interject. "You don't know half the story, Your Highness. He is also hoping to make her his wife."

The flames shooting from Hú Dié's eyes made me fear for my life, but if there was someone dying soon, it would definitely be my *former* best friend, Ding Māo.

"Gear up, we're on a mission tonight."

Hú Dié looked at me as if I were mad. "With your brother in residence? Aren't all your enemies lulled by the fact that his funeral is taking place in a few days?"

My father had meticulously planned a grand funeral ceremony as it was due to the crown prince. The casket would be sealed under the guise of possible contamination. He would, as the emperor, be giving a speech explaining how, due to his grieving, he would postpone the naming of the next heir to the throne for the usual mourning period of three years. Plenty of time for my brother and a whole lot of the ministers to either ingratiate themselves with my father or kill one another—maybe both.

"Just because they think he's dead, it doesn't mean our job is over," I said, flipping my white fan open in front of me. The air was hot and humid, turning my skin into a sticky surface that not even the breeze of the courtyard could alleviate. "I got word that Xian Lu is leaving the city tonight. He must be up to something. We must follow him, and I might need your special magic."

The corner of her mouth quirked up. "Who the hell is Xian Lu?"

Is she messing with me?

"Did you live under a rock for the past few years?" I snapped back and immediately regretted it when she winced as if I had physically slapped her. "He's the empress's only son and the one she wants to inherit the crown."

Whatever pain I had caused her with my comment was gone—or hidden away—almost instantly. "I was never in the habit of concerning myself with the lives of the rich and powerful. I've been too busy surviving."

And picking fights, I could have added. But I let it go. I hadn't imagined the pain that had clouded her eyes and paled her skin just a moment ago. No need to stir it up again.

"If he's leaving court right before my brother's funeral, it must be something important," I told her. "It would be in his interest to butter up my father in this time of grief. The fact that he's missing that opportunity tells me he's up to something big."

She eyed the steamed buns on the plate with longing before turning her face back to me. "Do I have time to eat?" she asked.

I almost laughed. Not for the first time, I wondered what kind of hardships Hú Dié had experienced in the past for her to stare at food that way.

"We leave in an hour," I said even though I wanted to be on the road as soon as possible. Who was I to refuse my brother's savior the time to do her favorite thing? I turned to the door. "Be ready by the back wall."

I left without looking back, but I could feel her pissed-off glare on my back and the typical rolling of her eyes as I walked away.

Damned fairy! Why does she make me feel so guilty?

An hour later I found her by the back wall, dressed in black gear from head to toe and with a large *bao* in her hand. She looked at me and then at the bun. "For the road," she explained, hiding the food inside her tunic. "You never know when you'll get hungry."

I chuckled quietly, hiding my smile with the black scarf bunched around my neck. The butterfly fairy was something else; she made me fume one minute and then laugh the next.

We went over the wall—our usual secret exit—and into the darkness of the bamboo forest that surrounded the compound. I was surprised she hadn't asked me where we were going, and I was reluctant to tell her. Not because I didn't trust her, but because in a petty corner of my mind, I enjoyed knowing I was privy to something she wasn't. Hú Dié had insinuated herself into my thoughts, my dreams, and—I hated to admit—my heart. This soft spot I had for her weakened me, made me vulnerable. I didn't like it a bit. I had spent the last ten years or so of my life building an impenetrable wall around me beneath an air of shallowness and vanity. The fucking butterfly had put a huge dent in my armor. So what if I liked withholding something from her?

"So where are we going?"

I sighed. Her silence was too good to be true. "Trust me," I said, not bothering to look at her. Our dark-clad bodies moved smoothly and quietly through a forest of shadows under the full moon's glow. For any onlooker we were practically invisible.

"I don't know what that is," she said, making me stop suddenly. She came to a stop mere inches from me. "What? I don't trust any-one—yes, not even you, Master. I have no reason to do so."

Despite myself I felt slighted by her words. "What do you mean? Have I given you any reasons to mistrust me?" I asked. "Have I mis-treated you? Lied to you?"

She shook her head, her eyes the only visible part of her face. "Not yet."

It struck me then. The fairy must have been wronged before. Many times.

But I will never hurt you, I promise.

Now, where did that thought come from?

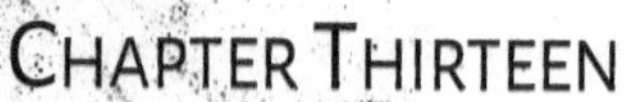

CHAPTER THIRTEEN

The Trap

Hú Dié

NOT KNOWING WHERE WE were heading set me on edge. The unknown had not served me in the past.

"Are you ever going to tell me where we're going?" I asked Shén Mì, who hadn't slowed down for the past hour as we dashed through the forest, the moon our only light. Thankfully, being a butterfly also provided me with better-than-human eyesight, or I would have crashed into a bamboo trunk a long time ago. I couldn't figure out how *shīfu* navigated through the darkness as easily as he did.

"Following my brother's track," he answered, veering sharply to the right to avoid a tree.

I'd be better in my butterfly form, but he had insisted I follow him on foot. A new way to torture me, I guessed.

"But how can you track him in the dark?" I asked, more confused than ever. We couldn't see anything.

He did stop then. He turned around, dug inside his tunic for a moment, and removed a small shiny object.

"A ball? How does that help?"

He stepped closer to me and handed me the iridescent sphere. As soon as I touched it, I felt it pulsing in my hand and almost dropped it.

"It's a tracker," he said.

I cocked my head to the side, and he explained, "An object imbued with magic that can track people."

Something that wondrous exists?

"Where did you get it?"

He snorted. "Haven't you noticed by now that I have an extensive network of contacts across the empire?"

Asshole!

"I acquired it a few years ago after a particularly difficult mission up north. I picked up a couple of other interesting magical artifacts as well."

"How does it work?" I couldn't help asking as I rolled the pulsing orb in my hand. Subtle colors of blue and orange covered its surface, fading only to reappear a few seconds later.

"The rhythm and tempo of the pulsing, plus the combination of colors, tell me which direction to go," he explained, a note of awe in his voice. "I just have to follow it."

I knitted my brows. "But you had it hidden inside your clothes."

"I can feel the vibration better that way," he said. "Once I feel its pulse, I pull it out and check the color combination."

As much as I hated to admit it, I was in awe. I had heard of a lot of magical artifacts, but never one like this one. I wondered how my master had got a hold of such a device. I opened my mouth to ask, but he swiped the globe from my hands, turned around, and took off running, not waiting for me to follow him.

"Wait for me," I yelled, running after the blur of his body moving between the trees. How could a mere mortal run so fast in the dark?

We must have run for over an hour before we finally exited the forest into a wide clearing. Without the cover of the trees, the moon's glow was stronger, bathing the world in its creamy, soft reflection. I wanted to stop for a moment and drink in the light to regenerate my *qi*, but Master had other ideas—he dashed across the clearing as if his life depended on it.

"Can we take a minute?" I yelled after him, but he didn't stop. Irritation swelled in my chest. My leg muscles were on fire, and my stomach cramped and growled from the lack of food.

I'll show him.

As fast as my body would allow, I morphed into my butterfly form and flew unnoticed over Shén Mì's head to alight a few yards ahead of him in my human form. That's when he saw me, and I couldn't have misread the expression of panic in his face as he screamed at me to stop.

My bewilderment only lasted a moment, for as my feet touched what I thought was solid ground, it gave up beneath me and swallowed me whole. It happened so fast, I didn't even have time to switch back into a butterfly—I dropped for what felt like a long time but was most likely only a few seconds. I hit the ground so hard, a cloud of dirt erupted around me, blurring my sight for a minute. I checked my body for injuries, but other than soreness, nothing seemed broken or twisted. I exhaled loudly, taking care not to breathe in the dirt. All I had to do was wait for the solid, dirty fog to clear, and I would fly out of this hole.

A few minutes went by before I was able to see anything around me. As the air became clearer, I realized I had been lucky, it seemed.

All around me there were wooden spikes sharpened to lethal lance-like points. For once, being small had worked in my favor as I fell between spikes and avoided becoming a human kebab.

A groan told me that someone else hadn't been so lucky. Master was lying not far from me, a spike through one shoulder.

"Fucking gods!" I yelled out unhelpfully, making my way to him between the spikes. "Why did you fall in?" He had been at a good distance from me when the trap had given in beneath me, so how had he ended up in the hole beside me?

"I was trying to catch you, fool," he barked at me, eyes glittering in a mixture of anger and pain. "You can't help yourself, can you?"

Not sure what he meant—it's not like I was in trouble all the time, was it?—I knelt carefully beside him, wedging myself between his body and the next spit to examine his wound. He winced when I touched it gently.

"That thing has to come out," I said. "It's going to hurt." No sense in hiding it.

"Do it."

Despite his determination, I hesitated. He did not seem too strong, more delicate than brawny.

He gave me a side glare. "What are you waiting for? Break it."

I repositioned myself and studied the bottom part of the wooden shaft. I'd have to break it close to the ground so I could then pull it from his shoulder.

"Can you hold it steady with your other hand?" I asked him.

He nodded, turning his body slightly in order to wrap his free hand around the spike directly below his underarm. I shuffled backwards as much as I could, holding the spit behind me with both hands. I took a deep breath and then kicked the offending spear as hard as I could.

The scream my master released could have awoken the dead, but the spike was now broken in two. I closed the space between us, and before he could recover from the shock, I held his shoulder tightly and pulled the sharpened point out. My ears would tingle for hours, I was sure.

I threw the bloody wood as far away from us as I could and leaned against the spike behind me again, waiting for Shén Mì to get himself together. He wasn't screaming anymore, but his breathing was ragged, and I thought he might pass out. Blood was gushing from the wound, but surprisingly not in the amount I would have expected for such an injury. It seemed as if the spike had not hit any major artery.

"Let me look at the wound," I told him once his breathing had quieted down. "I can't stitch it, but I can apply some of my powder to protect it and start the healing."

He looked up at me. His face was even paler than usual, his lips bluish and sweat covering his forehead. "Powder?"

After the life I'd had, I would never share this secret with anyone. But he was suffering and, despite his obvious enjoyment at putting me through hours of hellish training daily, he'd been good to me. Very good.

"It's a little-known secret," I admitted, scooting closer to him. "Butterfly powder is a natural anesthetic and antiseptic. It also speeds up healing."

He tilted his head, eyes searching mine. "Anything else you haven't told me about your powers?" he asked.

I avoided his eyes but still felt obligated to share one more piece of information.

"Well, it is also sought after as a powerful aphrodisiac." His look of horror made me add, "Not that you need that right now."

It would be nice if I could shut up once in a while.

Whoever had set up this trap wanted to make sure the animal was dead before they retrieved it. The wound on Shén Mì's shoulder was angry, with its long-reaching black branches snaking out in every direction.

Poison!

"Don't mean to spook you, but if we don't take care of this, you'll be dead in minutes," I told a very cranky man.

The top of his *changshan* gathered around his waist like a deflated balloon as he sat beside me, his arms tightly wrapped across his bare chest, he looked as pissed off as a trapped pallas cat.

"You are not sprinkling me with an aphrodisiac," he barked, pouting like a small boy.

Gods give me patience.

"It has a minimal effect when used to fight infection or the effects of poison," I explained, trying to restrain myself from doing what I really wanted to do at that moment: slap the crap out of him. "For it to work as an aphrodisiac, you have to ingest or sniff it."

The big baby didn't budge, his eyes turned away from me. "How do I know you're not lying?" he said.

I sighed in frustration. "For gods' sake, *shīfu*. Why would I want to give you an aphrodisiac? I have no wish to mate with such a...." My voice trailed off as I pointed at him, looking for words to describe him. "With such a vain, pretty man." It was the least offensive thing I could think of as anger bubbled inside me.

His head snapped around, golden eyes shooting daggers at me. "Vain? Pretty?"

His arms fell beside his body, and I had a first good look at him as the light of the moon flooded the hole we had fallen into.

He did not have the body of a spoiled, sheltered, vain male. He had the body of a warrior.

Something hot stirred in my belly. Yes, he was definitely beautiful, but not in a weakling kind of way like I had thought. Instead, his chest and arms were shaped by lean, subtle muscle that spoke of hard physical training rather than trips to the beauty parlor. That was no perfect skin covering the aforementioned muscles, but a surface marred by many scars and old bruises.

I had him all wrong.

I think my jaw dropped, and I must have stared at him for too long, because he shook me. "Did you go to sleep or something?"

I sighed, shook my head, and returned to our reality. His shoulder needed mending, and no matter how gorgeous the man was, he would be a very dead pretty man if I didn't take care of his wound soon.

"Try not to inhale any of the powder," I warned before releasing a heavy dusting of my butterfly powder.

He gasped and belatedly covered his mouth and nose with a hand as the small cloud of dust floated toward and around him before settling on his injury.

"Let it do its magic," I told him, spreading the iridescent dust over the open wound.

He winced, and I leaned closer to blow on his skin. The powder could sometimes sting. When I moved back, our faces were so close, I could have touched him with my lips. His eyes shone like gold and wouldn't release mine. Except when his gaze moved to my mouth. His tongue flickered over his full lips, his cheeks flushed, and I knew.

He inhaled some of the powder.

"Damn you, *shīfu*," I exclaimed, making as much room between us as the cramped space allowed. "You inhaled it, didn't you? Now we have another problem on our hands."

Despite the blood that still flowed down his chest, he scooted closer yet. I could always turn into my butterfly and leave him here until the effects from the aphrodisiac ran cold. But he was severely wounded, and one wrong move with his arm was all it would take for the wound to open further and make him bleed to death. I was a lot of things, but I wasn't ungrateful, and to leave him in this hole alone would be despicable.

Even if his eyes are undressing me as we speak.

Truth was, he was rather cute with his cheeks the color of peaches on a summer afternoon and his golden eyes so bright and shiny, they looked like tiny suns.

What is wrong with me?

"Control yourself." I couldn't be sure I was talking solely to Shén Mì as a slow burning fire erupted in my belly.

He, of course, paid me no heed, and, in an impressive move that belied his still-fresh injury, he grabbed my shoulders, pulled me to him, and kissed me.

I couldn't move at first in a mixture of shock and surprise, but then I began enjoying the pressure of his warm lips on mine a little too much. The insistence of his kiss as he gently but decisively pried my lips open and stroked me with his tongue sent bolts of energy through my body. One moment I wanted to slap him, and the next all I wanted was to melt into his arms and let him do with me whatever his altered, overstimulated libido wanted. Memories of when he told me he'd make me his wife came flooding in. Had he been serious then? Could it be that he really had feelings for me?

No! This is not him. It's my powder.

With a groan of frustration, I flattened my two hands against his bare chest and pushed him away. "Stop. This is not right."

His grin turned into a grimace of pain when I accidentally pressed on his wound. He yelped and let go of me. When his gaze returned to me, there was no hunger in his eyes anymore. Pain must have broken the spell.

"Gods, I'm sorry," he rushed to say, the creases on his forehead mirroring the pained look in his eyes. "I shouldn't have.... I don't know what came over me.... I'd never—"

With a thundering heart playing havoc inside me, I shook my head. "It wasn't your fault," I assured him, a tinge of regret escaping along with the words. "It was the powder."

He waved a hand. "No, even then I should have been in control," he said. "There's no excuse for my behavior. No excuse at all."

Shén Mì might be willing to take all the blame for that moment of brief and uncontrollable madness between us, but I knew deep inside that I had been a willing participant, eager even. Not that I would ever tell him that, but I had to admit it to myself; what I had felt when our mouths were connected and our hearts beat in unison had nothing to do with the fever induced by my butterfly powder.

As much as I hated to admit it, it went much deeper than that.

The question now was, what about him? Had the passion in that kiss been completely caused by the aphrodisiac, or was he—just like I was—harboring hidden feelings in his heart?

CHAPTER FOURTEEN

The Half-Demon

SHÉN MÌ

WHAT HAVE I DONE?

I wanted to dig a hole and bury myself in it. How did that happen? How did I lose all control and give in to my yearning for the butterfly, all else be damned?

When had I developed such feelings for Hú Dié?

"As soon as your wound is healed enough, I will figure out how to get us out of here," she told me as I avoided her eyes at any cost. Was she so used to this reaction from males that she didn't react anymore?

Still trying to look away from her, I focused on my own shoulder and was shocked to find the wound almost completely closed, a long, angry scar where the flesh had been opened a few moments ago. Her magic powder worked miracles despite the uncomfortable and unwanted side effects.

"Once I'm healed, I can get us out of here," I countered, finding my voice. "I just need to replenish my *qi* a bit." I ventured a glance in her direction, my eyes half hidden under my lashes. "And thank you," I whispered. "I know you could have just flown out of here, but you chose to stay and help me. I owe you big." *For more than one thing,* I added in silence.

She waved my gratefulness away with a click of her tongue. "It's only my duty, *shīfu,*" she said with a sheepish smile that belied the twinkle in her eyes. "But now you should rest for a while."

There was not much space for stretching out and resting, so we made do on our sides, curled around the spikes that surrounded us, and took a nap. At least I did. I had a sneaky feeling Hú Dié did not sleep a wink.

When I woke up, the sun was rising, long tendrils of young light reaching the bottom of the pit where we had been trapped most of the night. The butterfly was awake, studying me from underneath her thick, dark lashes as she leaned against one of the wooden posts. I blinked a few times before sitting up and checking my shoulder.

"It's healed," Hú Dié said, raising her gaze to me. "I just checked."

It was indeed fully knitted together, an already fading scar the only remnant of the injury. My *qi* was also strong, running freely through my body as I slipped my arms through the sleeves of my *changshan.*

"Let's get out of here," I told her, standing up and testing the strength of my legs. They were back to their normal selves. I lifted a hand in her direction. "Give me your hand."

With her eyes narrowed to mere slits, Hú Dié hesitated for a moment before giving in and slipping her hand inside mine. I pulled her closer to me, wrapped an arm around her waist, and jumped out of that hole with her.

We landed smoothly near the edge, and the butterfly gasped. "You can fly!"

I let her go, making sure she wouldn't fall back into the hole, and said, "No, I can jump really high, that's all." Even though that was not the whole truth, I wasn't sure I was ready to fully reveal my secrets to her. Part of me wanted it so bad, it almost hurt. The yearning to be close to her, physically and emotionally, was so intense, I wondered if her powder was still affecting my brain.

I deflected. "We should get going before the hunters come to check the trap."

I didn't wait to see whether she followed me and began running in the direction of the next town. The soft steps behind me confirmed she wasn't far, and I allowed myself to relax a little.

We weren't too far from Yumai, the town my wayward brother seemed to have chosen for his destination. Soon enough we spotted the makeshift gates made of bamboo that were guarded by two men who looked as if they wished to be anywhere but here.

We stopped behind a large bush as soon as we saw the gates to remove most of our black gear and stuff it into our bags. Without the black scarf around her neck and face, Hú Dié couldn't hide her beauty, her long black silken hair falling over her shoulders before she twisted it into a high bun.

I swallowed hard and tried to focus on my own clothing, a simple pair of black pants under a nondescript grey *changshan*. I pulled a wide-brimmed straw hat from the bag and set it on my head.

"How did you stuff all that in the bag?" the butterfly asked, wrinkling her nose.

"Magic," I said, not daring to look at her. "Let's go."

Hú Dié walked beside me, her attempt at being unnoticeable failing completely. Not even her simple black dress and plain hairdo made her look ordinary. There was an aura about her, a halo of light that enveloped her whole self. Others may not realize it was there, but they would certainly feel the draw. Even as we walked together through the gate, the eyes of every male followed her.

I didn't like it.

Am I fucking jealous?

No, it couldn't be that. Why would I be jealous of other men? But then what was that burning feeling in my gut, a heat that rose all the way to my face and choked me? Why did I have to fight the urge to put my sword through each and every male who dared to look at my butterfly?

Wait! *My* butterfly?

Oh, for each of all seven hells! I am *jealous.*

The inn we were staying in was on the other side of town, but I had to make a stop on the way there. No one seemed too curious about the two strangers walking down their packed-dirt streets, and I realized there were quite a few foreigners in town, people who clearly didn't belong here.

By the time we arrived at the humble building that housed the pharmacy I was looking for, I was restless—why were there so many visitors in such a tiny town? And why had my devious brother chosen to come here as well?

The inside of the store was dark, and the smell of a thousand different herbs assailed my senses. It was a mixture of pleasing and annoying scents that both caressed and tickled my nose. I threw a glance at Hú Dié and was surprised to see her sniff the air as if she was enjoying the flood of strong aromas. Shaking my head in disbelief, I turned to the person behind the counter, a young man with a mop of dark hair pinned in a messy top bun.

"When plums are ripe," I recited in a whisper.

The man raised his eyes to mine and said, "Jasmine sends out a refreshing fragrance."

The butterfly fairy stared at us as if we had gone crazy but didn't say anything. The man was one of my spies and the line from an ancient poem our security code.

"I have received the herbs you have asked for," my spy said loudly enough for anyone to hear. "I have them in the back room. Please, follow me."

We followed him around the counter and into a small back room. My man closed the door behind him and turned to us. His store-friendly smile faded, replaced by a much more somber expression.

"Xian Lu is in town," he announced.

It wasn't news for me, of course, but he followed with the information I was the most curious about.

"He came for a fertility drug."

Fertility drug? My wayward brother had left the side of my imperial father at a time when he could butter him up the most in search of a fertility drug. Why?

Hú Dié took the lead. "What for? Is he barren?"

The spy shook his head. "Not that we know. But this a special concoction that guarantees a male child."

Once I digested the news, I knew exactly why my brother was looking for such a drug. "He wants to make sure he produces an heir as soon as possible," I said. "With the crown prince out of the way, that's the best way to guarantee his own nomination as heir to the throne."

"Who is selling such a drug?" the butterfly asked, her voice strangely strained.

Did she know something I didn't?

"I will give you the address," my spy said. "But you are probably too late if you are trying to stop him from acquiring it. The prince has been here for a couple days already."

It didn't matter. The crown prince was alive and well, and my father wouldn't pick anyone else to fill his shoes. But Xian Lu didn't know that. That said, I would like to have a little chat with the man who could concoct such a wondrous drug. Who knew what else this person could come up with?

We collected the address, said our goodbyes, and left the pharmacy with several packs of herbs to diffuse the suspicions of anyone watching us. The butterfly was uncharacteristically quiet, a fact that should have worried me, but I was too focused on finding this miracle worker to pay much attention or wonder what she had stuffed inside her sleeve.

The streets were busy. People went in and out of stores, stopping at the small stalls that peppered the streets, the vendors' cries filling the air like off-key songs. Hú Dié walked beside me like a shadow as we meandered through town. When we turned the last corner before our destination, she suddenly stopped as if frozen in place.

"What's wrong?" I asked, turning around to look at her. "We're almost there."

She never got the chance to answer. A booming voice made me snap my head around.

"Little butterfly, you finally came back."

The man was huge, built like the imperial palace walls and just as strong. There was no hair on his large head, and his eyes were the color of dark, dull rubies.

A half-demon! A bàn mó.

I stole a glance at Hú Dié, who seemed glued to that same spot of the street, eyes rounded and filled with a panic I had never seen before. I could almost feel the fear wafting from her.

"Beauty, I missed you," the man continued, taking a couple wide strides toward us. "You've been very naughty, and now I must teach you a lesson."

Before I could do anything about it, the *bàn mó* vanished into thin air to reappear next to the butterfly. She yelped and tried to get away, but it was too late. The same woman who had never been caught unawares during her training seemed helpless against this creature.

The man roared as if someone had just told him the funniest joke, his tree-trunk arms clasped around Hú Dié's slim body. "You're mine again, beauty. I have great plans for you and your lovely powder."

It took me a moment to react. "Let go of her," I finally yelled, still finding it hard to believe the butterfly was not defending herself.

The *bàn mó* stared me down like I was an annoying mosquito, the snake tattoo on his cheek slithering as he clenched his jaw. "And who the fuck are you?" he asked, tightening his hold on the butterfly fairy.

"Someone you don't want to fuck with," I answered, anger beginning to boil inside me. "Let her go or you will regret it."

The creature laughed again. "Do you hear the pretty man?" he asked her. "He thinks he can hurt me. Will you tell him I am your master and that he better leave before I make him wish he did?"

Pure red-hot wrath wrapped itself into a ball of fire in my chest, and I knew exactly what would happen if that anger was released. "Don't be stupid, *bàn mó*," I warned him again, my voice low and dangerous. "Let. Her. Go."

"She's my most valuable source of fairy powder," the giant said with a grin. "I am not letting her go for you or anyone else. She's mine."

The fireball exploded then, and with it, one of my most-guarded secrets was fully revealed.

CHAPTER FIFTEEN

Secrets

Hú Dié

THE MOMENT THE *GUÀI* touched me, I was lost—fear took over like a pair of extra-strong hands holding me helplessly in place. Panic made me forget who I was and how I never went down without a fight, no matter how strong the opponent. I just froze, paralyzed as much by the fear that flooded my heart as by the Monster's ridiculously strong arms.

"Let. Her. Go." *Shīfu* growled, and my eyes automatically snapped to his.

Master was a lot stronger than he looked, but was he tough enough to go against the half-demon who had been my captor for years? A different kind of fear mixed with the old—I didn't want Shén Mì to get hurt.

I yelped, scared for my master, but the Monster didn't let go, his grip tightening around my waist.

Golden eyes met mine, and the anger I saw in them should have frightened me, but instead it calmed me down. There was something different about Shén Mì's eyes today. Something about his whole body felt strange, but in a good way.

When the half-demon didn't let me go, Master took a couple steps forward, and for a moment, I thought I was hallucinating. His whole being began to shimmer, blurring around the edges like the rays of the sun. His body elongated and so did his face, golden fur replacing his ivory skin as long, sharp talons grew out of his fingertips.

I was so stunned, I almost missed the moment my captor dropped his hold. The man I had worked for these past few months was no longer human but a dragon that stretched its long, massive body along the street before us, its huge golden eyes never once leaving the *guài* even as he released me.

"Get out of here!"

The voice was deeper, a roar of thunder, but I had no doubt it was my master's.

"Run, Hú Dié," he ordered.

Finally awakened from whatever paralysis I had been under, I ran to hide nearby but out of the way. The dragon—Shén Mì—slid closer to the half-demon, spewing fire, and the horror engraved on the Monster's face was so gratifying, I forgot my fear and surprise.

"Nobody touches my disciple," Shén Mì growled again, one step closer to the creature who had held me prisoner for so long. "Touch her again, and I will roast you with my breath."

The *guài* trembled and sputtered something incomprehensible.

"*Qù!* Leave!"

It took only a moment for the Monster to turn around and disappear around the corner as fast as his legs could carry him. A small crowd had gathered to watch the scene, and they all burst into applause as if what had just happened was nothing but some form of entertainment.

I left my hiding spot and rushed to my master's side, in awe of what he was.

"You're a dragon immortal." It was an accusation as I struggled between feeling insanely angry at him for hiding it all this time and equally madly happy he had come to my rescue. "Why didn't you tell me?"

He shook his massive head and threw glances around him. "We'll talk at the inn," he said. "I don't want anyone else to see my human form."

Well, it's a little late for that.

The whole town had seen him shift, and it was only a matter of time before his brother, who was somewhere in town, found out he was here.

"Hold your breath!" I yelled at him.

I changed into my butterfly and flew over the crowd, spraying them with herbs I had stolen from the pharmacy. I had planned to use them on Shén Mì later to make him forget the kiss, but this was more important. These people had to forget what they had seen.

Once I had dumped most of the herbs over the witnesses, I changed back to human form and pulled on one of the dragon's fur-covered ears. "Let's go," I told him, prodding him to follow me away from the square. "They won't remember a thing." There was something nagging at the back of my mind, but I couldn't focus long enough to figure out what it was. I'd worry about that later. I had more important things to do first; I had to make sure Master was safe and sound.

I ran in the direction of the inn, Shén Mì's dragon beside me. When I no longer heard the dragging of his long body on the rocky road, I knew he had changed back to his human form, but I didn't dare look.

I wanted to get to the inn as fast as I could and make sure my master was safe from prying eyes and wagging tongues.

Nobody showed any interest in us as we entered the inn, rented a bed, or when we walked upstairs to our room, but I still let out a sigh of relief once we were behind closed doors.

I stared at my master for the first time since the incident in the square. He was back to his nonplussed, smooth-as-silk mode—all elegance and no sign of his real strength. For a moment I asked myself if I had dreamed the whole dragon episode, but then I shook my head and dismissed the thought.

"Why didn't you tell me you are a dragon immortal?" *And why did I never realize it?* I knew how to read beyond mortal appearances, and yet I had never suspected he was an immortal.

He stood in the middle of the room, his clothes a little dusty from the road but otherwise perfect as usual. "Why should I?" he asked, pulling his white fan from a sleeve and snapping it open. "I don't owe you anything, especially my secrets."

For some weird reason, that statement stung. He was right, of course. I had my secrets too.

"Care to tell me about who that idiot giant was?" he asked, fanning himself, eyebrows raised. "I have never seen you so scared."

I wanted to yell out that I didn't owe him any secrets, either, but the man had saved me. Because of me he had exposed his secret to the whole town. I did owe him.

"It's a long story," I grumbled, dropping onto a chair.

He closed his fan, sat on the edge of the bed, and crossed his arms. "We have all night."

Gods, sometimes I hate my life.

How do you start a story that brings back so many painful memories and feelings? You distance yourself from it and tell it as if it happened to someone else.

At least that was the plan.

The reality was, I couldn't. Not completely. In fact, I couldn't even hide how I felt with every word I uttered.

"He specializes in rare and exotic drugs for all kinds of illnesses, and he charges his so-called patients a fortune," I started, my right eye twitching. "He used to have a bar in another town where he carried out his business. I guess he has now expanded outside his city."

Shén Mì shook his head. "He most likely came here to meet with my brother. Small town, no one would notice him."

When I didn't say anything, he cocked his head to the side and said, "Go on."

I swallowed a shard of glass before continuing, "In order to get his wonder drugs, he captured many minor immortals and harvested their magic." There had been at least a dozen cages in the backroom of the sleazy tavern he called his store, full of the unfortunate creatures he had hunted down and caught. Me included. "When he found out butterfly fairy dust can do many things, especially work as a powerful aphrodisiac, he set out to catch one." I chuckled bitterly. "Unfortunately for me I just happened to cross his path at the wrong time."

Master's eyes were closed to a mere slit. "He captured you?" It wasn't as much a question as a statement of fact. "How long did he keep you?"

"I lost track of time after the first couple years," I said with a shrug. A shiver went through me. "He kept me docile with *huǒ niǎo* ashes and extracted my powder almost every day."

Memories of those times hit me with the force of a hurricane. For the past few months, finally free from my captor, I had managed to keep thoughts of my captivity and daily torture contained in a dark spot of my mind. Telling the story brought forth all the pain and horror, the overwhelming sense of helplessness and despair that had filled my days then.

Shén Mì took a couple tentative steps toward me, and for a second, I thought he was going to hug me, but at the last minute, he stopped and crossed his arms behind his back. "I can tell it's painful for you to tell me this story," he said. "I'll call for some food, and we'll rest."

The simple show of kindness touched me, and I had to swallow a sob. He walked past me, squeezing my shoulders on the way. I stood there, head hanging and heart pounding, fighting the hot tears that burned in my eyes.

The door creaked opened, and I exclaimed without turning around, "Thank you, *shīfu*, for rescuing me from the Monster." I exhaled, deeply and slowly. "And for offering me a place to live and thrive."

He didn't say anything, but a long moment passed before the door clicked closed. I was alone, so I allowed the tears to roll freely down my cheeks and drown me. I dropped to my knees and bent over my own legs until my forehead touched the cold floor. The tears I had held in since I had been captured years ago fell, and somehow the weight of those memories lightened, morphed into an odd sort of relief.

Sometimes I still woke up believing I was in that cage, and I had to remind myself of how I escaped. I had waited a lifetime, but the Monster had finally got a little careless, leaving one of his sleazy minions in charge. My valuable powder proved to be too much of a temptation, so when he opened the cage and stuck his dirty hand inside, I flew out easily. The Monster always doused me with *huǒ niǎo* ashes before snatching me out of the cage.

This minion didn't.

I can't even remember how long and how far I flew until I reached the top of a very tall bamboo tree in the woods of some mountain and was able to rest and restore enough of my *qi* to change into a human again. The feeling of freedom that bloomed from the fear and anxiety of the flight is what always made my breathing slow down.

And what fueled my need for revenge.

By the time Master returned with a tray of food, I felt better. If he noticed my swollen red eyes, he didn't mention it. Instead, he set the tray down on the small table, sat down, and offered me a seat on the opposite side from him.

I lowered myself onto the red seating cushion, my stomach reacting to the wonderful aroma of the noodles in the steaming bowls he had brought in. Shén Mì poured tea for both of us and began eating, his chopsticks working faster than should be possible. I didn't waste any time and followed suit, the eggy noodles warming my throat all the way to my stomach.

Master was quiet for most of the meal, and I couldn't be more grateful for the silence. Inside my head there was chaos, the noise of years of pain and fear, of voices begging for mercy, sobs of desperation, mocking laughter and threats. The silence and the comfort food helped temper down a lot of the confusion inside my head and soothe my heart.

After the meal, Shén Mì offered me the bed and spread a blanket on the floor for himself. I didn't argue. The idea of a soft mattress was irresistible at that point. My whole body ached from all the tension and fear, and I couldn't keep my eyes open.

I quickly stretched out across the bed, not bothering to undress or even take off my shoes, dozing off as soon as my head hit the pillow.

No more monsters would come after me. I had a dragon beside me.

CHAPTER SIXTEEN

Unexpected

SHÉN MÌ

FLASHES OF HOW HER usual petulant, rebellious attitude had been replaced by that of a terrified young girl made my chest clench. If I hadn't seen it, I would have thought it impossible. Hú Dié was outspoken, painfully defiant, and stupidly brave most of the time, and yet, she had cowered before the Monster like a traumatized child, powerless and helpless. What had this Monster done to her? And for how long?

I should have killed him.

My mission came first, I reminded myself, anger bubbling in my throat. My brother and his right to the throne had to be my priority. Killing—even a monster everyone hated—in front of a crowd would jeopardize everything. Yes, Butterfly had somehow wiped the crowd's memories clean, but I couldn't risk it. I shouldn't have shifted in the first place, but I couldn't abandon my disciple. My dragon was a secret well-kept, even from most of my family. Of the whole imperial brood,

I was the only one who had inherited my father's dragon essence. Not even my father knew of my immortal side, and I wanted to keep it that way. Had he known I was a dragon like him, he would have named me the crown prince, an honor I really did not want. My brother would be a much better emperor than me.

Hú Dié moaned in her sleep, snapping me from my reverie. She was still wearing her shoes, stained from the mud of the streets. I sat on the edge of the bed and gently pulled her shoes off one at a time and then covered her with a silk blanket. She sighed—or sobbed—in her sleep, and I had the ridiculous yearning to wrap my arms around her and comfort her.

What's wrong with me?

Before doing something I would regret, I stood and stretched out on top of the blanket I had spread on the floor by the bed. I wasn't sure I'd be able to sleep. Shifting always made me restless, my dragon core wanting to fly, to explore, even as my tired human body protested the sudden burst of energy.

I cradled the back of my head in my arms and stared at the white ceiling, hating that it was so plain. Nothing to count or analyze. Even insects would be welcome, or maybe a lizard or two.

A gargantuan yawn escaped me.

I turned onto my side, my eyes immediately roaming towards the sleeping figure on the bed. Even in sleep Hú Dié was beautiful, her inner glow shining through loud and clear. Heat spread in my gut, and I shut my eyes tightly, hoping the desire would vanish with the sight of her.

Only it didn't.

Even in darkness, images of her danced in my eyes, spreading the fire that had erupted inside me. Was it possible these were lingering effects from her powder? Or was I utterly and insanely infatuated with the butterfly fairy?

A whimper made me snap my eyes open.

Hú Dié was tossing in bed, uttering words intersected with sobs, "No, stop! Let me go. Stop!"

I was up in an instant, desire forgotten and only one wish in my mind: to comfort her, to wipe that fear from her voice, to make her feel safe again.

I crawled in bed beside her and enveloped her in my arms. She fought me at first, her eyes still closed, stuck in whatever nightmare she was having. But as her ear rested against my chest, she calmed down, allowing herself to be cuddled, my heart beating against the side of her face.

"It's all right, Butterfly," I whispered, my lips skating over the top of her head. "I'm here. I won't let anything happen to you, I promise."

Anger erupted inside me again. What horrors had she been through that made her this helpless against the *guài*? A woman who was not scared of anything or anyone. The same fairy who had flown right to the heart of the palace, risking her freedom and even her life, to help my brother's cause.

I should have killed him.

I shook those thoughts off. I had to focus on the mission, not the fairy. But there was no denying that she had woven a permanent cocoon in my life, one that had merged with my own needs and wants, becoming part of who and what I was. There was no way out: she was just as important to me now as breathing.

She shivered and whimpered in my arms. Conjuring my dragon inner heat, I held her closer, letting the warmth soothe her nerves and relax her muscles, and soon her body loosened against mine and her breathing evened out.

My eyes, heavy with sleep, drooped closed, my head leaning on hers, and soon I followed her into the land of dreams.

Warm air blew on to my face, and I wiggled my nose. Sleep, heavy and languorous, clung to my eyelids, refusing to let me open them. In my half-asleep state, I snuggled into the solid but soft source of heat pressing against me. In the dreamy recesses of my mind, I was half aware that I had never felt this comfortable, this cuddled and safe. Even as a child, there weren't many hugs or cuddles to be had with an emperor for a father and a mother who had died when I was barely six years old. This, whatever it was, was heavenly, and I didn't want to move, didn't want it to end.

Then, reality hit me.

My eyes flew open to find Hú Dié's face so close to mine, I could feel her heat. She had one leg draped over my thigh and an arm firmly curled around my chest and back.

My heart burst into a manic race that made me choke.

What do I do?

The butterfly fairy looked so peaceful. Just a few hours ago, she had the tormented look of those who had been tortured, fear exuding from every pore. Now all of that was gone from her face, replaced by infinite harmony. How could I wrench her from such a good place? But the pressure of her body was bringing mine to life. Too alive for comfort.

I tried to wiggle myself away from her hold, but she was fiercely attached to me, and every time I moved, our bodies got a little closer. Sweat began to bead on my forehead, and I tried to steer my thoughts to something else, anything else—that disgusting dim sum the corner shop served, the time I had slipped and fell face-first onto a pile of dung—nothing worked. I was getting harder by the second and panicking.

What if she wakes up now?

As close as we were to each other, there was no way to hide how aroused I was. I started making mad plans of escape. I could turn onto my other side as soon as she woke up or even run out of the room. I was so into my own thoughts that I missed the flutter of her eyes, the slight movement of her lips.

I froze, each and every plan I had made rushing away from me. Her beautiful eyes opened, unfocused at first and she studied my face, moving from my eyes to my lips and back again.

She smiled. "Why are you here?" she asked, her voice still slurred by sleep. Then, her eyes opened wider, and her cheeks flushed bright pink.

Shit! She's noticed.

"Y-you were having a-a nightmare," I explained, stuttering like an adolescent. "Y-you held me here."

Gods! Now I sound as if I'm blaming her for my state of arousal.

With a quick glance at where her leg and arms were, she flinched back, freeing me from her grasp.

I was afraid to move and blinked like an idiot. "I'm sorry," I said. "Nothing happened."

For a moment she just stared, but then her lips began to slowly stretch into a smile that soon became laughter.

I was confused.

"Why are you laughing?" I asked, not sure whether to laugh along with her or be offended.

"You," she said, sitting up and pointing at me. "You look so guilty. Have you never been in bed with a girl?"

Heat flooded my cheeks. "I've been with plenty of women," I blurted and immediately regretted it. I sounded like a silly boy, the opposite of what I wanted her to see me as. I bounced up off the bed like a tightly coiled spring and sat on the edge, my back turned to her. "I was just wondering whether you're feeling better, but since you are mocking me, I assume you're fine."

Her soft chuckles tickled my ears for a few seconds before going quiet. I didn't dare turn around, instead busying myself with my shoes.

"Did you sleep next to me all night?"

Her voice was so quiet, I almost missed it. I nodded and grunted a yes.

Silence followed before she said, "*Xiè xiè*. Thank you for staying with me."

The knot in my throat grew bigger, and I coughed as I stood up and turned around to her. "You're welcome," I managed to say, struggling to keep my eyes on hers. "You would have done the same for me."

Her lips quivered in a sad smile. "Not sure I would," she admitted. "But I'm glad you did."

"I'll be downstairs getting breakfast," I announced, anxious to end the awkward conversation. "Join me when you're ready."

I left, closing the door behind me gently. The sun had barely peeked over the horizon, and the inn was as quiet as a tomb, the only sounds coming from the waking birds outside and the buzz of activity from the kitchen.

When Hú Dié joined me a few minutes later, the server had already brought out several platters of breakfast food: scallion pancakes, *youtiao*, and porridge. I poured her a cup of tea as she lowered herself onto the seating cushion next to mine.

We ate in silence for a long while, unsaid words hanging over us like vultures. But what could I say after what had happened? We had both revealed a side of us we had kept secret from almost everyone, bringing us closer together than I had ever been to anyone, including Mão Mão. Where do you go from that?

"You're a dragon," the butterfly fairy whispered suddenly.

My eyes shot up to hers, a porridge-filled spoon forgotten near my lips.

"Don't worry. I won't tell anyone." She studied me for a few seconds. "I assume not many do know." It was a question she already knew the answer to.

I nodded, lowering the spoon to the bowl. "Only Mão Mão and Su Lin know." I rushed to add, "And I want to keep it that way."

She nodded, not pressing for my reasons why.

I offered them anyway. "My power is an asset as long as I keep it a secret. It becomes a liability if it's made public. Right now, my enemies—my brother's enemies—are under the impression that I am harmless. Should they find out I'm not, things would be very different." I lowered my gaze and my voice to add, "And I don't want to inherit the throne."

"'Dragon emperors bring power and protection to the empire,'" she quoted, an old saying that was held as true and tested by every emperor before my father.

There had been four dragon emperors on that throne for the past couple centuries who had kept the nation stable and safe. I would be the first to skip the dubious honor.

"I can still protect the empire from the sidelines," I said, my gaze searching for understanding in her eyes. "A wise, smart, and dedicated emperor like my brother will serve the people much better than a reluctant one."

Hú Dié was silent for a minute, never moving her eyes away from mine. "There's a new concept for you," she finally said, her head cocked to one side. "A shadow emperor." She licked her lips as if savoring the words. "I like it."

I was being a fool, but those words—her approval—filled me with such joy, I wore a stupid grin for the rest of the day.

Chapter Seventeen

Dragon

Hú Dié

"THE PLEASURE GARDEN IS where you'll find them."

The information didn't seem to surprise Shén Mì, but it threw me for a loop. A brothel? Xian Lu was choosing a brothel as the place where all his troubles would be resolved? Was he planning on bedding every courtesan in the establishment until his seed took root? What about his noble wife and all the freaking concubines he had amassed for the past few years? If an heir hadn't sprouted out of all those feverish bedroom games, what made him think a prostitute could help?

"Why a brothel?" I had to ask. Curiosity was eating me up inside.

The young spy turned his face to me and blinked. "Well, the fertility drug he took does not last very long," he explained in a tone of voice that told me he thought I was an idiot. "He has to act while at its most effective. By the time he goes back to his wives, the drug will be a dud."

I refrained from the impulse to stick my tongue out at the informant. "So, he's just going to try to get as many women pregnant as possible before heading back.... Promiscuous, but effective, I guess." I scratched my head.

A stolen glance told me Shén Mì was holding off a smile, his lower lip stuck between his teeth. Was he laughing at me?

We bid the spy goodbye and left the pharmacy, carrying a few small herbal packages, including one with the herb I had used on the crowd that had witnessed my master's shift into a dragon. I had offered to steal it—because it was so expensive—but Master insisted on paying for it himself. Who was I to argue with the rich?

"Let's have something to eat," Shén Mì suggested as we wandered down the main street of town. "How does dumpling soup sound?"

I stared at him, shocked that he was asking for my approval. "That sounds good, but can we grab a couple *bao* on the way there?"

He chuckled, tilting his chin up in the air. "I forgot how much you love *bao*," he said. "*Hǎo de*! Let's find a good *bao* vendor."

For the next couple hours, we roamed the streets in search of good food, eventually settling on a small street restaurant that served passable, if not excellent, *bao* and dumplings. It offered the added benefit of a great view of the human river that weaved up and down the road.

"What are we going to do about Xian Lu?" I asked, my cheeks swollen with the soft, warm dough of a pork *bao*. "And don't the courtesans take some sort of birth control? How will that even work?"

He slurped a dumpling from his spoon and wiped his lips on a napkin. "As I understand it, this drug he took overrides any barriers to conception, including other drugs."

I pursed my lips and wrinkled my nose. "Courtesans also have drugs to end pregnancies," I mused. "How is he going to prevent that from happening?"

He gave the soup a stir. "My guess is that he will leave some of his people at the brothel to avoid any glitches."

We sat and ate for a while longer, enjoying the strange variety of people who walked by. I caught myself staring at him when he wasn't looking, in awe of how handsome he really was and wondering why I had ever thought of him as a dandy. The man might be pretty and elegant, but there was a definite strong masculinity to him in the straight bridge of his nose, the dark eyebrows crowning his golden eyes, and the determined set of his full lips. I couldn't take my eyes off his lips, remembering how warm and exciting they had felt against mine when we were stuck in that pit.

I want to taste them again!

I straightened my back with a jerk. "We should be going, don't you think?" I asked, suddenly in a hurry to move. "It will be dark soon." There were at least another couple hours before sunset, but I needed an excuse.

His forehead furrowed between his eyes. "What's the rush? The brothel doesn't get busy until much later."

That caught my attention. "We're going to the brothel? To do what?" It wasn't as if we could stop his brother from buying sex at a house of prostitution where the motto was always *have money, will fuck*. At least that's how it was in the brothels I was made to visit as part of the *Guài's* "business." He often took pleasure in displaying *his precious butterfly* to his clientèle.

"While you were busy stealing herbs at the pharmacy, I was busy collecting another type of drug."

My face flushed with heat. Shit, he had spotted my stealthy snatching of a few more rare herbs from the store. Not much seemed to go unnoticed by my master.

"The herbalist guarantees that a drop or two of this liquid in anything Xian Lu puts in his mouth will take care of things."

I studied the small white vial. Could such an herb exist? Despite myself, I was intrigued, always curious about medicine and herbology. "How does it work?" I asked, sniffing the bottle. There was a definite tangy smell wafting from it. "That stuff must be bitter."

He cocked his head, narrowing his eyes. "You can tell that just by the smell?"

I mimicked him, tilting my head to the side. "I'm a butterfly, remember? How else would I be able to find the right nectar if I didn't have a very sharp sense of smell?" That and the fact I was female. In my long life experience, I had found that females of any species seemed to have much more sensitive olfaction than males, but I wasn't about to ruffle his manly feathers.

He nodded. "The pharmacist did mention that it would have to be disguised with something sweet or Xian Lu would suspect foul play," he said. "My brother is a great fan of plum wine. I think it is sweet enough to disguise the tartness of the herb, don't you think?"

I did not like that Xian Lu and I had a common love for the very sweet and fruity *méijiǔ*, but I had to agree, it was a good choice. "And how do you make sure he drinks the right wine?" I asked, making a mental note to change my preference to another type of wine.

"We're going to Qīchóng Tiān Winery to buy the best plum wine the town has to offer, and then we will have to improvise."

I was all for improvising, but in this case, it felt as too much of a risk.

"And if by some miracle Xian Lu does get a girl pregnant, it's not as if the real crown prince is really dead, right?"

Right. Then why come all this way and risk our necks if there was no chance in hell Xian Lu would ever be made the imperial heir?

A side glance at my master answered my silent question: like a young boy, Shén Mì was having fun throwing daggers at his brother's plans. Plain and simple!

"That should do it!" I slapped my hands together with a self-satisfied grin. My plan was pure genius.

Shén Mì didn't crack a smile, his arms crossed as he leaned against the wall of the room I had just exited. "Your confidence makes me very nervous," he said. "What exactly did you tell the courtesans in there?"

I had managed to gather all the brothel's prostitutes in their madam's office for a chat. "You are not going to believe it, so I may just keep it a secret. Let's just say, I found an ingenious way to feed the potion to your disgusting brother without him ever finding out."

He raised his eyebrows. "You got the ladies in on it? How did you convince them to help us?"

I rubbed my thumb and forefinger together. "Money talks."

He cocked his head, a question in his eyes.

"I don't have much of that, so I used yours."

Master dropped his arms and took a step toward me. "How much money are we talking about?" he growled. "And how did you get it?"

I took a step backward and pointed at his waist. "Check out your money pouch." I knew he wouldn't find it because I had swiped it when he wasn't looking. Butterflies can be very sneaky.

He brushed a hand along the length of his face with a groan. "You didn't use all of it, did you? Because we need money for the way back."

I shook my head. "Of course not," I said, feeling slighted. "I'm not dumb. Just generous."

"With other people's money, obviously," he said. He wiped his hands on his tunic and smiled. "So what exactly did you convince them to do? Are they going to serve him the plum wine?"

"That's just part A of the plan," I told him, interlacing my fingers behind my back and walking past him. "Part B is a lot more creative and interesting."

He followed me as I walked toward the stairs. Madam Yang Xi had set us up in a room upstairs, next to the one Shén Mì's depraved brother would be using.

"Are you going to tell me what part B is?" he asked, falling into step with me.

I climbed the stairs two steps at a time, enjoying stringing him along. "Let's just say, it will involve lacing a particular anatomical female part with the herb," I said once I reached the top, Master right at my heels.

I headed toward the room, but he grabbed hold of my arm, stopping me. "Did I hear that correctly?"

Turning around to face him, I tried to assume an innocent look. "Why, you know his mouth is going to be busy, so why not take advantage of it?"

The look of pure shock he gave me made it all worthwhile. "You didn't!"

I opened the door to the private room and walked in. "I sure did," I threw back at him. "Aren't you proud of your acolyte?"

A grumble came from behind me. "Proud wouldn't be the word I'd choose. Terrified of your evil and slightly immoral creativity? Absolutely."

I chuckled, taking his words as a compliment, and threw myself on top of the bed. There was another hour or so before the brothel opened its doors to the public, and a nap might just be on the menu.

Shén Mì sat at the table where we had laid out a few snacks we brought with us and stared at me with his unsettling golden eyes. "You're just going to lie down and sleep?"

"Why not? There's nothing better to do," I said, cradling the back of my head on my arms.

He pointed at the chess table by the window. "We can always play *Xiangqi*. Unless you're scared I'll beat you."

I could never say no to a challenge. Besides, chess was something I excelled at. Years in a cage with nowhere to go had given me ample time to practice my strategy.

"I'm game," I said, jumping to my feet. "Let's make it interesting, shall we? A bet?"

Shén Mì stood up, too, and walked to the chess table. "Sure, what should we bet?" he asked, turning around suddenly.

Without enough time to slow down, momentum threw me at him, my hands flattening against his surprisingly hard chest, my forehead almost touching his lips.

I flushed, heat coursing through me like an out-of-control fire. I tried to disentangle myself from him, but he held me steady, his hands on my upper arms and chin against my head. It was an uncomfortable situation that felt so good, I had to wonder if I hadn't lost my sanity somewhere along the way.

"Well? What do we bet?" he whispered, his lips moving against my hairline like a caress.

I cleared my throat, pushing him away a bit more forcibly than before. He dropped his hands, and I backtracked a few steps. "You give me a two week break from our morning practices," I said, voicing the first thing that came to my head.

"*Hǎo!*" he agreed without hesitation.

"And if you win?" I asked, avoiding his glance. "What do you want?" I was betting on triple practices, but I could be wrong.

He pretended to think about it, tapping his chin. "Can't think of anything right now," he said. "Just promise you will do as I say if I win."

It was a dangerous game he was playing. Knowing him, he would increase the daily torture to unbearable levels. But if I said no, I would be admitting two things: that I was sure I would lose and that I was too scared of him.

I reached out my hand. "Done. One wish granted," I uttered, swallowing the knot of apprehension that had lodged itself there.

We shook on it and sat to play a game, the heat of his hands on my arms still burning my skin.

Damn you, Shén Mì! Why do I react like this to your touch?

To distract me from my thoughts, I immediately made my move with a black piece. No reason to be nervous. This was my game. I always won.

Except, and against all odds, I lost.

"*Hǎo*, I admit defeat," I said, my hands shaking a little. "What's your wish?"

He threw me a side glance, one corner of his lips rising into a devilish half smile.

"Too early for that," he said, placing the marble chess pieces back in the small basket. "I will let you know when I decide."

For all the fucking gods, he's going to make me suffer!

Evil master that he obviously was.

CHAPTER EIGHTEEN

The Brothel

SHÉN MÌ

S OMETHING HAD SHIFTED INSIDE me. The moment I beat Hú Dié at chess, the invisible hand that had been holding me back slackened and let go. If before that moment I had been more than hesitant to give in to my obvious attraction for the butterfly fairy, now I was open to all possibilities.

"Your brother is a noisy lover," she commented, busting the fantasy bubble I had been in for the past few minutes.

She had her ear to the thin wall that separated our room from the one inhabited by my half sibling and the current courtesan—the third one in the last hour or so. That fertility drug he had taken was obviously also a strong aphrodisiac.

"This is fun."

I sighed. Fun was not the word I would use to describe an hour of listening to my greedy brother moaning and screaming while having sex. Boring—and slightly disturbing—would be a better word.

I have to do something else.

I stood, determined to go for a walk, maybe grab something to eat down in the restaurant. Anything other than listening to the lascivious sounds.

"Where are you going?" the butterfly asked me, throwing me a suspicious glare. "They're not finished. I heard he has a couple more ladies lined up next."

I raised my eyebrows at her in a question.

"I may have dusted his wine with some of my powder too."

Well, that explained a lot. I shook my head and opened the door. "I'll be downstairs eating your favorite *bao*."

It was meant as a lure, and Hú Dié didn't disappoint; she swallowed the bait, hook and all. "I'll go with you," she said, pushing herself away from the wall. "All this sex is making me hungry."

I stepped aside to let her go through. "You have no shame." One of the many reasons she had wormed herself into my heart.

"And proud of that," she said, skipping down the hallway.

We sat at the restaurant for a while, enjoying the good food the brothel had to offer and drinking some wine. By the time we climbed up back to the rooms, my partner in crime was already a little tipsy, giggles escaping her lips every other wobbly step.

I reached out to steady her, my hand wrapped around her upper arm as she tripped over the last step. "Are you all right? You shouldn't have drunk so much."

She turned around suddenly, nearly crashing into me. "I can hold my alcohol," she declared, a hiccup belying her statement. She turned around again and moved toward our room. "I'm just tired."

With another sigh, I followed her closely, afraid she would fall or accidentally walk into somebody else's room. Just as we were a few steps away from ours, the door to my brother's room opened, and a disheveled, half-naked Xian Lu stepped out to call for another courtesan. Afraid of being spotted, I grabbed the butterfly, spun her around, and crushed her between the wall and my body.

"What the hell are you doing?" she asked, startled into sobriety.

I whispered over her lips, "My brother. He can't see me."

She took a quick peek to the side and nodded.

"Just follow my lead."

I don't know what came over me. Not sure if it was a real plan to disguise us as two other lovers in that house of sensual pleasures, or if I was just giving in to the yearning that had been eating me up since our adventure in the pit....

I kissed her. Hard. Desperately.

Lips locked, tongues entangled, and bodies so close together, it was a miracle we could breathe, we—or maybe just I—forgot about Xian Lu, his whores, and his schemes. I forgot time and space. I forgot who we were. All that existed was that connection, the warmth of her soft lips yielding to me, her wine-flavored tongue dancing with mine, her softness against my hard muscle.

My kiss softened as I nibbled on her lower lip, kissing the corner of her mouth. My lips moved across the line of her jaw to her earlobe, her neck, the hollow of her shoulder. I wanted to wrap my hands around her hips, lift her up, and make her mine right there against that wall.

You're in public, idiot.

I dropped my hands and stepped back. "Oh gods, I'm sorry," I uttered, forgetting to check for my brother. "I'm so sorry, Hú Dié, I don't know what came over me. I saw my brother and...."

As if reading each other's minds, we both looked toward my brother's room, but he had gone inside. We were safe.

I looked her in the eyes, afraid of what I may see there: disgust, disappointment, maybe anger. But there was none of that in her dark brown eyes. Instead, there was softness, longing.

"Are you really that sorry, or do you want to continue this in the privacy of our room?" she whispered, leaning closer to me, her fingers closing around my shirt. "I'd like to continue, but if you don't want to—"

That's all it took. I held her hand and pulled her inside our room, slamming the door behind us.

I'm not even sure how we got to the bed, but one moment I was holding her against a wall, and then the next, my butterfly was pinned between me and the hard mattress, her legs wrapped around my hips and her hands busy untying my tunic.

"Are you sure you want this?" I asked in a voice I barely recognized, desire choking me.

In response, she captured my lips in a kiss that spoke a million silent words. "Does this answer your question?" she asked in a whisper.

I think I smiled like an idiot, but I couldn't be sure because my need for her had overwhelmed everything else. The world outside that small space in bed had ceased to exist, and all I could think about was making love to her.

But I needed to be sure. "You didn't sprinkle your magic on me, did you?"

You couldn't be quiet, could you?

With a mighty shove, she pushed me off her. Surprised, I lost my balance and fell on the wooden floor. When I looked up, Hú Dié was sitting on the edge of the bed, looking less like a butterfly and more like a tiger. A very pissed tiger.

"You really cannot envision yourself wanting me because of who I am and not because of my magic powder?"

Gods, she was angry, and my yearning for her grew. She was gorgeous when she was mad.

"I thought you were different, but it turns out you're just another insecure, pompous male who doesn't know what he wants." She glared at me, her eyes nearly popping out of her sockets. In a whisper she added, "Or what's good for you."

Shit. I was screwed. And not in the way I had hoped for.

Hú Dié gave me the silent treatment all the way back home.

After taking a very cold bath and tidying up a few loose threads with my local spies, I left my sibling—half comatose after his nightlong sex marathon—and packed the few items I had brought with me while the butterfly simmered on her perch by the window. I could almost see the storm clouds gathering over her head as she sat, arms tightly crossed over her chest, sling pack ready and gaze firmly aimed at the street below us.

Now that we were quickly approaching the compound, those clouds had almost solidified, and I could have sworn I heard thunder coming from her more than once. Gods, I was in so much trouble.

As soon as we passed through the gates, she ran into the building and disappeared inside. I stood there for a few minutes, staring and maybe hoping she'd come back and smile at me. Or even snap at me. Anything but this pregnant silence that was eating me up inside. All I had wanted was to make sure I was not forcing myself on her—she had drunk a bit too much, and I wasn't sure how long the effects of her powder lasted—but instead, I had given her the impression I felt I was

being the one being coerced into it. Too long without a relationship had made me careless with my words.

"Daydreaming?" Ding Māo's voice snapped me out of my
trance. "What exactly are you staring at?"

I shook my head, finally awake, and swallowed the bile gathering in my throat. "Nothing. We had a disagreement."

Ding Māo glanced toward the butterfly fairy's rooms and then
back at me. "You and Butterfly?" he exclaimed. "What happened?"

I turned around and resumed my way to my rooms. "Never
mind. It will blow over." I hoped. "Let's talk."

My friend chuckled behind me. "Trouble in paradise, then?"
he asked, falling into step with me. "What did you do? Not that
it takes a lot to make that firecracker mad."

I had no wish to share my foot-in-my-mouth incident, so I kept
quiet. There were more pressing matters to discuss. As soon as we
were settled in my room, tea in hand, I relayed all the happenings
to do with my half brother, carefully avoiding anything that involved Hú Dié.

"Gods, who knew your brother had that much... vitality," Ding
Māo said with a snort.

"He had a little help from our home fairy," I admitted, wondering whether my friend was aware of her powers.

"What do you mean?" he asked, confusion clouding his eyes.
He did not know.

Satisfaction swelled in my chest as I explained.

"Who knew? Our fairy is full of surprises, isn't she?"

She was indeed. But I would jealously keep the rest to myself.

"Do you think it's safe to say he won't produce an heir even
after all that fucking?" my crass friend asked.

I shrugged. "It doesn't really matter, does it?" I took a sip of the hot tea, enjoying its descent down my throat. "*A Duì*, how's my brother doing?" I asked, suddenly remembering the reason for all this.

"He's doing great," he answered, playing with the few drops of spilled tea on the table. "It won't be long before he's on his feet. You should go see him."

Alongside Ding Māo, I crossed the courtyard to where my brother's rooms were located in a humbler corner of my compound, the last place anyone would suspect of harboring royalty and quiet enough for him to be able to recover in peace.

But quietude was not exactly what awaited me.

As we turned the corner to the smaller courtyard, the sound of laughter reached us, loud and raucous. I only had time to steal a glance at my friend before we were both dashing inside.

"Mì Mì, you're here," my convalescing brother exclaimed between chuckles. He wiped the tears from his eyes. "Gods, *gē*, Hú Dié is hilarious."

The butterfly fairy's grin turned into a scowl at the sight of me. What was she doing here?

"She was telling me about your adventures at the brothel," Wang Li continued, still brushing tears from his eyes. "Who would have thought Xian Lu capable of such vigor?"

I swallowed the knot in my throat, unable to say anything as her eyes burned me to the ground.

Ding Māo approached the bed where my brother was lying and sat on the edge, next to Hú Dié. "I heard he was pretty loud," he said to her with a wicked grin.

She snorted. "That's an understatement. The man sounded like a pig being slaughtered," she said.

I cringed even though what she said wasn't far from the truth.

"If he fucks as well as he screams, he's a fabulous lover."

"Hú Dié! Stop talking like that." My exclamation came out a lot louder than I'd planned. All three of them stared at me. "You're a female. You shouldn't be talking about these things with males."

Gods, I sound like an idiot. I just don't want her talking to other males about this.

She crossed her arms in her favorite stance. "How prudish of you," she said, a mocking smile dancing on her lips and in her eyes. "As an immortal I have been around long enough to not heed any of those silly social conventions. Or listen to those who do."

Ouch!

Ding Māo was having fun, as his toothy smile attested. "I don't remember you being so... proper and all, Mì Mì," he said. "I mean, you're the one who started the rumors about your sexual preferences by sharing detailed accounts of your—albeit imaginary—romantic dalliances."

Heat climbed up my neck and invaded my cheeks. "That was a necessary evil." I stumbled over my own excuses. "And I am a male, so it doesn't look as bad when I say things like that."

Shut up, just shut up!

My brother came to my rescue. "All right, you guys had your fun embarrassing the man," he said with a soft chuckle. "He's only trying to protect his charge, that's all."

"I don't need his protection," Hú Dié snapped, her eyes still shooting fireballs at me. "I am perfectly capable of doing it myself."

Of course she was. I knew that. I loved the fact that she was fierce and more capable than many of my own hardened spies. I still wanted to protect her, to make sure no one picked on her or caused her any pain.

I love her. I do. I love her.

The realization hit me harder than an enemy punch straight in the gut. I was in love with this fairy. Me, the one person who had not given his heart to anyone since childhood. The same man who lived for his mission and nothing else.

This couldn't be good. I couldn't afford distractions. But how do you tell your heart to fall out of love?

You don't, you fool. You just don't.

CHAPTER NINETEEN

Awakening

Hú Dié

I MUST HAVE WALKED the length of my room a hundred times, torn between fuming at *shīfu* and hating myself for it.

What was wrong with me that I'd snapped at what he'd said in a moment of vulnerability? The old me would have ignored it and proceeded to have sex with him. The old me wouldn't have cared that he may think I'd drugged him. Hell, my old self would have laughed and felt flattered by his assumption. After all, trust and care for no one if you want to survive. Trust only yourself if you want to protect your heart. The old me knew that.

What the fuck happened to my former self? When did this creature who listens to feelings she knows to be dangerous overcome the cold-hearted me?

I yelled, frustration getting the best of me. A walk would do me good, I decided. Outside in the fresh air of the night where my thoughts could clear and my irritation could dissipate.

I opened the door and walked into the dark, feeling the chill cover my arms in goose bumps. Restless, I began pacing the covered walkway that ran along the whole row of buildings in this courtyard.

His courtyard.

Now, why would I think about Shén Mì again? By now, he was fast asleep after feasting with his brother and friend. He had more important things to think about and do than staying up late ruminating on what had happened between us. He was not the sentimental type.

But he was not as coldhearted as he wanted everyone to think he was. I had seen a gentler side of him, revealing someone willing to do anything for what was right.

Someone who is willing to save you at any cost.

Fuck! He *had* saved me at a huge risk to himself and his mission. He hadn't hesitated to reveal his immortal form when I froze at the sight of the *guài*, incapable of coherent thought or action. He had rescued me from the Monster and myself.

I stopped in my tracks, closed my eyes, and cursed myself. Loudly. How ungrateful of me to bite the hand that not only fed me but that had also protected me from the one creature I feared the most.

Determined to make amends, I strode across the yard to go knock at his door. Nobody answered.

Was he ignoring me, or was he already asleep?

"Master is at the hot spring," a little voice said from behind me.

Yushu, who apparently never slept, lowered her eyes as soon as I turned to her.

"In the White Lake," she added.

I braced my hands on my hips. "Yushu, please look at me when I speak to you," I told her, hoping my voice sounded gentle enough not to scare her. "We're equals, you hear? Until I came to live here, I was homeless, living out in the streets, and begging for food."

The young woman raised her eyes to mine, blinking.

I smiled. "That's much better. Now, do me a favor and go fetch me a towel. I think I will join *shīfu* in the lake."

She turned around and shuffled across the yard as quickly as her short legs could carry her, but I couldn't miss her giggles. Shit, I hoped she would keep this between us, or by tomorrow, rumors of what we may or may not have done in the bath would be all people talked about.

Soon enough I was at the lake, large white towel in hand and the glorious moon peeking from behind a cloud. I saw him right away, his back turned to me, white-jade skin bathed by the moonbeams, a stark contrast to the raven silk of his long hair. A shiver went through me, and it had nothing to do with the chilly air.

I took a deep breath.

You're not backing out now. Be brave.

Silently, I navigated along the edge of the water all the way to the opposite side of where Shén Mì was. His eyes were closed, the dark crescents of his eyelashes black against his skin. I watched him for a while, his strong shoulders crowning lean but muscular arms and chest, a surprise for anyone who had only seen him inside his elegant silky clothes carefully tailored to make him look more delicate than brawny.

I lingered one moment too long, or maybe I let out a sigh at the beauty of him. His eyes snapped open and homed in on me. I froze for a second under the weight of his gaze, but it was only a fleeting moment before his stare softened.

"What are you doing here, Butterfly?" he asked, a smile on his lips.

"I came to join you," I said and then hurried to add, "If that's all right."

He nodded, his hands still submerged under the hot water. I began peeling off my clothes. He blinked, the only sign of his surprise, but he never took his eyes away from me. I wasn't shy. No one who had lived a lifetime in a glass cage could be shy. But the heat of his golden eyes on me made me blush as I removed each and every piece of my clothing before sliding into the warm water.

Naked and stupidly nervous, I waded my way forward until I was standing before him, shivering like an idiot, the water barely covering my breasts.

The jerk smiled.

I should have got pissed at him making light of my vulnerability, but I smiled instead, my nerves smoothing out at the sight of his grin.

"I thought we'd finished what we started the other night," I said, much calmer now, my determination coming back full force.

He took a moment to answer. "You're sure?"

I threw my head back with a grunt. "Shén Mì, stop asking me that," I said. "I'm not your pure virgin who can't decide one way or another. If I am here, I *am* sure, no question about it."

He moved so fast, I didn't realize what was happening until my body was flush with his, his hand curving around my waist, pulling me even closer.

"You're naked," I said, narrowing my eyes.

"I *am* taking a bath," he countered, a wicked smile lifting the corners of his mouth. "And so are you, in case you forgot."

I chuckled, shamelessly rubbing myself against his hard muscles. He moaned, and I reached through the water between us to touch him. He captured my lips with his and made me forget who I was for a second, his tongue tracing the edges of my mouth before dancing with mine.

"I'm sorry," I whispered over his mouth, our hot breath mingling. "I shouldn't have said the things I said."

He nibbled on my lower lip. "I'm sorry too. I said the wrong thing. I know that." He bookended my face with his hands and looked me straight in the eyes. "Do you forgive me?"

"It depends," I said.

He raised an eyebrow.

"Can you make me fly?"

His smile widened. "I'm certainly going to give it my best, Butterfly."

I was a butterfly, used to flying wherever I wanted. I had never flown high enough to touch the stars, though.

Until now.

Shén Mì was as good and dedicated at making love as he was with everything else in his life. His touch was magic, making my blood run hotter and faster in my veins, turning my body simultaneously as heavy as the earth beneath us and as light as the air above us.

"Say the word, and I'll stop," he said again, his lips touching my earlobe and sending a thousand little caresses rushing through my body.

Why was he so afraid I didn't want this? Wasn't it painfully obvious by my moans of pleasure and the enticing whispers and touches that I very much, undoubtedly, absolutely wanted to make him mine?

I nibbled on his ear. Well, more like an actual gentle-ish bite. "Stop asking me that," I told him, brushing his dark hair from his eyes. "Once and for all, the answer is a giant yes. Make love to me. Please."

He chuckled against my neck. "I like that."

I furrowed my brow. "Like what?" I played with the hard ridges of muscle on his back. He might not be bulky, but every inch of his beautiful body was covered in solid, corded muscle.

"That you want me to make love to you," he whispered, brushing his lips over the hollow of my neck.

What did he mean?

"Not that you want me to fuck you."

Comprehension hit me. Now that he mentioned it, I was also surprised with my choice of words. Not one of my past lovers had been asked to make love to me. Ever. I knew that it was always a meeting of the flesh, a distraction, an itch to be scratched. So I always called it what it was. Nothing more and nothing less.

Then why am I calling it love?

I stiffened for a second, and he lifted his head to look at me, the water sloshing between us. "I'm not saying it means anything, I just like it," he assured me.

I softened against him again, relishing the feel of his warm body—warmer than the heated water—against mine. I wasn't sure what to say, so I didn't say anything, focusing instead on running my thirsty fingers all over him.

My mind flew to other realms, and I was caught by surprise when he closed his hands around each side of my waist and pulled me out of the water. Before I could say anything, he settled me on the very edge of the rocky wall of the natural pool and pried my thighs apart.

"I promised you I'd make you fly," he explained, a wicked twinkle in his eyes. A shiver weaved its way through my being, my wings temporarily materializing behind me as what he was about to do dawned on me. He chuckled softly. "No need for your wings."

He settled himself between my legs and shattered every inch of me with a flick of his tongue.

I moaned. Or at least I think that sound of utter delight came from me, but the bliss his warm mouth was stirring had made me separate myself from everything else. All I knew, all I felt was his touch and the waves of pleasure each stroke of his tongue, each suckle of his lips roused in me.

It didn't take long for his promise to be fulfilled as stars exploded inside me, making me soar higher than I had ever been, higher than I ever thought possible. I lay all the way back, my hot skin meeting the cool grass as tremors ran through my body, Shén Mì's hands still flat on my upper thighs.

"Are you all right?" he asked, his voice a caress.

I chuckled. Was I all right? Was there even a word to describe how I was feeling at that moment? I settled on a nod as a response, gathering my strength to sit up again.

When I finally did, I was struck by what I saw in his eyes. I couldn't name it, since I had never seen it before, but it blew me over emotionally. There was such intensity, such longing and warmth in his gaze, it made my heart tip-tap. Whatever that emotion was, I liked it.

No. I love it.

I had never been sentimental. I couldn't be, having been a prisoner in a cage for more than two mortal lifetimes. What was there to be sentimental about? But this gooey, fuzzy, and overwhelming feeling brought tears to my eyes.

"Why are you crying?" Shén Mì asked, gently wiping a tear with his thumb. "Did I hurt you? Did I do something to make you uncomfortable?"

I couldn't voice the words, all choked up in my throat as they were, so I wrapped my arms around his neck and pulled him against me, pressing my mouth to the side of his head in a kiss. He hesitated for a second before wrapping me in his embrace.

"You didn't hurt me," I managed to whisper against his silky hair. "These are good tears."

He let out a loud exhale as if he had been holding his breath, and that simple gesture made me cry even more.

You're a fool, butterfly. Remember? Don't trust anyone.

But I did trust this dragon. He had more than proved himself worthy of my trust. Despite my own efforts to the contrary, I had full confidence Shén Mì had my best interests in mind. And even more surprising was the fact that I *wanted* to trust him, I wanted to keep him in my heart forever and protect him from all those who wished him ill.

For fuck's sake! Am I in love with this man?

CHAPTER TWENTY

Love

SHÉN MÌ

Y USHU WOULD BE LIVID when she saw the trail of water Hú Dié and I left on the bamboo floors of my room. We didn't bother drying out or even dressing. I swept her into my arms and carried her all the way to my room, water dripping from our hair and our bodies across the courtyard, up the few steps, and all the way inside.

Slick with the warm water of the natural pool and the early dawn's dew, we stood face to face, my hands on her shoulders, hers on my hips. Hú Dié was a whole head shorter than me, the top of her head barely crossing the line of my chin. She tipped her face toward me with a smile, and I swore the floor moved underneath me.

"You're so beautiful," I whispered, longing to trace the elegant lines of her eyes with my fingers.

"You're beautiful too," she said, sliding her hand lower to my upper thigh.

A shiver ran through me as my body reacted to her touch.

After a moment of silence she added, "We should dry off."

I blinked, not sure what to do. I didn't want to move. At least not in any way that would pull us apart.

"We don't want to wet the bed," she explained with a wink.

I'm not even sure where I got them from, but in no time, we were wrapped in soft towels, dry and cozy. Butterfly sat on the edge of the bed while I dried her long hair with another towel, the heat rising with each stroke, my longing shamelessly obvious against her back.

She leaned back and gasped. I froze, afraid my physical response would scare her away. She'd been in a cage for a lifetime, and gods only knew the indignities she had to suffer under the control of the *guài*. I had to be gentle, careful, respectful.

She turned halfway toward me, the ends of her hair still caught between the towel in my hands, and looked up. "I'm not fragile, you know."

My heart skipped a beat, and I dropped the towel.

She stood up, letting her towel slip all the way to the floor before divesting me of mine. "We should make love before Yushu wakes up," she said, running her hand slowly from my neck down to my navel. "And I have it on good authority that girl doesn't sleep much."

Her fingers stopped teasingly shy of my erection, her eyes twinkling with mischief. I think I grunted with a mixture of frustration and excitement, and then I took a step closer, taking her lips with mine.

This was not a gentle kiss. It contained all the hunger, desire, fear, and love I had kept inside me for the past few weeks, refusing to accept the fact I was in love with this fairy. Refusing the idea that I was indeed capable of loving anyone but my siblings and my mission. I had foregone love many years ago as a teenager, a direct result of realizing I was a prize to be had, not someone to be loved.

Hú Dié had changed all of that.

I softened my kiss and scooped her up in my arms to lay her down on my bed. My butterfly fairy was beautiful even if her body was marred with scars left by years of physical torture and all the fights she picked. Her immortal body had healed most of them, but there were a few left.

"They're reminders," the fairy whispered as if she had read my mind. "I didn't want them all gone. I wanted to keep reminders so I didn't get careless or too trusting."

I clenched my fists. "Can you trust me?" I asked even though I was terrified of the answer.

I knew how hard it was to open up yourself to people after getting pushed down so many times. I was lucky. I had my siblings and Mão Mão, plus a group of others I could at least trust with my life if not necessarily with my heart. She had nothing, nobody to lean on to, no shoulder to cry on. How could I ask her to open up to me?

She waited a few heartbeats, swallowed, and said, "I do. I really do."

I'd never heard any words that made me as happy as hers did. I slid over her, my skin still damp and warm from the pool water, all my hard spots melding with her soft ones. I braced myself on either side of her to kiss her again, gentler this time, slowly enough to savor every second of her sweet flavor but deep enough to fan my desire.

I dropped onto my side, reaching to find her small breasts. I cupped one, then the other. Encouraged by her whimper, I rubbed the pink bud between my fingers, making her moan and wiggle while I swelled against her leg. I followed my hand with my mouth, swallowing one of the soft mounds, teasing it with my tongue and my teeth until I thought I'd explode. I slid my hand down her belly and slipped my fingers between her legs, softly brushing them against her folds. She curved her back, pressing her lower body against my hand, demanding more pressure, more speed.

I obliged, on the verge of losing control. I needed to be inside her.

As if guessing my thoughts, my fairy flopped over so that she was now straddling me, her heat against mine. It was my turn to groan as she raised her bottom and lowered herself onto my arousal. I buried myself inside her, screaming as I did, pleasure exploding in every inch of my body, inside and out. She gyrated her hips faster and faster until I felt I couldn't hold it any longer.

"Let it go," she ordered, breathless, her hands flat on my chest. "Let. It. Go."

So I did. For the first time in who knew how long, I just let it all go: seed, body, heart, and soul. For the first time in my adult life, I felt like a free man.

If anyone had told me before that I would be in tears after having sex, I would have called them crazy.

Yet, here I am, crying.

With my face buried in the crook of Hú Dié's neck, I wept. Gods, those tears just kept coming, dampening her skin and the silk of the pillow beneath her head.

After taking me up to the heavens and back, my fairy flipped us over so I was now on top of her, hoping I wouldn't crush her with my weight and incapable of stopping the stream of hot tears from rolling out of my eyes.

Why am I crying?

Hú Dié curled a hand over the back of my head in a gentle, comforting caress. "It's all right," she cooed in my ear. "Let it all out."

But what was I letting out, anyway? I was happy, still basking in the aftermath of our flight together. So what exactly was making me cry like a child?

"It can't be easy for you," she said, her other hand flat on my back. "Pretending to be something you are not, always acting, always hiding your true self. I may have been imprisoned for most of my life, but I was at least allowed to be me—a very unhappy, fearful, and belittled me, but still myself."

I hiccupped against her shoulder.

"You, on the other hand, can never be your true self, not even in front of your father."

Gods, she had hit the target spot-on. These tears were not about making love to her or how I felt in that moment. They were all about realizing how good it felt to be allowed to be who I was, how freeing it was to know I didn't have to hide anything from her. She had seen me at my best and my worst. She had seen my secret dragon self and hadn't uttered a word about it to anyone. For the first time in my life, I could be Cheng Shén Mì, Dragon Prince of Lóngzhī Dìguó, even if for her eyes only.

I don't know how long we stayed like that, bodies entwined and voices silenced, my heart half exploding inside me but soothed by the contact, the warmth of her breath, the beating of her heart against my chest. It was a lullaby, and eventually I must have fallen asleep.

"Shén Mì." Her voice echoed quietly in my ear. "I have to get up. Can't feel my legs anymore."

It took me a moment to clear my mind and understand what she meant. Gods, I was still lying on top of her, my body easily double her weight. Could she even breathe?

I rolled off her. "Sorry. Did I hurt you?" I asked.

She laughed. "No, I'm fine," she said, turning onto her side to face me. "How are *you*?"

I was surprised that her question didn't embarrass me. After all, I—a grown man who had been running a spy-warrior network for years—had poured my heart out onto her delicate shoulder. Instead, I felt happy, comfortable in the knowledge that she had seen that side of me and had not run for the hills—or at the very least, laughed in my face. I had seen her at her weakest. It was only fair to show her mine.

"Are you hungry?" I asked, dodging the question.

Her stomach growled even before she could answer, and we burst out laughing.

"I guess you are." I swung my legs over the edge of the bed and offered her my hand. "Let's sneak into the kitchen and see what Cook has in the cupboard."

Her eyes opened wide. "Ooh, you have a mischievous side," she said, a twinkle glinting in her eyes. "I like it."

She took my hand, and we half dressed, half kissed our way to the door, a sight to be seen in our disheveled state, and for once I didn't worry about being caught doing something that might be considered fun and immature by one of the servants or one of my spies. For once, I didn't care if my reputation for being coldhearted and somber among my people shattered into a million pieces. I was so very happy, and I wanted the world to know it.

As we opened the locked door to the kitchen, we giggled like two children up to no good. I grabbed Hú Dié by the waist and pulled her back against me to kiss the top of her head. "What do you want to eat?"

She spun in my arms to face me, her hands clasped behind me. "What do you think?"

A smile curled my lips. "*Bao*, of course. Silly question." I dropped a kiss on her tiny nose. "I love how you smell."

My fairy laughed harder. "Of mud and sweat?" she said. "You have a strange sense of smell, *shīfu*."

"You always smell of flowers, no matter how much you've trained or dragged yourself through dirt." It was true. Maybe it was her nature as a butterfly to always carry a flowery scent. Not an overwhelming, strong perfume but rather a subtle, barely-there bouquet. It was lovely. It was intoxicating.

Fuck! I love her!

So why was I not panicking at all? Why was there this irrational joy in my heart?

My world—the world I had created so carefully throughout the years—had cracked like an egg, spilling out the gooey innards. But after all, wasn't the inside of an egg what fed and delighted us?

"Any news from the brothel?" I asked, half preoccupied with a loose string on my sleeve.

Ding Māo walked beside me, cracking pistachio nuts with his teeth and throwing the shells behind him. "No pregnancies that we know of," he mumbled while chewing. "But one of his concubines just gave birth to another girl."

I wasn't worried about my sibling producing a male heir. After all, the crown prince was alive and getting healthier with each day he rested in my house. There was no real threat there. However, some petty part of me wanted to make sure Xian Lu got no satisfaction whatsoever from his whole crooked plan to take the throne.

"Where's our beautiful warrior?" my friend asked, flinging more shells over his shoulder.

I froze.

Ding Māo, unaware I had stopped, continued walking for a few more feet. When he realized he had left me behind, he turned around, the skin between his cat eyes furrowed. "What's wrong?"

"She's not *your* beautiful warrior," I growled, irrational anger making me choke on my own words.

He opened his eyes wide, a tiny smile trembling on his lips. "What?" He could barely disguise his amusement. "It's just an expression. She *is* beautiful and she *is* one of our spies, isn't she?"

I swallowed, feeling ridiculous for the sensation that something was about to explode out of my chest. "I repeat: she's not yours!"

My friend raised his hands in appeasement. "*Hǎo, hǎo,*" he said, a poorly veiled smile on his face. "She's not mine. Never was, never will be. She's all yours."

I growled again, my dragon fighting to surface. "She's not mine either. She doesn't belong to anyone." I meant it. Butterfly was free to do as she wanted and no one, not even me, had the right to restrain her in any way. I would deal with anyone who tried.

"*Gē,* you are bewitched," my friend said with a chuckle, crossing his arms over his chest. "You have it bad."

"What do you mean?" I knew what he meant, but damned if I was going to admit it.

"You're in love with the fairy."

As if I didn't know that already.

Ding Māo clicked his tongue. "The cold, supposedly *duan xiu* prince and spymaster has fallen in love. I wouldn't believe it if I didn't see it with my own eyes."

I had no response. What could I say? That he was lying? That I didn't love the butterfly? This was my best friend, closer to me than any of my own siblings. He could read me like an open book. I sighed loudly and resumed my walk toward my brother's quarters.

Ding Māo snickered behind me, and I waved a dismissive hand at him. "Think what you wish," I said.

Fuck, I am pathetic.

As we turned around the bend into what was currently Wang Li's courtyard, we both came to a halt. Hú Dié was leaving my brother's room, a wide smile on her face and an obvious spring in her step. My dragon roared inside me, fighting to come out. I inhaled deeply, trying to calm down.

What's wrong with you?

Was I jealous? Of my own brother?

"Are you all right?" my friend asked, patting my shoulder. "You're very red right now."

I took off with a quick stride as soon as my fairy disappeared around the corner. Wang Li's door was not closed, a cool breeze blowing inside in my wake.

"What was Hú Dié doing here?" I asked even before I reached the bed where my brother sat.

Wang Li looked up at me, furrowing his brow. "Good morning to you too, *gē*," he said, a hint of sarcasm tinting his words. "She came to visit, what else?"

I knew I was being stupid and unreasonable, but I couldn't stop myself. "She looked awfully happy when she left your side."

Gods, please stop me from making a fool of myself.

Ding Māo caught up with me, a little winded. "He's jealous," he said, shaking his head.

I turned my face to him. "I am not." If I kept going like this, I'd be breathing fire soon.

My brother flipped the sheets from his legs and sat on the edge of the bed. Even in my anger, I was amazed by how well he was recovering.

"I have no designs on your butterfly fairy," my brother said, amusement twinkling in his eyes. "And she has no interest in me, I promise you."

Anger burned in my throat. "How do you know that?"

He chuckled and ran a hand over his face. "Because she spent the whole time she was with me talking and asking questions about you."

My anger dissolved as if by magic and a strange titillating glow spread over me.

"I think it's fair to say that your... admiration for her is reciprocated tenfold."

I couldn't stop the idiotic smile that stretched my lips. "You're sure?"

He shook his head just as Ding Mão burst out laughing.

"The girl is besotted with you. I don't understand why, but she is," my brother said with a snort. "It's not like you're handsome or smart. Or even interesting at all."

I pretended to punch him. "Not as much as you, anyway," I said, my dragon finally back to sleep. "How do you feel?"

He stood up, a little shaky still. "Much, much better," he said, taking a couple steps toward me. "Getting stronger every day."

I offered my arm for support, which he took with a smile, and we walked to the table where one of the servants had set up a tea tray. Steam wafted out of the blue kettle, filling the air with the tantalizing scent of good tea. I led my brother to a chair, and we all sat around the table.

"So, *gē*," Wang Li started as I lifted the teacup to my lips, "when is the wedding?"

Needless to say, the tea spurted out of my mouth like one of the northern lands' geysers while laughter echoed through the room.

The funny thing was, the idea of marrying the fairy didn't feel that outlandish anymore. In fact, it left me with a lingering sense of anticipation and joy.

But did Hú Dié feel the same? Or would she skewer me with her sword if I asked her in earnest?

CHAPTER TWENTY-ONE

Danger

Hú Dié

YUSHU FUSSED WITH MY overdress in a perfect imitation of a mother hen. "Hú *xiǎojiě*, the sleeves are askew," she said as I continued to walk, forcing her to skitter behind me in a huff. "Let me fix them."

I waved a hand, throwing her a glance. "Will you stop worrying about my dress?" I told her, not slowing down. "Who cares?"

She shuffled beside me, clutching the edge of her cloak. "You must look proper for the sake of the master," she said, her pretty face twisting with concern. "Master prides himself on his looks and fashion sense, and he expects all of his people to do the same. Even the servants."

I had noticed the high standards of Shén Mí's dress code for his household. I now knew it was but a ruse to throw off any onlooker's suspicions. He wanted to be thought of as a shallow man with an overinflated interest in expensive silks and other luxuries. The prince was smart and cunning, but most only saw his shiny shell.

Reluctantly I stopped and allowed her to fix my outerwear to her very high standards before continuing our walk. We were heading to the night market in town. It was rare for it to be held in the area and was rumored to offer an exquisite range of goods for sale—from beautiful silks from the far edges of the empire to the most magnificent blades. I was equally excited about both ends of the array and couldn't wait to get there, fueled by the irrational fear they would be sold out before my arrival.

At first, Shén Mí had planned on coming along. The town people expected him to show his face—a frivolous man out to buy things to feed his vanity. But Ding Mǎo had arrived with urgent news from the palace, and the two of them were sequestered in talks with the crown prince.

I don't care. I want a new blade and a new dress.

Freedom was sweet, and I was quickly getting a taste for those small luxuries I had only been able to dream about for years. I might have lots of shortcomings, but vanity was not one of them. However, I did enjoy the feeling of good silk against my skin and the weight of a well-forged sword on my back.

"You are to buy yourself something pretty too," I ordered Yushu, the chill of the night making me shiver. Maybe the girl was right about proper attire. I pulled the edges of my coat tighter across my chest. Maybe I could find some good furs at the market to make a better, warmer coat for the impending winter.

As soon as I spotted the lights of the market lanterns in the distance, I set out at a trot, much to Yushu's dismay.

"Wait for me, Hú *xiǎojiě*," she yelled out from behind me.

I barely recognized the town I had visited so many times in the past couple months. Red and gold lanterns hung from poles posted along the main street, lending an otherworldly mood to the whole market. Legend claimed that many, many centuries ago, before mortals came to inhabit this world, there was a magical realm where all immortals lived. I'm pretty sure this is what it looked like.

People dressed in their most festive clothes meandered along the main thoroughfare and its many branches, chatting, checking out the colorful wares underneath the white canopies, and snacking on candied hawthorn berries or sugar sculptures on a stick.

I yelped and clapped in delight. "How beautiful. How fun."

Without delay, I skipped from one stall to another, dragging poor Yushu behind me. There were so many wonderful things, I wasn't sure where to start.

When I stopped by what I thought was the last stall on the street, a blinking light beckoned from around the bend. Curiosity piqued, I cocked my head to one side, narrowing my eyes and wondering. The light was more of a glow that ebbed and flowed, changing colors and bathing the alley in a rainbow of light.

What's that?

The butterfly in me couldn't resist the yellow-and-red glow, so I dropped the hairpin I had been studying and turned around to follow the light.

"*Gūniáng*, you're not taking the pin?" the merchant yelled after me, but I was too curious now, instinct taking over my common sense.

I hurried to the end of the alley, Yushu pitapatting behind me.

"Hú *xiǎojiě*, don't," she kept saying, grabbing my arm in an attempt to physically stop me. "It's too dark in this alley. It's dangerous."

"Stop fussing, Yushu," I snapped back, my glance glued to the glow around the corner. "I'm not helpless, you know."

"But—" She never finished, and that alone should have set off all my alarms. But I was too hypnotized by the pulsing light to notice.

It wasn't until I turned the corner that my common sense made a return, and by then it was too late; I had a bag over my head and shoulders and couldn't move.

Instinct took over, and I started morphing into my butterfly form. Except I couldn't. No matter how much I tried, my human shape stuck like tree sap to the bottom of a shoe.

Magic!

I was stuck inside an immortal-subduing artifact, helplessly incapable of using any of my magic or strength. My thoughts went to poor Yushu. What had they done to her?

"Who's this? What do you want?" I yelled, struggling to free myself from the burgeoning constriction of the magic bag. "Let me go!"

"Stop fighting, little butterfly. You can't get away."

My heart stopped and my body went cold. Arctic cold.

I knew that voice all too well. "My master should have killed you," I said, hating the weakness in my trembling voice.

The *guài* roared with laughter. "The dragon?"

Fuck, in the chaos of the whole thing, I had forgotten the Monster had gotten away before I wiped the crowd's memory.

"My new boss will take care of him. No need to worry."

What does he mean by that?

Was his boss who I thought it was? The conniving Xian Lu?

Gods, Shén Mì is in danger.

I threw myself against the constraints of the bag, but all I succeeded in doing was making it snugger. Every time I moved to free myself, the bag got smaller and tighter to the point that I could barely breathe.

"Let me go!" I yelled in vain. No one would hear me while the sounds of the night market filled the air, but I had to try. "Somebody help me!"

Strong hands grabbed me around the waist, lifted me up, and threw me over a hard shoulder. "It's time to go home, little butterfly," the Monster said in a mock tender tone. "I have lots of customers waiting for your powder."

My thoughts went flying. I could guess where he was taking me—I was sure he still had a cage reserved for me. But strangely enough that wasn't what I was worried about. Instead, I kept thinking of my young maid and *shīfu*, worried about what might happen to them. Frustration brought tears to my eyes. I knew they were in danger, and yet, there was nothing I could do about it as the *guài* carried me like a bag of turnips to whatever prison he had magicked for me this time.

Gods, please protect Shén Mì. Don't worry about me. Just take care of him.

I couldn't allow the first person ever to care for me—and whom I loved—to be harmed in any way.

I will find a way out, I promise.

That was a promise I couldn't afford not to keep.

The place reeked of human feces and sweat, an odor combination I was familiar with. Too familiar. As soon as the bag was removed from my head, other equally familiar sights and sounds hit me so hard that I stumbled.

"And don't try to change to a butterfly," the *guài* warned me as he closed the door to my cage. He pointed at the plain metal rods that formed the walls of my jail. "These bars are imbued with immortal-subduing potion."

Frustrated and angry, I turned around and dashed to the door, then grabbed a couple of the bars. Just as I closed my fingers around the thin cylinders, pain rushed through my arms and spread to my whole body as I was thrown backwards to the center of the cage. I fell on my back and hit my head hard on the metal floor.

Laughter echoed around me. "Oh, and yes, I have added a little lightning juice to the bars as well, just to remind you of what kind of pain you will be in if you try to escape again," my jailer said.

I blinked, trying to focus my eyes, but the room wavered around me every time I moved. I pressed a hand to the back of my head where I could feel a growing heat mixed with the pain. There was blood on my fingers. For a moment I gave in to the pain, the exhaustion, the sense of helplessness, to lie there, still and silent.

What do I do?

After the blow to my head and the bolt of electricity that had gone through my body, I couldn't think straight. My thoughts were muddled, flying around like leaves in the wind with no particular reason or direction.

Rest! Heal and regroup.

The first rational and cohesive thought I'd had, and a good one. That's what I'd do: allow my body to heal so my brain could think and come up with a plan.

I closed my eyes, and within seconds, the image of my master appeared, so clear that it was hard to believe it was only a dream. He smiled at me, nodded, and then whispered something I couldn't hear.

In my dream I leaned closer, straining to make out his words. His lips—those beautiful and warm lips I so enjoyed kissing—moved, but no sound came out. Then, before I could lean even closer, someone wielding a sword came from behind him. I screamed, but Shén Mì didn't hear me and stood there, looking at me, confusion in his eyes. The sword came down in a sweeping arc, slicing through Master's neck.

I yelled again, and this time, my own scream woke me up from one nightmare straight into another.

I sat up slowly, my head still dizzy but steadier than before, and looked around me. From between the bars of my prison, I could see many cages of different sizes housing other unfortunate immortals who, like me, had been captured by the greedy and unscrupulous *guài*. My ears were assailed by a wave of moans, yelps, sobs, and pleas for help. My stomach dropped, and bile rose to my mouth.

I was a prisoner again, to be exploited for my magic and beaten regularly to keep me docile. But this time the Monster was out of luck; I had experienced kindness and love, and no amount of cruelty was going to make me bow down to a bully ever again. I knew that something wonderful awaited me outside these bars, and I would do whatever it took to escape.

I studied the space around my cage which was larger than the one I'd been kept in before. The Monster had moved. This was not the same back room of the tavern he used as a shop front for his illicit deals. It was bigger and had no windows at all.

He must have moved his operation to Lóngzhī Dìguó. It made sense if he was now, as I suspected, being sponsored by Xian Lu.

Fuck! If the Monster remembers about Shén Mì's dragon, then Xian Lu knows as well.

I really had to find a way out of this prison, and the quicker the better. My master—my love—was in mortal danger. If his brother was indeed aware of his secret, Xian Lu would do anything to eliminate him from the equation. A harmless, shallow sibling was not a threat, but one with the power of a dragon definitely was.

Inside the cage closest to mine there was a crane immortal. She sat, her back to the bars, cradling her head on her bent knees. In a room where the sounds of suffering and despair were thick in the air, she was the only one who sat in silence, maybe broken like I was before my escape.

"*Hè Xiǎojiě,*" I called her. "Are you all right?"

She didn't answer, so I called her again. Her head moved just enough for me to know she had heard me.

"Why are you here?" I asked. Cranes were known for their long lives, but I had never heard of any other magic properties attached to them. "Are you a doctor?" Shén Mì's doctor was a crane immortal, so maybe the Monster kept her here for medical reasons.

The crane turned her face to me, and I gasped. Dark, almost purple bruises circled her brown eyes, which were too big for her face. Her cheeks were hollowed as if someone had carved the flesh out of them, her skin so pale, I could see all her veins through it.

"You're new," she said in a voice she obviously hadn't used in a long time.

I didn't contradict her even though I had most likely been a prisoner longer than she had. I didn't remember her from before.

"Ever heard of immortality powder?"

I shook my head.

"It's the main ingredient in a *wugu* recipe guaranteed to make your life last a very long time," she explained, sad eyes searching mine. "Do you know what that ingredient is made of?"

I shook my head again.

She sighed and paused for a moment as if catching her breath. "It's made of the bone marrow of a crane."

After spending a lifetime trapped in his grasp, I was sure nothing about my jailer could shock me, but her words hit me so hard, I felt sick. How could anyone, human or demon, be so cruel?

"The Monster has been harvesting my bone marrow for months now," she continued, ignoring the utter horror in my expression. "He's giving me a break now because I almost died last week. As soon as I heal enough, he'll start again."

My shoulders slumped. I had to get out of here.

I had to make sure the *guài* was stopped for good. Even if it killed me.

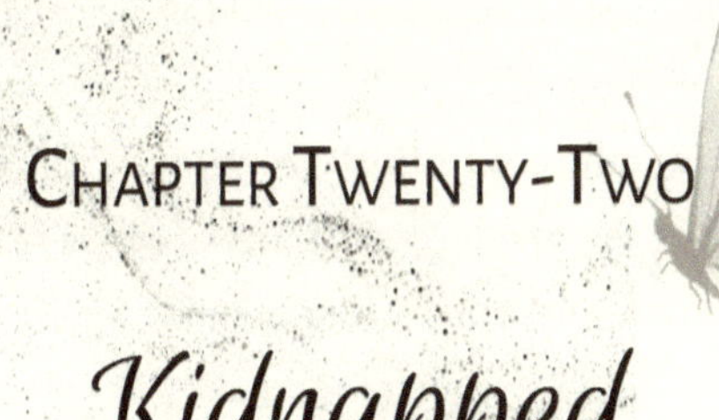

CHAPTER TWENTY-TWO

Kidnapped

SHÉN MÌ

"WHAT DO YOU THINK it's going on?" Ding Māo asked me as we exited my brother's room where we had been all night, discussing the information my spies had gathered.

News that Xian Lu had dispatched a group of his men back to Yumai a few days ago may not at first look suspicious—after all, it was only natural for him to send people to where he was hoping to produce an heir. However, the fact that they had come back with a full caravan comprised of several closed carts containing unknown cargo was indeed worrisome. Xian Lu was up to something, and I needed to find out what.

"Hard to say," I confessed, shaking my head. "We need to find out what's inside those carts. Was there anything else our spies noticed?"

My friend thought for a moment, playing with his nonexistent beard. "Oh yeah, my men told me there was an unknown giant of a man with them. It was dark and they couldn't see details, but apparently the guy was huge."

"Hm," I said unhelpfully. In all the years I had been following and investigating the comings and goings of my half brother, I had never encountered someone who fit the description. "Who could that be?"

"You could send the fairy to find out," Ding Māo suggested. "She'd be the only one who could get in and out undetected. They took the caravan to a compound outside the city walls." He cocked his head in a catlike fashion. "And they left quite a few guards around the perimeter. Whatever's been hidden there has to be important."

The idea of sending Hú Dié into a potentially dangerous situation was not one I relished, but Ding Māo was right; of all my spies, she was the only one who could do it.

"Let's go talk to her," I said, changing direction. "I haven't seen her since she left last night. She must be in her room."

The doors to her quarters were wide open, so after calling out her name, we just walked in. She was nowhere in sight, and even stranger, neither was Yushu, who was always somewhere near.

"*Qíguài*," I whispered, checking behind the dressing screen as if the fairy might be hiding there. "Odd," I repeated, a strange pressure growing in my chest. Something was not right. "Let's go ask the cook if he saw them." My butterfly was a frequent visitor to the kitchen, where she had somehow made friends with the very cranky cook.

The cook hadn't seen her since the day before. I was going into panic mode. There was no way Hú Dié would have missed breakfast with her insatiable hunger for *bao* and porridge. Something bad had happened.

Anticipating my thoughts, Ding Māo said, "Let's go into town and look for them."

He didn't have to say it twice; before he had even finished the sentence, I was already striding to the stables.

It took us only ten minutes to get into town, where the merchants were dismantling their stalls from the night before. The streets were cluttered with the signs of a busy, well-attended event: torn paper, discarded candy and kabob sticks. Even a couple children's bamboo toys littered the packed dirt street.

But no sign of Butterfly or her maid.

"You look on the side streets to the left," I told my friend, my heart trying to jump out of my chest as I climbed down from my horse. "I'll look on the ones to the right."

The small town had been built as a simple but organized structure: a main street from which all others stemmed, spreading to the slightly more chaotic meandering of the outer town, where the houses had been built under or against the protective wall.

I scoured each and every side street from the main gate up the main street, stopping only to ask the merchants if they had seen the two women. It had been a busy night, and nobody seemed to remember them,

At the very end of the main street, I addressed an old vendor who was finishing packing up his wares. "*Shūshu*, have you seen two young women last night, one with a sword across her back...?"

He didn't let me finish. "Yes, she was looking at my hairpins and left without buying anything. The younger one followed her into that alley." He pointed at a narrow street I had missed on the right. "They never came back to buy the pin."

A second look at the alley made my heart thump even harder. It was a narrow strip, hardly a street, which would have been pitch-dark at night. Anything could have been hiding around the bend.

I thanked the old vendor and called Ding Māo. "Someone saw them going down this alley," I explained, my voice choked with anxiety.

"What are we waiting for? Let's go," my friend said, frowning.

I knew I should be running down that street, but my feet wouldn't move. I was frozen with the fear of what I may find, afraid of the worst.

Ding Māo gave me a shove. "Snap out of it, *gē*," he said, running his hands through his hair. "Go!"

Frustrated with my lack of reaction, he grabbed my wrist and pulled me behind him toward the alley. After the first steps, my legs and my brain began to function again, and I was soon running before him, examining every inch of the alley. Too soon we arrived at the end and turned into a brighter street full of abandoned houses and piled trash. As soon as my eyes adjusted to the sudden brightness, I saw what looked like a pile of light-colored clothes and rushed to check them out.

My stomach dropped. This was no heap of clothes. Young Yushu lay motionless in a puddle of what I assumed was her own blood.

"Here," I yelled at my friend. "I found Yushu." Quickly, I touched underneath her nose with my fingers, but in the breezy air, I couldn't tell whether she was breathing. I dropped to my knees and placed an ear against her chest and waited.

A faint but definite beat echoed in my ear. "She's alive," I said, relief flooding my whole being. "She's alive."

It took a few minutes for reality to fully register in my brain. Yushu might be alive, but where was Hú Dié, and was she alive as well? If her maid was so badly hurt, what had they done to my fairy?

And who exactly were *they*? I couldn't shake the feeling that Xian Lu had something to do with it.

If you hurt one hair on her head, I will kill you myself, Xian Lu.

Dr. Ming clicked her tongue as she straightened up from examining a still-unconscious Yushu. She stood for a moment, her arms crossed over her chest, her white robes giving her the look of an ethereal creature from the heavens.

"She'll live," she pronounced, her head cocked like a bird's.

Impatience made me fidgety. I stepped forward and asked, "But when will she wake up? I need to ask her what happened to Hú Dié."

The doctor turned a frowning face to me with a heavy sigh. "I know that the butterfly fairy is very important to your mission, but the life of this young woman is of no less value," she chided me.

I flattened a hand on my chest, looking at my feet. "I don't value Yushu less than anybody else, I promise you." I raised my eyes to her. The good doctor was tapping her foot and glaring at me still. "I'm just afraid that time is of essence to save the fairy."

Ding Mǎo, who had not left my side except for an hour or so to go instruct our spies to scour the land for Hú Dié, spoke up in my defense. "The fairy is important to Mì Mì for more than one reason," he said.

The doctor moved her reproving glance to my friend. "Ah, I see," she said, her stance belying her words. "So, I suppose it's all right to ignore this child's health."

Her sarcasm was so thick, I think I could touch it if I tried.

"Of course not, doctor," I protested, my impatience and frustration rising to alarming heights. "I was just wondering, that's all."

As if summoned by our worry, Yushu fluttered her eyes open and mumbled a few incomprehensible words. I was at her side faster than a hummingbird's wings, leaning over her mouth to try to make out what she was saying.

"They took her," she whispered in my ear. "A... gi-giant."

I sat up and looked at my friend. "Didn't you tell me there was a giant with the caravans?"

Ding Māo nodded.

"Was he bald?"

He nodded again.

"With a tattoo of a snake on his right cheek?"

My friend blinked a few times, his mouth slack. "How did you know that?"

I jumped to my feet. "Fuck! That's the *bàn mó* who had her imprisoned most of her life. He—"

Realization flooded all my senses. Had the half-demon been there when Hú Dié erased the crowd's memories? I closed my eyes, trying to summon a clear picture of that moment, but sometimes when I shifted into or from my dragon form, memories got murky.

I sat on the bed and bent down to Yushu again. "Yushu, did the giant have a snake on his face?"

Her eyes widened and she nodded.

I patted her arm and thanked her. "You rest and get better. I will find Hú Dié."

She closed her eyes, and I stood.

"How many men?" Ding Māo asked, anticipating what my plan was.

"All of them," I said. "Bring Wang Li's trusted men as well."

The next hour or so was a whirlwind of activity distracting me from the fear that had wrapped itself around my heart like a boa constrictor, squeezing and suffocating. By the time I was on horseback, riding toward the mysterious compound where we were certain this half-demon was holding my fairy, the tendrils of fear had morphed into thick tentacles stretching into every part of my body, holding me hostage.

You have to stop this. Hú Dié needs you to be clearheaded and strong for her.

I swallowed the bile, took a deep breath, and urged my horse to go faster. Behind me, Ding Mǎo led a small army of warriors, most of them my own. My brother had quickly agreed to lend us all of his trusted soldiers to go rescue the woman he viewed as his savior. I had insisted on leaving four behind to protect him, but the other eight skilled soldiers were now mixed with mine and more than willing to risk their lives to save Butterfly.

Once we were close enough that we could walk, we hid the horses in the bamboo forest and began our way to the compound, staying out of sight and on padded feet. The half-demon had no idea whom he had messed with. Even if he knew about my dragon, he had no way of knowing that I employed many powerful immortals.

Half of my men circled the building to position themselves in the back, while the other half attacked from the front. I tugged on Ding Mǎo's sleeve and whispered, "I'm staying behind."

He nodded, knowing what I was planning to do without me having to explain.

At my signal, the small army advanced in silence, quickly and quietly subduing the guards that stood by the gates and peppered the whole perimeter. None of the guards were any match for my experienced and magical warriors, as I suspected. Soon they were breaching the gates and pouring into the compound, still lethally silent.

I waited until all my men were out of sight and summoned my dragon. I was going in there with fire, and this time I wasn't leaving the half-demon alive. He was going to pay for daring to touch my butterfly.

Just as I was getting ready to take flight, my long body itching to soar, I heard someone—one of my men—yelling, "They have immortal-subduing shields inside."

If I could, I would have smiled. They may be able to keep magic in check inside their building, but I was coming from above with heavenly fire at the ready. They couldn't—wouldn't stop me.

With an undulating push, I took to the sky up above the tall bamboo trees, the rush of wind against my head and body making my scales shimmer in delight. The urge to let out a mighty roar was powerful, but I didn't want to alert the enemy of my presence just yet. My men had seen my dragon a few times in the past when things got more dangerous than expected, but if they suspected it was me, they had never mentioned it. They were thankful for the dragon power behind them, and that's all they cared about.

I rolled, coiling and uncoiling up above the buildings, studying the ground structures. There was nothing unusual or distinctive about the buildings inside, but one stood out from the others, not because of its uniqueness but because of its size—a rectangular structure with no windows and only a closed door. The shimmer around it told me it was protected by a shield of some kind.

First target acquired.

I circled the building one more time, watching as my men captured more of the people inside, but I hadn't spotted the giant *bàn mó* who had kidnapped Hú Dié. Where was he?

I'll find him later.

Right now, I needed to make sure my fairy was safe and sound. So with a mighty growl, I dove just enough to reach the shield with my fiery breath. I was almost disappointed that it didn't offer much resistance.

I dove again, this time aiming at the straw roof. I had to make sure it burned without falling inside, so it took longer than I had hoped. As soon as there was a hole big enough for me to peek through, I dove lower.

That's when I heard Hú Dié scream, "It's a trap. Don't come in."

At the speed I was going, there was little chance I could stop before it was too late. But no matter what, I was saving my butterfly.

Even if that meant my death.

CHAPTER TWENTY-THREE

Rescue

Hú Dié

I THOUGHT MY HEART would escape from my chest, the way it was throwing itself against my ribs. Shén Mì barreled toward the trap the *guài* had set up, and it didn't look as if he would be able to stop in time. The Monster had placed an immortal-catching net along the inside walls and ceiling of the building, and even though I wasn't sure it would be powerful enough to kill my master's dragon, it would definitely incapacitate him for long enough to put him in danger.

"Stop, Shén Mì," I yelled yet again, angry that that's all I could do, helpless in this cage. "It's a trap. Stop."

I watched in horror as Master dove toward me at great speed. As much as I wanted to look away and not witness what was about to happen, I couldn't take my eyes away from the magnificent creature heading in my direction, hellbent on rescuing me. Suddenly he veered away—or tried to. But his momentum and weight kept him speeding in my direction.

He's not going to make it.

I did close my eyes then, dropped to the metal floor, and drew my knees to my face, waiting to hear the great crash of magic against magic.

But it never came.

I opened one eye and then the other, terrified of what I was about to behold, but it turned out that all I could see was the bright blue sky.

Where did Shén Mì go?

A growing clatter of metal and voices snatched my attention. All around me, cages were opening, and the creatures inside were slowly walking out, turning their heads this way and that, as if awakening from a dream. The shields had been destroyed, or maybe just temporarily disabled.

As I realized that I may not get another chance to escape, I cautiously stood up and touched the bars, bracing myself for the same pain and shock I had felt earlier, but nothing happened. The bars were just metal rods with no magic in them whatsoever.

The magic was gone, but the door was still solidly locked. I closed my eyes and pushed against my magic, trying it out. Finding no resistance, I began transitioning to my butterfly, hesitantly at first, not quite believing in my luck, but faster and confidently a few moments later. With the transformation completed, I flew between the bars and into freedom.

It felt amazing. The first time I had escaped and flown away, my wings had been sore, stiff from not being used for so long. I was so scared I'd be caught, I couldn't enjoy the feeling of freedom until much later. But now my wings spread out and joyfully trembled with each flap, soaring through the air over the other immortals as we all made our way out of the building and into the fresh air.

A big black cat waited outside, pacing from one side to the other, growling in either anticipation or anxiety. As soon as I flew through the doorway, his body began to shimmer, and in less than a minute, Ding Mǎo stood there, a huge smile on his face.

"Fairy, you're safe," he exclaimed, stretching out a hand so I could land on his wrist. "Mì Mì is going to be so happy."

Where was my master? I scanned the area around us, searching for him, but couldn't see him anywhere.

Ding Mǎo lowered his voice to a whisper. "He's changing back in the woods. He's not hurt."

He had barely finished talking when a winded Shén Mì came racing down the path, his long hair loose over his shoulders and an unmistakable frown of worry on his face.

Desperate to ease his distress, I turned into my human form, forgetting I was perched on Ding Mǎo's hand and almost falling face down on the dirt. Master's hand stopped me from falling all the way to the ground, and I held on to his wrist for dear life.

"Dié Dié," he whispered, bending down to hold me better and to turn me to face him. "Are you all right? Does something hurt?"

I straightened within his arms, tilting my chin up to look into his eyes, a tremulous smile tickling my lips. "I'm fine, totally fine." I wrapped my arms around his waist, pulling him closer to me, anxious to feel the heat of his body against mine.

He closed his arms around me, too, and lowered his mouth to mine. "Gods, I thought.... I was afraid...." The man who was never want for words seemed to be speechless. "I was so worried."

I whispered, "The *guài* knows about your dragon. I think he told Xian Lu about it."

Shén Mì nodded as if the thought had already occurred to him. "It's all right," he said. "We'll figure something out."

I pulled back a few inches from him. "But now he knows you are not the weak brother he thought you were," I protested. "You're in danger."

"I can handle him."

I was not about to give up on my own anxiety. "But we need to come up with a plan, don't you—" I didn't finish. Master's lips claimed mine, desperate and hungry. It took me a fraction of a second to respond as passionately.

"Shouldn't you get a room?" Ding Māo asked.

We ignored him and continued to explore each other's mouths, our bodies melding into each other, completely oblivious to the chaos developing around us.

Ding Māo coughed. "I hate to interrupt this very touching reunion, but we should probably get out of here before your brother sends in reinforcements."

He was right, of course. At any moment Xian Lu would receive news of our attack and descend on the compound to protect what he undoubtedly viewed as an investment in his future. Given his mercenary soul, the chance at lining his pockets with the money from illicit magic was irresistible.

Reluctantly, we parted, eyes still on each other's, our bodies alight with a mixture of joy over being alive and well and yearning.

"We'll continue this at home," Master said before draping an arm over my shoulders and walking me away from that prison.

It was then that it hit me: Shén Mì had called me Dié Dié.

Silly as it sounded, that made me giddy with happiness. Master had given me a nickname.

As much as all I wanted was to curl up in bed, wrapped around a very naked Shén Mì, there were more important matters to take care of. Matters that related to the whole empire, not just our selfish desires and needs. So, after I had checked on Yushu, we gathered in Wang Li's room to discuss what we thought was happening and brainstorm how to fight it.

"The damned *bàn mó* is still alive somewhere," Shén Mì growled, a cup of steaming tea on the table in front of him. "I want him dead."

I did, too, and, even though I wouldn't tell him that at that moment, I would be the one ending his life, not anyone else. I needed that closure, and that was the one thing I wasn't willing to give up for my master.

"He's too cunning," I said, sitting on the chair beside him. "I'm sure he built escape routes for himself in case something went wrong." Thankfully, Shén Mì and his men had rescued every fairy trapped in that building and relocated them to a safe place. My heart was happy even if not fully satisfied.

Wang Li, who had left his bed to sit with us around the table, rubbed his chin. "But he's not the main problem," he said. "We have to deal with our brother. Now that he knows about your dragon, Mì Mì, he will do everything in his power to eliminate you."

I agreed. Shén Mì was in great danger.

"He thinks he killed me," Wang Li continued, "but he will view you as a threat, since you are the only other dragon in the family. He knows Father would make you crown prince as soon as he found out."

It was complicated. I knew Shén Mì didn't want to reveal the truth to his father exactly because of the fear that he would insist on making him the heir to the throne, an honor he did not want. On the other hand, he couldn't very well tell his father Xian Lu was trying to kill him for no good reason.

"We set up a trap," Ding Māo suggested, taking a whiff of the tea. "We don't have to be afraid that he will reveal your secret to the emperor. He gains nothing from it, but he would most definitely lose any chance at the throne. So we lure him into thinking he's got us where he wants us."

We all looked at him, waiting for him to tell us what.

"We leak news that Shén Mì was injured and is recovering in the Whispering Caves. Alone."

We all must have had the same question: how was that going to help us in any way? Yes, it would draw Xian Lu's attention and tempt him to show up to kill his brother, but knowing how cowardly he was, he most likely would send someone else to do it for him. Also, we had to both figure out how to stop Xian Lu from plotting against his brothers and the Monster from kidnapping and enslaving poor immortals for his own financial gain. Luring Xian Lu in that way wouldn't solve either problem.

Ding Māo sighed. "Are you all just stupid?"

Shén Mì threw him a warning glance, and his friend chuckled.

"*Hǎo*, I'll tell you," he said, his hands up in surrender.

Our heads all drew together over the small round table as the cat-warrior whispered his plan to us. It was a good plan—risky but doable. The fact that it ended with the death of the Monster scored bonus points for me.

"*I* will kill him," I declared with great emphasis on the pronoun and daring anyone to contradict me.

They all nodded, and Master seemed to be holding back a smile.

"I'm not joking, *shīfu*. You better let me do it."

He reined in his smile even further and said, "Of course. I wouldn't have it any other way."

Now that we had a plan, we needed to start putting all the working pieces in their right places for it to work. We all agreed to go visit the Whispering Caves the next morning to survey the area and plan where exactly everything would go. Crown Prince Wang Li tried to convince his brother to let him participate in the ruse but was quickly shut down by everyone in the group.

"First, you're supposed to be dead," Ding Māo said. "Second, if you really die, we'd have all risked our lives for nothing."

Shén Mì nodded emphatically.

"You are staying here with double protection."

It was final even if coming from someone in no position to give orders to a future emperor. To his credit, Wang Li didn't fight him, and after a moment of pause, he nodded in agreement.

Master clapped his hands once. "Well, that's that for today. Let's eat something, and then I suggest we all rest."

I hoped that resting part would include some vigorous naked interaction between Shén Mì and me, but I was indeed very hungry. The idea of warm, soft *bao* made my mouth water. I hadn't had anything to eat since the previous night, before the Monster had kidnapped me, and my stomach felt as if it was glued to my back.

It was a lavish meal lovingly prepared by Lǎo Cōng and his small kitchen staff and brought in by a couple servants who were temporarily replacing Yushu. I stuffed my face with all kinds of food while the men wasted their time talking. When everyone went suddenly silent, I stopped chewing and looked up, my cheeks swollen with food. I met three pairs of male eyes staring at me as if I had grown an extra head.

"What?" I sputtered, little bits of food flying out of my mouth along with the words.

They exchanged glances and then burst out laughing.

"What's so funny?"

Their laughter was contagious and try as I might to be offended by it, I couldn't help myself; I swallowed the food in my mouth and joined them.

It was an amazing feeling to be part of something wholesome. It was amazing to feel I belonged.

Shén Mì glowered at me, his arms crossed over his chest. "Are you ever going to stop eating?" he asked.

When you spend a lifetime having access to only the crappiest of foods, you become very attached to a meal. "I'm hungry," I said, my cheeks still puffed up with bits and pieces of the delicious veggies Cook had prepared.

The other men at the table snickered. They had all stopped eating a while back, but I couldn't get myself to send all the wonderful leftovers back to the kitchen. Like the child that I wasn't, I stuck a very dirty tongue out at them, hoping some of the food still in my mouth would fly over to erase their grins.

Master stood up, dragging the stool back with a screech of wood on stone and came around to stand beside me. "That's it," he said as if that meant anything at all. "We're leaving."

I furrowed my brow. "Leaving—?"

I didn't have time to finish the sentence. Shén Mì turned my chair around, grabbed me by my waist, and draped me unceremoniously over his shoulder.

I spat out the food I still had in my mouth before screaming, "What the fuck, *shifu*! What are you doing? Put me down."

Even though I couldn't see them, I could hear Wang Li's and Ding Māo's chuckles.

You're both so dead.

"I'm warning you, *shīfu*, put me down," I growled, hitting his back with my fists.

He turned around so I could see the chuckling fools at the table. "Say good night," he said.

I scowled at the two other men. "Good night? It's barely evening," I protested. "I'm not sleepy."

"Who said anything about sleeping?" he said, patting my butt with his free hand. "I have something much more active and exciting in mind."

Had I been a proper maiden, I would have blushed at the insinuation, but I was no lily-white virgin, and the blood that should have gone to my face gathered in much lower parts of my body. I stopped fighting him, relaxing against the hard bone of his shoulder and within his tight hold on my legs.

"Now we're talking," I said, my heart beginning a vigorous jig inside me. "What are you waiting for, then? Let's go."

The crown prince and Ding Māo wiggled their fingers in the air in a mock goodbye wave and smiled—not the amused, teasing grins of seconds ago, but ones of encouragement, of support. The smiles of people celebrating their friend's happiness.

I could have waved back, shown them how touched I was by their acceptance, but I was who I was, so instead I yelled out, "Don't be jealous. I hear the brothel in town makes home visits." I winked at them, and Shén Mì pinched the back of my leg. "Ouch, you better be nice to me, *shīfu*. This mouth can be used for pain as much as for pleasure."

He pinched me again.

Shameless jerk.

He carried me over his shoulder all the way to his room on the other side of the compound, periodically readjusting his hold on my legs. Every time he did that, he would move his hand a couple inches up my thigh, hiking up the skirts of my tunic with it. By the time we entered his courtyard, his hand was on my bare skin, the tips of his fingers teasingly stuck between my inner thighs, making me tremble with yearning.

After kicking his doors open, he carried me across his room to the bed on the opposite wall and, without a word, dropped me gently on top of the silken covers. I was afraid that if I moved, I would come undone, so I lay still, braced on my elbows, watching him as he removed all his clothes one piece at a time.

I was still surprised how I had once thought of him as a vain, pretty man. Underneath those layers of elegant clothing, there were no delicate features. He was indeed a beautiful man, each of his many scars adding another layer of beauty and strength to his lean, tall frame.

I shivered, running my eyes over his entire body as he now stood bare and vulnerable before me.

"Are you just going to lie there?" he asked, a crooked smile lifting the edges of his mouth.

I shrugged. "Just waiting for someone to undress me like a proper lady should," I answered, deadpan even as my whole body tingled in anticipation.

Hurry, fool!

He cocked his head to one side, licked his delicious lips, and stepped forward. Low in my belly, every single muscle clenched so tightly, it hurt. A quiet moan escaped my lips despite my determination to look cool and indifferent.

The jerk smiled.

Master took one more step and paused to free his long, black hair from the clip that kept it up in a messy bun. Silky strands of liquid midnight cascaded down over his bare shoulders, making me whimper.

Shit, he's so beautiful!

I was shaking now, incontrollable quakes running through me in waves. I dug my fingers into the softness beneath me as Shén Mì took yet another step toward the bed and stopped, studying me as if trying to decide where to start.

He began with my shoes, gently pulling them one at a time from my feet and then carelessly throwing them over his shoulder. My socks came next before he leaned over me, one knee resting on the edge of the bed, to untie my overdress and peel it off me in agonizingly slow motion.

After that, I couldn't tell exactly what happened, my brain so muddled by desire and the fire that had replaced blood in my veins. But at some point, I had nothing on me other than my own skin, and his face hovered over mine, bodies mere inches apart, seconds away from melding into one.

Shén Mì's eyes burrowed into mine, and I swear he touched my soul.

"Want to know something, Dié Dié?" he asked, the use of the endearment turning me into a mushy puddle.

I nodded, hungry for his body, heart, and whatever he needed to tell me. He paused for a long while, his desire hard against my thigh and something deeper in his dark gaze.

"What?" I finally asked, feeling I could explode at any time, take my butterfly form, and fly to the skies.

He smiled, pecked my lips, and said, "I love you, Hú Dié, my sweet butterfly."

Just like that, the darkness filled with a million shining stars all blinking at me.

CHAPTER TWENTY-FOUR

The Cave

SHÉN MÌ

I'M GOING TO KILL him.

Who was daring enough to wake me up from the best sleep I'd had in years? Ding Māo's voice crossed the barrier of the door, confirming what I suspected. It could only be my friend.

"Go away," I yelled out, nestling my head further into the crook of Hú Dié's neck. She groaned in protest. "We're sleeping."

"We have to go check the Whispering Cave," my friend said, his voice muffled by the distance and the wooden door. "Get your ass out of bed, *gē.*"

I stretched my legs, reluctantly rousing myself from that half-dreamy space, cuddled against my butterfly fairy. "Dié Dié, we have to go," I whispered, shaking her gently.

"Go without me," she replied.

I chuckled. She was obviously still asleep. She would never in a million years not want to go with us.

She fluttered her eyes open and licked her lips. "Wait, where are you going?"

"The Whispering Cave," I told her, half sitting, supporting myself on one elbow and waiting for her reaction. "Māo Māo and I can go without you."

She sat up so suddenly, I barely had time to move my head out of her way. "You're not going without me." Hú Dié was back from slumberland.

It didn't take long for us to get dressed and ready to go, as Hú Dié's excitement seemed fueled by the idea of exploring the cave.

Less than an hour later, we were all at the bottom of the mountain at the entrance to the Whispering Cave, our hands on our hips, staring at the giant dark maw and questioning the wisdom of walking through it.

"It looks like the mouth of a sea monster," Ding Māo said. "Are you sure it won't swallow us whole?"

"Don't be stupid," the butterfly said. "It's just a cave."

Ding Māo barked out a laugh. "Just a cave? This is a magical place, which is the main reason we picked it for our plan."

Hú Dié's eyebrows met in the middle.

"We came across this cave a few years ago," I explained. "No one else knows about it. Once you're inside, you'll realize exactly how magical it is."

"You just stumbled on it while on a walk?" My butterfly sure could take sarcasm to new levels. "How lucky."

"Not really," I replied, biting my lip to avoid falling into her sarcasm trap. "It belonged to a nine-tailed-fox clan, and it was kept a family secret for generations. But through the years, the members of the clan died out to the point when there was only one fox left."

"How's that even possible? That they all were just gone?"

I didn't blame her for the disbelief. It didn't happen often, but once in a few generations, something happens—infertility is inherited by too many clan members, or a war decimates most of the young ones—that wipes out an entire population within an immortal group.

"The surviving member was understandably tired of being alone, so he decided to sell whatever was left of the clan's material possessions and join another clan up north," I said. "He sold us everything, including this cave."

My acolyte and lover tilted her head like a bird. "What kind of magic?"

"Trickery magic," Ding Māo answered. "It was a nine-tailed-fox cave, after all. Trickery and seduction."

Butterfly opened her eyes wide. "Seduction?"

Was she thinking about what had happened in that pit a while back?

"Not just sexual seduction," I rushed to explain. "Any seduction. Anything that will make it almost impossible to refuse whatever proposition is on the line. It'll be easier to understand when you see it," I told her. "Just remember that it's all an illusion. Don't give in to it."

She nodded, not looking fully convinced. Knowing her, she had to see it to believe it. I couldn't stop the smile that erupted from my lips.

Damn, I am so fucked. I love this fairy.

I took the lead, anxious to hide the glow of adoration that I was sure had taken over my whole self. I'd never hear the end of it if Ding Māo noticed it. As soon as I stepped inside the cave, I could feel the pull. It was a strange but pleasant sensation, but I knew that for others, it could be brutally cruel. The fox had once told me that the cave could read people's character and desires and then play with those.

"Those who are pure of heart don't have much to worry about," he had said.

Were we three pure of heart? I wasn't so sure. But I had been in the cave before, and nothing terrible had happened as its magic threw all kinds of temptations my way. One time, my father had suddenly appeared before me, his arms wide open in an invitation for a hug.

"I'm proud of you, son," he'd said, a smile dancing on his lips and his eyes. "I'm so happy you're my son."

The desire to believe it had been so strong, I cried like a baby, curled up in a fetal position on the hard cold ground of the cave for hours.

I shook my head, dispelling the memories. I had learned to resist the pull of the magic since then. It had required many visits to the cave with my friend, but eventually we both grew half immune to the magic. Hú Dié was not.

Daring the wrath of my fairy, I laced my fingers through hers and held her hand tightly in mine. I wasn't going to let her wander alone. Gods only knew what temptations the cave would throw at her.

She stared at our joined hands and then glanced back at me, her brow furrowed. "Is this one of the illusions?" she asked.

I almost laughed, my heart melting at the thought that she would think of such an intimate gesture as a temptation. "No, it's real. I don't want you to go off alone."

She nodded, and we pressed on deeper inside the cave.

The cave was not huge, but the magic made it feel like it was. You could walk for hours and never feel you'd reached the end when, in reality, you were walking around in circles between the four small chambers that surrounded the larger central hall.

"He's here," Hú Dié whispered, stopping suddenly.

I stopped a couple steps ahead of her, our arms stretched out across the empty space. "Who?"

"The Monster," she said, her skin cold and clammy. "He's here."

I had hoped she would be immune to the magic, but she obviously wasn't. Her first illusion had just crawled out of her imagination, her wishful thinking, and had been made real.

What I couldn't understand was how the *guài* she feared more than anything else in the world could be part of any desire she had.

If I was expecting Hú Dié to freeze like she had that first time we had come face to face with the *guài,* I would have been utterly disappointed. Instead of cowering like she had before, my fairy's eyes shone with excitement, a wild sort of grin stretched along her lips. I glanced in the direction she was staring, but of course couldn't see anything. Whatever she was seeing was all in her head.

"What do you see?" I asked gently, afraid of triggering some strong reaction from her. "What are you looking at?"

She turned her face to me, narrowing her eyes. "You can't see him?"

I shook my head.

"The Monster is in a cage."

What? She is seeing the guài *inside a cage?*

No wonder she looked rather pleased with the whole thing.

"Oh good," I said, holding her hand tightly in mine. I was afraid she would take off running and get lost in the cave. Besides seduction, the magic here could trick you into believing you were lost or prevent you from finding whoever you were looking for. "So, we can go."

She gave me such a dirty look, I shivered. "Go? Not a chance, *shifu,*" she said. "He's helpless now. I have to take advantage of the situation and kill him."

I pulled her closer to me and wrapped my arms around her shoulders. "There's no *guài*, remember? It's the magic, Dié Dié," I whispered in her ear, hoping she could feel the very real beating of my heart against her. "Focus on my heartbeat. That's where reality lies. Listen to it. Feel it."

She wiggled in my arms, trying to free herself from my embrace. "Let me go, *shīfu*, I have to kill him. I have waited a lifetime to do this."

"And you will—when we meet the real monster, not this illusion your mind is creating," I told her, not letting her go. "Focus on our heartbeats."

For a moment she obliged, standing still inside the circle of my arms, her ear against my chest. "But I see him," she said at last. "My eyes can't deceive me."

I dropped a kiss on the top of her head. "But the magic can and *is* deceiving you," I said. "The cave is making you believe you have the one thing you want the most: the opportunity to kill the demon who had you enslaved for years."

She went quiet again, her breathing slowing down. "Let's get out of here, then."

I didn't need to be told twice. Grasping her hand tightly, I pulled her behind me in the direction of the exit. The quicker we got out, the better.

Once we were outside, she shook her head as if trying to get rid of her thoughts. "Wow, I now understand the power of that magic," she said. "I really thought the Monster was there and that I could finally get rid of him."

Ding Māo, who had been leaning against a large boulder, waiting for us, stood and came to join us. "Weird, right?" he asked.

We nodded. Weird didn't even begin to describe it. I had long learned how to resist the magic, but even now the pull of it always made me shiver in a mixture of fear and wonderment.

"But I don't understand how this magic will help us with Xian Lu," Hú Dié said. "How is that going to play into catching him red-handed?"

Hú Dié was still breathing hard, so I walked her to a flat rock and told her to sit down. "Remember when I told you I had picked up a few interesting magic objects on a mission?"

She nodded.

"One of those artifacts is a word-catcher."

Cocking her head, she rubbed her eyelid before looking at me, her palm half covering her mouth. "What is that?"

I hadn't brought it with me, so words would have to do. "It looks like a crystal funnel with a twisted narrow neck that can collect words and play them back later."

"What good will that do?" she asked, ever the doubter. "And how can you be sure he'll even say anything incriminating?"

Ding Māo snorted. "Wow, have a little faith, pretty butterfly."

I threw him a don't-you-dare glower and then chided myself for being jealous of my best friend.

He was unaffected by my visual warning. "For someone as beautiful and smart as you are, you sure are stupid sometimes."

My fairy sprung to her feet so fast, I had no time to react before she had her dagger against Ding Māo's throat.

My unwise friend only laughed. "You have a seriously feisty one here, Mì Mì," he said, pushing the dagger's sharp blade away from his skin with a couple fingers. "I just meant that you speak before thinking."

Hú Dié pulled back, stashing the knife away inside her tunic. "So, oh smart one, can you explain it to this stupid butterfly, then?"

He cleared his throat as if about to make a speech. "Once we get Xian Lu inside that cave—which we will, one way or another—the magic will latch on to his strongest desire, which is to be the crown prince." He leaned against the rough trunk of a cherry tree, his head resting on a large branch that grew outwards. "We can't be sure what the cave's magic will conjure up, but we can be pretty certain it will have to do with his plan to take the throne."

I stole a glance at my butterfly. She had lowered herself into a crouching position, her arms resting on her upper thighs, and I could almost see her thoughts churning.

"So, chances are, he will say something that we can use against him." It sounded more like a question than a statement.

Both Ding Mão and I nodded.

"And you'll take the word-catcher to the emperor and let him decide what to do with your not-so-lovely brother."

We both nodded again.

"My father is a great man, but he has an unreasonable trust in his children." Except when it came to me. Not that my father totally distrusted me, but he certainly didn't have much faith in my personality and abilities. "He needs solid proof that one of his sons is plotting against the others—possibly even against him as well—to take action."

The fairy paused for a moment, deep in thought. "And how are you going to convince Xian Lu to come here?"

My eyes must have glittered, because Hú Dié smiled. "We're going to make him an offer he can't refuse."

She rose to her feet, crossing her arms over her chest. "What offer?" she asked me.

I exchanged a glance with my friend before returning it to her.

"We're going to offer him the throne."

Chapter Twenty-Five

Whispers

Hú Dié

W HAT THE HELL DID he mean by that? How could they offer Xian Lu something that was not theirs to give? And I doubted that the emperor himself would be willing to play this game.

"The throne? How can you possibly offer him the throne?" I asked, my mouth open in disbelief. "That makes no sense at all."

Ding Māo pushed himself off the tree trunk. "Think, woman," he said. "Where did you leave your brains today?"

"Say one more thing like that and I *will* kill you," I snarled like a rabid dog.

He chuckled.

Idiot!

Shén Mì pulled me closer to him. "Ignore him," he said. "The cat in him loves teasing."

"The cat in him will be a very dead cat if he keeps sharpening his claws on me," I warned, pincushioning him with my eyes.

Master laughed softly, his arm draped over my shoulders as if protecting me from his friend's barbs.

"We are going to leak information that one of his prostitutes is pregnant with his son," Shén Mì explained. "Since he's unaware that Wang Li is still alive, he will see that as a sure way to become the crown prince, the chance he's been waiting for. But he'll want to make sure there's no competition at all, so he'll go after me, the only other obstacle to his plan. When he finds out I'm 'recovering' at the Whispering Cave, he will be here faster than we can blink."

"But he'll bring his men with him," I said, nestled comfortably against his chest. "He's too cowardly to come alone."

"No matter," Ding Mǎo said, shrugging. "He's going to want to confirm Mì Mì's death, so he'll come along. He can bring a hundred men. It won't make a difference. Once they go inside the cave, they will lose touch with reality, and we will be the only ones in control."

I wouldn't be satisfied until I was one hundred percent sure no harm would come to my dragon. "There's a very good chance that Xian Lu knows about Shén Mì's dragon. Won't he be too scared to face him even with backup?" I asked, the pulse of my prince's heart vibrating on the side of my face.

The annoying cat had the gall to roll his eyes at me. "He'll think Mì Mì is hurt and can't defend himself properly," he said. "That alone should be bait enough for him to come running into our trap."

I hated to admit it, but it sounded like a solid plan. I also hated that I didn't seem to have much of a role in the operation.

"What about me? What am I supposed to do while this whole thing is going on?" I asked, tilting my chin up to look into Shén Mì's eyes. "Am I supposed to stay home, drink tea, and entertain the crown prince?"

Golden eyes met mine, soft and warm. "Would that be so bad?" he asked with a ghost of a smile. "He needs someone to watch his back, too, and you're the right warrior to do it."

I knew he was buttering me up, but I still melted a little. "Give me something more to do, please," I begged, steepling my hands in front of my chin.

Shén Mì laughed in earnest then. "All right, fierce butterfly, we'll give you something else to do," he said with an exaggerated sigh. "We'll figure something out, I promise."

On our way back to the compound, we stopped in town to look at some new swords being forged by a local artisan. The swordsmith, a tall and willowy middle-aged man, was working on several blades, one of which immediately caught my eye. I was more of a dagger woman. As a butterfly, I favored smaller weapons that I could carry easily and hide even better. But this sword was calling me.

Without even realizing it, I drew near the bench where the sword lay and began running my fingers over the simple but elegant hilt decorated with subtle details—a pair of silver wings.

"Do you like it?" Shén Mì asked, startling me.

He had silently approached from behind, and I was so dazed by the beauty of the sword, I hadn't noticed him. I nodded, the distinct impression that the weapon was calling my name covering my skin in goose bumps.

"It's yours."

I spun on my heels to face him. "Mine? What do you mean?"

He lifted my chin with his finger and bent down slightly so our eyes were level. "Yours to keep," he said. "I had it made for you. It's time you have a better weapon than that puny knife you carry with you at all times."

I didn't waste any time diving in to pick it up from the bench. As soon as my hand closed around its pommel, I felt it: energy that spread quickly through my body and mind.

"*Give me a name,*" it whispered inside my head.

It's a live sword!

I looked up at Shén Mì, the question in my eyes. He gave me a half smile and a shrug. "I thought you might need something to keep you company when I'm not here."

Cheeky bastard.

I ran my hand along the shiny silver blade in a caress. "Báiyín," I whispered back to the sword. "Silver."

The female voice whispered back, "*Báiyín. I like it.*"

I slid it into the plain white scabbard lying beside it and turned to my dragon once more. His face was glowing, and I had to stop for a moment, relishing the fact that someone in this world cared enough for me to feel such pleasure in my happiness.

I smiled and wrapped my arms around his waist to pull him in for a very public hug. "Thank you, *shīfu*. I love it."

He squeezed back, his chin resting on the top of my head. "I'm glad you like it, but don't you think it's time you stop calling me master and start calling me by my name?"

I thought for a second before answering, "If you insist." I pulled apart from him far enough to look into his eyes. "A-Shén it is."

The smile that stretched across his full lips was like a warm blanket on a winter day. I sighed.

All was well in the world at that moment.

Being a butterfly immortal had its perks. One of them was being able to fly almost anywhere undetected. On the rare occasion I was spotted, people generally didn't try to harm me, for butterflies were widely believed to bring luck and prosperity.

I was nevertheless anxious when flying to places I didn't know or where I knew danger lurked. When Shén Mì asked me to fly to his brother's palace in the imperial compound, I was tempted to say no. So much depended upon this mission, however, that I made myself face my fears and go.

The idea was to watch Xian Lu closely and alert our people when he finally left to the Whispering Cave.

I hovered over his rooms for almost an hour, my wings burning with the effort. Eventually I perched on a nearby peach tree from which I had an unobstructed view of his doors. I had lived a very long life, most of it within the constraints of a cage just big enough to hold my sitting human form, and yet this wait outside the palace's doors felt like an eternity.

Servants came and went, rushing with baskets and trays of food, freshly washed clothing, and tea. One girl servant walked a funny-looking dog for a while before returning him inside, and a couple soldiers walked in with some report. But the blasted prince never left. My eyes were getting heavy with sleep, and my butterfly body was begging for a good roost somewhere warm and safe.

It wasn't until dusk that a hooded figure, who couldn't be anyone but the prince, left the rooms, closely followed by two burly men—his bodyguards, no doubt. Sleep vanished, and I was suddenly buzzing with energy. I took flight and followed them from above as they were joined by a second pair of guards at the exit from the courtyard. I would follow them for a while longer to make sure they were heading to the Whispering Cave, and then I'd fly ahead to warn my prince.

When I was sure they could not be headed anywhere but the Whispering Cave, I left them behind and sped ahead to go let Shén Mì and Ding Mǎo know.

I was barely out of my butterfly form when I yelled, "They're on their way here."

Both men looked at me as I was still wavering between butterfly and human.

"How far?" Shén Mì asked.

"Less than an incense stick," I told them. "Maybe half an hour."

Now fully human, I stepped forward into my dragon's strong arms. He took me in, no questions asked, wrapping me in his warmth.

"I have to get things ready, Dié Dié," he whispered. "You go hide somewhere safe while we do this."

"But I want to help you." Translation: I want to keep you safe.

He gently pried me from him, holding my shoulders and searching for my eyes. "I will be fine, believe me," he said.

I did believe him, but I didn't trust his half brother. I opened my mouth to protest, but he interrupted me.

"Go. It's an order. As soon as we have what we need, we'll leave the cave. Meet us at the crossroads ahead."

I didn't want to be so far away while he risked his life. I knew he was much more powerful than Xian Lu, and with Ding Mǎo beside him, he was almost indestructible. But I still worried, wanting to stay nearby just in case. Like a butterfly would be able to do much against a group of trained warriors.

"Do you hear me, Dié Dié?" he asked again, giving me a soft shake.

I nodded. "All right, I will meet you at the crossroads, in the restaurant."

Shén Mì smiled at me and then turned to his friend. "Let's go."

I watched them both enter the cave, an overwhelming sense of helplessness invading every inch of my body.

I can't just leave.

Looking around me, I found a hidden outcrop in the mountain, just above the entrance to the cave. I would hide there and be close at hand in case things turned sour. I had brought a sleeping powder from the infirmary. If all else failed, I could fly over the enemy and put them all to sleep.

I flew to the hiding place, turned into a human again, and perched on the outcrop's edge, ready for everything and nothing at all.

Sooner than I expected, the sound of galloping horses reached my ears. My heart raced and thumped against my chest bone. What if things went horribly wrong? Life without my prince was unthinkable. When the horses with their riders appeared around the bend of the road, I thought I'd choke in my own bile.

Calm yourself down, butterfly.

I watched them approach the Whispering Cave, slide off their horses, and confer with each other for a few minutes as my heart tried to escape through my mouth. Then the hooded prince uncovered his head. The arrogant bastard hadn't even removed the golden coronet that held his hair in a top bun and marked him as an imperial prince. The same two men who had followed him from his room bookended him, a wall of muscle on either side of him.

"You've got me if you need me."

The whisper almost threw me off the ledge. I had forgotten my new sword, Báiyín, hanging comfortably in its scabbard across my back.

The words comforted me somehow, as if knowing my live sword was there with me, ready to help me intervene if things went wrong, made all the difference. I reached behind me and patted the scabbard in a silent thank you.

Two of Xian Lu's guards placed themselves on either side of the cave entrance, legs braced apart and trunk-like arms crossed over massive chests. The other two followed their prince into the cave. I allowed myself to breathe easily. There was nothing I could do while they were inside the cave.

I had counted more than three thousand ants crossing the sparsely grassy ground in front of me when I heard a yell. With every sense on alert, I got on my knees and peeked over the edge of the outcrop. Shén Mì and Ding Māo had exited the cave and were in the middle of a brawl with the guards.

Báiyín grew hot against my back. "*What are you waiting for, Butterfly? Let's go,*" the female voice said.

I jumped from the outcrop, not bothering to change into my butterfly form. I couldn't jump up that high, but I certainly could plunge down without a hitch. I landed hard and rolled to prevent my ankles from cracking, and in mere seconds I was up on my feet again, sword at the ready.

The fight was going on a few yards away from me, so I dashed forward, Báiyín throbbing with excitement in my hand.

Shén Mì saw me first and yelled, "No, stay away. We can take care of this ourselves."

I knew they could, but I just had to do something, anything to help them. Being idle was not a part of me. One of the guards saw me, too, and charged toward me, leaving the other to deal with my prince and his friend.

I was ready for him.

It wasn't much of a fight. Báiyín knew what it was doing, and my hand was being guided by it rather than me guiding it. In less than a few strokes, the sword went through the man's chest, the sickening sound of metal cutting through flesh making me gag. The guard dropped his sword. He stared at the metal protruding from his body and then at me with unbelieving eyes, blood beginning to drip from the corners of his mouth. He didn't say anything; he just stood for a moment, a stream of blood flowing from the wound in his chest and soaking his dark tunic, and then tilted backward and fell.

Báiyín's voice burst in my ears. "*Take that, you giant oaf.*"

I like this sword.

I turned quickly to go help Shén Mì, but that fight had also ended, the second guard lying on the ground in a puddle of his own blood. Ding Māo was holding his left arm where a bloody stain was spreading.

"Let's get out of here before Xian Lu comes out," Shén Mì said, grabbing my hand and pulling me behind him.

Still holding my sword, I followed him. They had hidden their horses in the bamboo forest, just a little over a *li* from the cave. I sheathed my sword and mounted my prince's horse before he did, and we wasted no time riding home.

"Did you get what you needed from Xian Lu?" I asked him, raising my voice above the wind that buffeted our faces.

"Yes, we got him," he said, dropping a kiss on the side of my neck. "But you were very foolish, facing that guard like that."

Báiyín's voice rang in my head. "*Fuck him.*"

I burst out laughing.

"What's so funny?" Shén Mì asked.

He had no idea he had given me a sword that was even more trouble than I was.

Ding Māo yelped, pulling his arm out of my grasp. "Are you trying to kill me?" he asked, glowering at me.

I crossed my arms and tsked. "You're such a fucking baby," I told him. "You should be ashamed of yourself."

I had been trying to take care of his wound for almost an hour, but each time I tried to clean it, he would moan and groan as if I were branding him with a hot iron.

"You don't let me take care of that, it will fester and rot," I told him.

He was an immortal, so the chances of that happening were remote, but it was true that he would be in a great deal of pain if the injury was left untreated.

Shén Mì walked in the room, carrying a small pile of bandages I had asked him to fetch from the infirmary. "You better do as she tells you, *gē*," he said, poorly disguising a smile as a frown. "She'll make you suffer if you don't."

The cat immortal looked crestfallen, his glance bouncing from his friend to me. "Promise you won't hurt me," he begged me, a silly childish expression on his face.

I nodded.

"All right. Do it, then."

He stretched out his arm to me as if making an offering, and I supported it on my lap. The wound was not deep, but it looked rabid.

"I think there was poison in that sword," I told him after careful examination. "You'll need some of my powder."

"Oh no, you don't," Shén Mì said, dropping the bandages on top of the small table beside me. "You are not giving him your aphrodisiac dust."

My jaw dropped at the insinuation. "The only reason it affected you that way was because you breathed it in," I protested.

Ding Māo looked up, his wound suddenly forgotten. "Wait! When did you give Mì Mì an aphrodisiac? And what did you do afterwards?"

I poked his wound for his nosiness, and he screamed. "Just hold your breath for a few seconds, and it will be fine," I said.

"Hold on," Shén Mì said, turning around and placing himself behind his friend with a couple of thick bandages on his hand. "I will cover his mouth and nose while you do it."

I chuckled as he muffled his bedraggled friend while I sprinkled a little of my dust over the injury. "You can let him breathe now," I told my prince.

Shén Mì let go of his friend, who gasped, trying to catch his breath. "Holy shit, *gē*, you almost suffocated me."

"I should have," my prince muttered under his breath.

While they were bickering like idiots, I was watching Ding Māo's skin knitting itself back together. Good thing he was distracted, because the process was fast but unpleasant, and I had forgotten to give him an anesthetic. After a while, the pain must have finally registered in his moronic male brain, because he suddenly turned his glance to his arm and grimaced.

"Fuck, that hurts," he whined, watching in disbelief as the wound closed. "What the hell did you do, Butterfly?"

"I've healed you, ingrate," I snapped back, beginning to collect all the bloodied bandages into a wooden bowl. "Nobody said it would be painless, did they?"

As I walked away and out of the room, I heard him yell, "I bet you did it on purpose, didn't you?"

It was mostly an accident.

I chuckled to myself, bowl in hand. There was a rather ugly trash container beside the dainty gazebo in the center of the courtyard. I dropped the dirty bandages in there, having no wish or motivation to wash them, and then turned around and walked back to the room.

"It didn't take long for him to talk, did it?" Ding Mão was saying.

"I gather Xian Lu sang like an off-key bird," I said, pulling a chair to sit closer to the two men. All my attention had been focused on checking the cat's injury, so I hadn't asked about what happened in the cave yet.

Shén Mì reached for my hand and held it in his. "It didn't take long. Not sure what he saw in the cave, but he gave us all the proof we needed," he said. "He sat on a rock as if on a throne, an expression of total bliss on his face. Assuming he believed he had been crowned emperor, I asked him to tell me how he'd managed to do it. 'It was easy,' he said. 'I will become the crown prince once I eliminate you after killing Wang Li.' He even laughed and boasted about how he had procured the poison that killed the crown prince and planned to use it on our father."

"Wow, he really tied the noose around his own neck, didn't he?"

My prince nodded. "I just don't understand how the four of us were brought up together in the palace and turned out so different from each other."

"Humans are evil," I said and immediately regretted it. I didn't believe that. Not anymore, anyway. Shén Mì and his crew of men and women of all walks of life had shown me a different side of humanity, both mortal and immortal. I could no longer profess my general hatred for the species. "All right, there are a few good ones," I conceded with a shrug.

They laughed, and I rolled my eyes.

"So what's the plan now?" I asked, anxious to move their focus away from me.

"We prepare a grand show which includes greatly exaggerated rumors of my death," Shén Mì said, much to my surprise.

"What?" I exclaimed, jerking my hand away from his. "What do you mean?"

He grabbed my hand again. "Calm down. It's all part of the game," he said in a soothing voice. "We spread the rumor that I am very dead, killed while recovering from an injury in the Whispering Cave." He brought my hand to his lips and kissed my knuckles, sending a frisson of pleasure up my arm. "He won't remember most of what happened in the cave. In fact, chances are, he believes he killed me in there, since that was his original wish."

"I don't see how that helps our case, though," I said, fighting the urge to pull his handsome face to mine and kiss him.

"He will make a big fuss about comforting my grieving father, and that's when we hit him."

His smile lit up the room, and at that moment, all I really wanted to do was to kick Ding Māo out of the room and make love to my dragon.

But instead I said, "Hit him with what?"

Ding Māo, who had been nursing his arm in half pain, half wonder, looked up and said, "With the truth. Truth is like vinegar: very hard to swallow."

"Tell me I will be allowed to watch," I said with a pout I hoped was charming.

Shén Mì cupped my cheek with his free hand. "Dié Dié, my sweet fairy, I wouldn't let you miss it for the world."

I wasn't sure what they were planning, but judging by their grins, it was going to be epic.

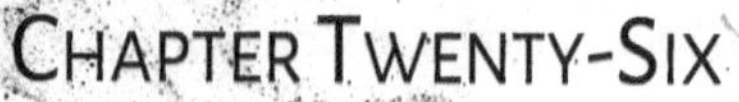

Chapter Twenty-Six

Revelations

Shén Mì

MY FATHER, THE EMPEROR, could be intimidating. Terrifying, even.

I stood before him, feeling just like I had felt when I was ten and planned to tell him I didn't want the crown. I couldn't do it back then, and even now, facing him across the dais where his throne was perched, my mouth was dry as the desert sands and a nervous sweat dampened my brow and my hands.

"What do you mean Xian Lu is coming to announce your death?"

His booming voice echoed inside my head and my soul.

"You're obviously very much alive." He waved a hand in my direction. "Can you stop your silly games and act like an adult?"

I sighed, gathering patience and courage to explain to my father that one of his sons was a traitor and a murderer. He didn't think much of me, I knew. My fault, after all. To make my cover as a *duan xiu* truly believable, I had allowed my father to think I would never bed a female and never produce an heir. Despite his position as the ruler of a massive empire, Father had not shunned me because of that.

"You bed whom you like, my son, and love whom your heart desires," he had told me then. "I won't love you any less."

What had broken the camel's back was my second layer of deception: leading the apparent life of a shallow and useless prince who only cared about fine clothes, brothels, and all things material. *That* he hadn't been able to ignore or forgive. He might still love me, but he would never trust me.

Now, standing at the bottom of the two steps leading to the top of the imperial dais and looking up at my father as he sat on his elaborate golden throne, I felt as if I had shrunk to my ten-year-old self.

I made myself speak, my voice shaking slightly. "I am not playing a silly game, Father," I said, the words scratching my throat and my tongue. "Whatever else you think of me, believe me when I tell you this is very serious, and I can prove it to you."

The dragon sculpted into the wood of the throne peered at me, judging. "Prove what exactly?" my father asked, narrowing his eyes.

I took a deep breath. This wasn't going well. "That he was the one who had Wang Li poisoned and tried to kill me a few days ago in the Whispering Cave." There, I had said it.

He went quiet and still. I knew he was thinking, putting the pieces of the puzzle together, hoping they wouldn't fit. He was too smart, too sharp to not have been suspicious before. Xian Lu was not the brightest of his children and wasn't too hard to read.

"I won't believe that one of my sons would do something like that to his brothers," he said finally, still hanging on to the hope that I was making up stories.

"Father, I hate to bring you pain," I said quietly. "I know you love Xian Lu as much as you love Wang Li." I wondered if he noticed

I hadn't mentioned my name. "But he wants that crown, and he's willing to do whatever it takes to get it. I'm not asking you to believe me without proof."

My father's golden eyes darkened, a veil of sadness dulling their shine. "How will you do this?"

I climbed the two steps, my legs wobbly beneath me, and handed him the word-catcher. "You can hear it from his own mouth, Father."

The emperor took the magic item and turned it in his hands. "A word-catcher," he whispered. "I haven't seen one of these in years." He looked up at me. "How do you turn it on?"

I bent down and whispered, "Open," over the funnel-shaped item.

And the words wafted out and surrounded us, menacing and heartbreaking. Even my father, muddled by his paternal love, couldn't deny what he heard. His wide shoulders stooped with every word it released, the corners of his lips drooping, adding years to his face. My still-young and vital father was an old man by the time the word-catcher emitted the last syllable.

I didn't dare say anything, giving him time to process the enormity of what he had heard. One of his sons had betrayed everything he had ever taught us, and all for the sake of inheriting a crown he didn't earn or deserve.

After what felt like hours, Father raised his eyes to me, tears rolling down his cheeks. "What do you need me to do?" he asked.

So I told him.

It was quiet. Too quiet.

Even Hú Dié, standing beside me, was silent. Once in a while, she squeezed my hand, whether offering me comfort or taking it, I couldn't be sure. We had been waiting around in a hidden niche in the throne room, well protected from prying eyes by the high dais where my father sat half slouched on the imperial seat. On a padded chair across from us, wearing his crown prince coronet and dressed in his princely clothes, Wang Li sat quietly. Neither of us relished the idea of what we were about to do, however needed and deserved. Xian Lu was our brother whether we liked it or not, and what was about to happen had to be the most difficult thing for a father to do to his own child.

So we waited.

And waited.

When one of the guards announced my half brother, we all let out a collective sigh of relief. The time was now.

"Father, you've summoned me." Xian Lu's voice reached us loud and clear, courtesy of the room's excellent acoustics. I could be imagining things, but he seemed to have a new spark to his voice. "What can I do for you?"

My father cleared his voice. "I haven't talked to you in a while," he said, his voice steady despite everything. "I thought we could catch up."

My father ordered his eunuch to bring a chair next to the throne and serve tea and pastries. I could hear the strain in his voice as he proceeded to make small talk.

"Lord Wang Tāo requests an audience," a guard yelled out.

I tensed up. Wang Tāo was one of the most trusted men in my half brother's circle. The show was about to begin.

The sound of Wang Tāo's boots against the marble floor echoed throughout the room, amplifying the sound of the single pair into those of a small army.

"Your Imperial Majesty," he said. "I'm afraid I have terrible news."

There was silence, and then Xian Lu asked, "What's the news? Speak!"

"Prince Shén Mì was recuperating from an injury in the Whispering Cave," Wang Tāo continued, his voice wrapped in a mournful tone so believable, it could have fooled me. "He was attacked by bandits and killed."

I had made sure to spread the news of my demise to the right people, those who I knew would immediately bring it to my brother.

"What? My son is dead?" My father had hidden talents, apparently, for his acting was impeccable. "You must be mistaken. You *have* to be mistaken."

"Unfortunately, I am not," Wang Tāo continued. "It's been confirmed."

There was a long pause, and then Xian Lu said, "It's tragic, Father, but he wasn't much of a son, was he?"

Bastard.

"You must pull yourself together and think of the empire."

What a crock of shit! The sniveling son of a bitch.

"I always think of the empire, Xian Lu," my father replied. "But I just lost yet another son. You're the only one left now."

"Father, you know you can count on me to do whatever you need me to," the liar continued. "It's my filial obligation—to you and to my nation."

The bastard was so sure he had already won the crown, he could barely contain his excitement. Father had no one else to inherit the throne. Xiao Bin was adopted, and all my father's brothers had passed. He had no nephews or even male cousins. His one and only option was Xian Lu.

Or so my brother thought.

This was Hú Dié's cue. I gave her hand a squeeze and tried to smile. She smiled back, that reckless side of her coming through in the lift of her lips and the glint in her eyes. She stood up and walked around the dais to where both Xian Lu and my father could see her.

"Your Imperial Majesty," she said. The muffled sound of her voice told me she was kowtowing. "Can you give me the honor of listening to me?"

I would have paid a fortune to see my brother's reaction to her appearance. He most likely thought she had perished in that building where the *guài* had kept his slaves. After all, it had burned to the ground once we had freed every fairy and taken them to safety.

"Stand!" my father said. "Who are you and what are you doing in my palace?"

My father's acting skills impressed me again. He had met my butterfly before, of course, and we'd sat with him just a few days prior to concoct this trap of sorts for Xian Lu.

"I came to lodge a complaint against a member of the court," she said, loud and clear.

By this point, Xian Lu must have started to sweat profusely.

"What kind of complaint?" my father asked.

"Someone in this court hired a monster to kidnap and enslave me."

"This woman must be insane, Father." Xian Lu's voice had gone up an octave. "Monster? What monster?"

"Let her talk," my father said. "Under my rule, everyone has the right to air their grievances. You know that, my son. And if you are going to be the next emperor, you must remember that."

"Next emperor?" Hú Dié squealed in mock surprise. "How can he be the crown prince when Prince Wang Li is still alive?"

My brother sputtered, and for a moment, I was afraid that he would succumb to the shock and die. But he collected himself after a few seconds.

"Everyone knows that Wang Li died of poisoning a few weeks ago." The unsteadiness in his voice spoke volumes about how nervous he was getting.

My butterfly snapped back, "Oh really? Poisons have antidotes, don't you know?"

"We even held a funeral for my brother," Xian Lu threw back, his pitch getting higher. "The antidote for *Hēimógū* is very rare and hard to find, anyway. How would anyone get a hold of some without knowing what poison he had taken?"

Silence fell so quickly and so thickly, the throne room felt like the inside of a tomb.

My father was the first one to break the silence. "How did you know that's the poison that killed your brother?"

I was probably imagining it, but it seemed as if the room suddenly reeked of sweat and fear.

"It wa-was just a guess, ju-judging by the symptoms," Xian Lu stuttered. "I-it might have been some other poison, of course."

"No, you are correct," Hú Dié replied in that flippant tone I loved so much. "That's exactly what killed your brother." She paused for a moment. "Correction: what *would* have killed him if we didn't find the antidote," she added. "On a side note, never trust a mercenary shaman who will sell you out for the highest price."

When Wang Li stood up and walked to the front of the dais, I couldn't hold it anymore. I needed to see Xian Lu's face when his two dead brothers appeared in front of him, resuscitated and healthy. I followed him.

My wayward half brother didn't disappoint—his chin fell so low, I thought he had dislocated his jaw, and the little color he had in his face drained away. With his eyes bulging, hands shaking, and sweat dripping from his forehead, Xian Lu stumbled backwards and was caught by Xiao Bin, who had stealthily entered the room after him. Close behind him was Su Lin, dazzlingly dressed in golden silk. A show of brotherly love, the kind Xian Lu was not acquainted with.

My father stood, white knuckles on the arms of the throne. I could only imagine how he felt.

"Guards," he called.

Several men ran toward the dais and stood at attention, waiting for his orders.

"Take this man to the dungeons," he said, pointing at Xian Lu. "He is no longer an imperial prince. I hereby remove all his titles and the rights that go with them."

Xian Lu let out a small screech, like a rat caught in a trap.

"I will deal with this commoner later today." He waved a hand dismissively and averted his eyes. "Take him away. I don't want to see his face."

"Father, I'm innocent," Xian Lu yelled as the guards held him by his arms and pulled him toward the doors. "No, Father, please...."

Faced with his resistance, the guards doubled their efforts and dragged him out of the room, screaming and kicking.

Hú Dié wiggled her fingers at him in a mock goodbye before turning and latching on to my arm. "Victory," she whispered.

But looking at my father as he dropped into the throne seat, eyes moist with tears, it didn't feel like a victory at all.

Chapter Twenty-Seven

Redemption

Hú Dié

S HÉN MÌ HAD LEFT the palace with me in tow so that Wang Li could talk with his father in private.

"Shouldn't you be part of the conversation?" I asked. "After all, you were instrumental in the whole thing, and you *are* his son as well."

He didn't look at me as he strode across the courtyards as if late to an appointment. "He's the crown prince. There are matters of state no one else should be privy to," he said as I sped up to catch up with him.

"I can't believe your father wouldn't want you there and involved in the conversation," I insisted, unwilling to accept that the emperor was that disconnected from his own child.

We passed through the palace gates into the stone-paved streets of town, Master still rushing ahead and me trying to keep up.

"Trust me, he wouldn't want to share anything important with me," he said, eyes still firmly on the ground before him.

Men could be so thick. "He has no reason to think you are a useless idiot now," I snapped back, irritated that he was still caught up in that deceit. "He knows that you are loyal and perfectly capable of defending what's right. Shit, you basically saved your brother."

"I'm still a disappointment," he grumbled.

I groaned in frustration but didn't say anything else, following him on his frantic walk home. By the time we arrived at the compound, I was sweating and probably smelled like the sewer. He made a straight line to his rooms as if intending to lock himself inside it alone, but I wasn't about to let him do that.

I didn't give him the chance to shut the doors in my face—I was a butterfly and could be as fast as the wind. He blinked, and I was inside, standing behind him.

"Fuck, Dié Dié, go to your room," he said when he realized I was in there with him. "I want to be alone."

"No chance," I said, taking a step forward and beginning to undo the ties of his tunic. "We're going to soak in the hot spring."

He made as if to stop me but then gave in, allowing me to disrobe him one piece of clothing at a time until he was left wearing only his long white underpants. I didn't wait for him to undress me. I was bare in a blink.

"You're going to go naked?" he asked me, still not cracking a smile.

"Do you have something against it?"

"What if someone shows up?" he asked.

Ding Māo did have a bad habit of popping in on us when we were bathing.

I shrugged. "They'll get an eyeful," I said. "Let's go."

I covered myself with a thin robe for the walk to the spring, and we strolled to the pool at the foot of the hill, hand in hand. Shén Mì was too quiet for my liking, but I didn't interrupt his thoughts.

The water was hot and bubbly as we sat neck deep in the pool, feeling each and every muscle relax. I sighed in contentment and sought Master's hand underneath the water. We interlaced our fingers, the side of my body glued to his. I wanted to smooth out the sad creases on his face, erase the grief in his eyes, and kiss his frown away.

"You look like salted mackerel soaking in water."

We twisted around to look at Ding Māo, who had appeared on the edge of the pool behind us, his hands braced on his hips. We were surprised to find he was not alone. Su Lin and Xiao Bin were standing beside him, amused smiles on their faces.

"Can we have some privacy?" I asked, not completely annoyed by their presence. Shén Mì needed company from those who loved and appreciated him.

"Stop being so selfish," Xiao Bin said, beginning to undress. "That's a huge pool. Plenty of room for all of us."

I started protesting, but all three of them started removing their clothing. When they were all down to their undergarments, they slid into the pool. Ding Māo waded in our direction, a grin on his lips.

"Stop right there, Māo Māo," Master yelled, stretching a hand out in front of him. "Don't come any closer."

"Why not?" the cat immortal asked.

"Because—"

He couldn't say it, so I did. "I'm naked."

Everything stopped. It was strange how even the crickets and the cicadas seemed to have gone quiet.

We stared at one another in an impasse, no one willing to be the first one to break the sudden silence and paralysis.

"Oh for all that is holy, you've never seen a naked woman before?" I finally said. "Su Lin, you are a woman yourself."

She chuckled. "But I'm not the naked one here," she said. "We'll stay on this side of the pool."

They settled against the opposing wall, and I nestled closer to my prince. "What are you all doing here, anyway?" I asked.

"We came to see our favorite hero," Xiao Bin said, his lips curving into a half smile.

Shén Mì smiled at that. "Thank you for saying that, but I'm no hero."

With a snort, Su Lin exclaimed, "Who said anything about you being the hero? We're talking about your butterfly fairy."

Silence fell again for a few seconds before an explosion of laughter broke through the darkness of the night.

We were called to the palace the very next day. Neither of us had slept much, finding solace in each other for most of the night, but we got dressed quickly and left for the imperial compound.

"What do you think this is all about?" I asked my dragon as we rushed through the forest, hand in hand.

He shook his head, worry creasing his forehead.

"Maybe he has found the Monster," I said wistfully.

Whatever it was, it couldn't be bad. Could it?

One of the imperial guards announced us into Emperor Cheng's private chambers when we arrived at the palace. Surprisingly, the room was very simple and frugally furnished. It seemed as if the man went in for comfort over luxury.

He was sitting on a chair, dressed more like he had been the first time I had met him than as a powerful ruler, his hair free of any ornaments. He smiled at us, and we bowed.

"No need for ceremony," he said, gesturing at the two chairs next to his. "Sit. Let's talk."

We did as we were told and waited for him to tell us the reason for this unexpected summons. He ordered tea to be brought to us and started a chain of pleasantries that felt out of place for an imperial summons.

Maybe he didn't call us as the emperor but as a father.

"Father, I thank you for this invitation." Shén Mì's hand, still in mine, trembled. "We're honored, but could you tell us why?"

Emperor Cheng looked confused for a second. "For all the seven heavens, did I make you nervous?" he asked.

We didn't have the heart to deny it.

"I just wanted to see both of you and have a chance to thank you both for your selfless service to the crown."

Shén Mì stiffened. "We did what was right."

"No, you didn't," the emperor protested.

We both stared at him, not sure what to think. Was he saying we hadn't done the right thing?

"You did so much more."

I exhaled in relief.

"Hú Dié, you risked your life to save Wang Li, and, as I understand it by what Su Lin and Xiao Bin tell me, you also saved Shén Mì. I can't thank you enough."

I exchanged a glance with my dragon, who looked stunned.

"You asked us here to thank Hú Dié?" he asked.

"And to thank you, my son," the emperor continued. "You went far above what I could expect from you."

Shén Mì's eyes darkened. "You never expected much from me, did you? I have always been an embarrassment to you and the empire."

He was quiet for a moment, but then the emperor stood up and came to stand by his son, placing one hand on the prince's shoulder. "Child, if you think you had me fooled all these years, you must think me an idiot."

My jaw dropped.

"What do you mean, Father?" Shén Mì asked, looking as confused as I was.

Emperor Cheng chuckled. "As an emperor, don't you think I have reliable sources who keep me informed of—well, everything?"

My brow furrowed, eyes glued to the older man.

"I have always known about your cover."

Slather me in honey and throw me into a beehive.

Shén Mì wasn't giving up the pretense just yet. "I don't understand. What cover?"

"You run the most efficient and successful spy business of the empire," the emperor continued, an amused grin on his face. "To make sure there were no suspicions about your covert activities, you created the illusion that you were *duan xiu*—that was a brilliant move, by the way. Congratulations."

What the fuck is going on here?

My dragon looked as if he had been frozen in time, neither frowning or smiling, eyes as round as the full moon and uncharacteristically speechless.

"You may ask yourself why I went along with the deceit and even validated it in some way," he continued. "You're my son. I love and trust you despite what you have undoubtedly thought all these years. In order to help you make your cover believable, I pretended I accepted it as the truth."

He paused for a second, a tiny smile lifting the corner of his mouth. "And yes, I did believe it at first. But it didn't take long for me to realize what you were doing. After all, I had taught you well." He winked at his son, and I couldn't help it; I smiled.

"So you knew all along?" Shén Mì said, narrowing his eyes. "You let me think you didn't trust me so my cover would not be blown."

It was more of a question than a statement. He seemed to be trying to convince himself of what his father was telling him. So many years believing he was the black sheep of the family couldn't easily be erased.

Emperor Cheng nodded. "I'm sorry, son, for letting you think I was disappointed in you," he said, the smile replaced with a frown. "But I wanted to both help you and protect you. The least number of people who knew of the deception on either side, the better it would work."

They locked eyes, and for a long moment they just stared, eyes suspiciously shiny, their chests quickly rising and falling. I didn't dare interrupt.

The emperor broke the silence first. "Do you blame me, A-Shén?"

It was the first time I heard the man address his son by a nickname. My heart melted a little.

Shén Mì shook his head, tears erupting from his eyes and rolling down his cheeks. "No, I don't."

"I did all of this because I love you and wanted to support you in whatever you want from life," his father said. He paused and then opened his arms wide, an invitation for a hug.

My dragon didn't hesitate, and in a couple strides, he was wrapped in his father's arms, his face buried in the side of the man's neck. They were almost exactly the same height, I realized. In fact, they were very alike in every way, age the only thing setting them apart.

We stayed for a while, drinking tea, eating sweet pastries, and talking. Without his heavy coronet and all the other imperial trappings,

Emperor Cheng was a modest, easy-to-talk-to man. Not a total surprise for me, since I had met him at his most vulnerable during the time his son was dying, but it was still a wonder that a man that powerful could be so... normal.

When we finally stood up to leave, the sun had already started its descent in the sky. We said our goodbyes, held hands, and prepared to go out the doors. The emperor had another surprise for us, though.

With our backs turned to him, we heard him say, "And by the way, son, I know you are a dragon."

Just when I thought we couldn't be any more surprised!

Monster

SHÉN MÌ

M Y FATHER KNEW I was a dragon like him—the only one amongst his children—and yet he had just officially made Wang Li the crown prince.

I didn't know whether to laugh or cry that I had gone through so much trouble to hide it from him so he wouldn't insist on me being the heir to the throne for naught. He accepted my decision to remain just an ordinary prince pretending to be shallow and unwilling to produce progeny. The latter point was going to be tricky now that Hú Dié had entered my world. I fully intended to make her my wife—not that I'd asked her seriously already—and maybe even have children if she was willing, but to continue my pretense of being *duan xiu* while married to her was not going to be an easily accomplished feat.

We stopped in town on our way back from the naming ceremony, leaving behind a crowd of noblemen and women far more interested in ingratiating themselves to my brother than anything else. One of the many reasons I had moved out of the palace so young.

"Let's stop at the clothing store," my fairy suggested.

For someone who didn't much hold on to mundane things and wore her all-black *changshan* most of the time, she sure loved a pretty dress.

I indulged her.

The store was not busy, since most of the usual customers—those who could afford the expensive materials—were still at the palace. The owner let out an expansive yelp when he saw us and came around the counter to greet us.

"Welcome, Your Highness," he said, rubbing his hands together as if he had just spotted a bowl of delicious noodles. "Can I interest you in the latest silks from the North? They would make a stunning overtunic for you."

I'd been an avid patron to his store for the past few years, another way to keep my cover as a shallow man who loved all good and rich material things in life. I had to tread carefully not to bust that secret.

"Master Guan Xi," I greeted him with a nod. "Can you help my cousin find something she likes?"

The look Hú Dié gave me could melt jade. She turned to the tailor and forced a smile that looked more like a grimace. "Yes, can you help this poor cousin of His Highness?"

The man bowed deeply. "Of course. Let me show you our latest acquisitions," he said, pointing at the back of the store where bolts of new fabric were leaning against the wall.

I amused myself looking at some pretty ribbons in a display on the counter, contemplating buying one for my fairy.

The tailor's fussy voice rose into a pitch. "But, *gūniáng*, that fabric is for a wedding dress."

I turned my head around so fast, I swear I heard my neck bones pop. What was the butterfly up to now? From the short distance, I saw her steal a glance at me as if making sure I was listening.

I definitely am now. Wedding dress?

"Well, Master Guan Xi, you see, I expect to be betrothed very soon, and I like being prepared," she said, as deadpan as possible.

I cocked my head to the side as she called on me.

"Shén Mì, isn't it true? That I am going to be married soon?"

Was she just joking around, or was she sending me a message? I waited, studying her for a moment. She winked and raised her eyebrows.

She wants me to ask for her hand in marriage.

The revelation was too overwhelming. I choked on my own words, and it took me far too long to reply, "Yes, that is true. My cousin is to be married soon."

Hú Dié's smile was the sun on a rainy day. Of course I would marry her and strive to make her happy for the rest of our lives. Which, considering we were both immortals, could span a few centuries. I couldn't envision ever being tired of her feisty, even belligerent, personality.

The tailor returned his attention to my fairy, excited by the chance to sell very expensive red silks to the young woman in front of him. I sat on a corner stool and watched as Hú Dié picked the fabrics and then gave strict orders on how she wanted the dress decorated.

"I will bring in my best seamstress," the man promised, holding on to the huge bolt of fabric as if to a lifeline. "She does exquisite embroidery. I think you'll love it, *gūniáng*."

When we finally left the store, I wanted to wrap her in my arms, kiss her, and voice my feelings for her, but we were in public, and there were appearances to be kept up. So I waited until we were in the middle of the bamboo forest to pull her into the shelter of the trees and the low brush and kiss her long and hard.

"What was all that about?" the little minx asked, holding on to my neck. "Not that I'm complaining."

There was a knot in my throat, so I kissed her again, hoping to regain my speech soon. My lips lingered over her mouth, prying hers open to explore it with my tongue. I loved the way she tasted, sweet and tart in equal measures. So I took my time, enjoying the heat, the feeling of headiness I always got from her touch.

As soon as our lips drew apart, I whispered, "I love you, Dié Dié. I love you so much."

This wasn't the first time I told her this, but why had I waited so long? I'd known it almost from the beginning that this reckless, impudent fairy was the one for me.

I felt her smile rather than saw it, our faces still so close, I could taste her breath. "That's it?" she asked.

I pulled her away from me a little so I could see her clearly. "What do you mean? Isn't love enough?" I asked, knowing all too well what she wanted.

"I did just buy a wedding dress," she said, tilting her head sideways.

I chuckled and pulled her against me again. "All right, I surrender," I told her. "Do you remember when I won at a game of chess? You gave me the right to one wish." She nodded. "Well, it's time to pay up. Please marry me, Hú Dié."

It was her turn to draw away a few inches, her eyes searching mine. "That's better," she said. "Yes, I will marry you."

I hugged her so tightly, we felt like one body, one soul. "I love you," I told her again, my lips brushing her ear.

"I love you, too, my prince. Now and forever."

It was not the wedding expected for an imperial prince. No pomp or circumstance. No large crowds of nosy people. But then again, I couldn't have a public wedding. I'd still be posing as the unmarried prince so no one suspected me or my spies.

Yushu and Hú Dié had turned my compound into a wedding venue, red bows and bunting festooning every corner, tree, lamp, and eave. The gazebo in the middle of the main courtyard was staged to be the place where we exchanged our vows and became husband and wife. Cook had enlisted a group of servants—and possibly some of my spies too—to help in the kitchen, and the wonderful smell of hot food wafted to every corner of the compound.

Su Lin had disappeared with the butterfly for "bridely business," and Xiao Bin had joined forces with Ding Māo to thoroughly drive me insane under the guise of helping me get ready. When we finally arrived at an agreement on how I should wear my hair—we settled on a simple coronet to hold it into a top knot—we left the room to join the few people in attendance.

My father, dressed in his plain clothes, was seated next to Wang Li. They both looked up when we approached.

"Son, you look like a proper groom," my father said with a grin.

Even the years of wearing bright, showy clothes didn't prepare me for the deep red of the wedding *changshan*. I had insisted on a mostly unadorned tunic to contrast with the flashy garments I had worn throughout the years. I wanted to go into this marriage as myself and not the character I had created for everyone else.

When everything went silent, I turned around and was rendered speechless. My bride was standing at the end of the pebble path, bookended by Su Lin on one side and Yushu on the other, a vision of beauty and power. She had been very secretive about her wedding dress, and now I knew why.

I watched entranced as she walked slowly toward me, two large rosettes made of bright red fabric in her hand. She looked exquisite in a dress that was uniquely hers. Over a plain red dress, she wore a crisscross black brocade tunic with red accents and trimmed with an unadorned red band. The tunic was cinched at the waist by the same wide red belt she had worn the first time I had introduced her to my men. Unsurprisingly, her face was not covered by the traditional veil, and she wore her hair defiantly loose over her shoulders, a few strands gathered on top by a simple but pretty golden butterfly clasp.

I rushed toward her in a very undignified way to hold her hands in mine. "You look beautiful, Butterfly," I told her.

She smiled, handed me one of the rosettes, and said, "Let's get married."

The rest was a blur. I have only a foggy memory of our walk toward the gazebo, holding the connected rosettes side by side, the three obligatory bows that bonded us as husband and wife, and my father's trusted eunuch declaring, "You are now married." I only remember the kiss and the warmth it caused inside me while our friends and family yelled in celebration.

Someone brought two chairs and directed us to sit and receive the gifts from our guests. Other than my family, none of the people attending were wealthy, but they still offered us heartfelt tokens of their love and respect: homemade pastries, embroidered handkerchiefs, and small wood carvings.

When the procession of gift-givers ended, Hú Dié turned to me and asked, "What do you have to give me as a wedding gift, my husband?"

I had waited a long time to do this, so I paused for a moment, savoring the anticipation. Then, I turned to the side where Ding Māo stood and said, "Is everything ready?"

He nodded.

"Tell her, then."

My friend stepped before us, a mischievous grin on his lips, bowed briefly, and said, "Hú Dié, your new husband has prepared a very special gift for you."

She looked around, searching for the promised gift. "Where the hell is it?" she asked.

Ding Māo chuckled. "Not here," he said. "It's too big and too...." He searched for the right words. "Inappropriate for the occasion," he finished. "It's currently being held in the palace's dungeon just waiting for you to do with it as you will."

Hú Dié perked up. "In the dungeon? What is it, exactly?" she asked.

"Dié Dié, we actually caught him a couple weeks ago, but I thought this would be the perfect wedding gift for you, so I kept it a secret."

She was getting annoyed by all the secrecy, her hands on her hips.

"We caught the *guài* for you," I concluded.

She jumped from her chair, sending it flying behind her. "You caught the Monster?" she exclaimed. "For me?"

I nodded, laughing. "You can do whatever you want with him. The bastard was trying to enlist new slaves south of here so Ding Māo tracked him down, and I used my special gift to catch up with him. Let's just say he got a fiery surprise he won't soon forget. His butt might be a little crispy."

In a fluid move, she wrapped her arms around my neck. "I love you," she yelled, almost busting my eardrums. "Thank you, thank you."

"You're going to kill me, woman," I said, still laughing.

She let go of my neck.

"What do you want to do now? Dance? Eat?" I winked. "Go to our room?"

"Are you joking?" she asked. "Yushu, go get my sword."

The girl didn't hesitate, taking off at a trot toward our room.

"You all have fun dancing and eating," she said, and then for my ears only, whispered "I'll see you in the room later."

Yushu came back and began helping my wife tie the scabbard across her chest and back, much to my father's confusion.

I knew what she was about to do, but I still had to ask, "Where are you going with your sword?"

She shifted the scabbard into a comfortable position and smiled. "I, my husband, am going to slay a monster."

And she ran to the stables to get a horse.

I love my butterfly, my not-so-sweet wife.

<<<>>>

Glossary

Pinyin (Mandarin) to English

A Duì = *by the way*

Báichī = idiot

Báiyín = silver

Bàn mó = half demon

Bao = *steamed meat bun*

Changshan = traditional Chinese long robe for men

Dāngrán = sure, of course

Duan xiu =cut sleeves

Duì = *yes*

Duì ma = *right?*

Gē men = brothers, bros (colloquial)

Gē = *brother, bro*

Guài =monster

Gūniáng = young woman

Guqin =traditional string instrument

Hǎo = *good, all right*

Hǎo de = Good! OK

Hēi mógū = Black Mushroom

Hòu = queen

Huǒ niǎo = firebird

Jiǔ = wine

Lǎo Cōng = Old onion

Lǎo tiě = *old man*

Li = 0.31 of a mile

Lóngzhī Dìguó = Empire of the Dragons

Méijiǔ = plum wine

Mèimei = younger sister

Nǐ Hǎo = *hello*

Qi = *life energy*

Qiánbēi = Cheers

Qīchóng tiān = Seven Heavens

Qi gong = *type of martial art*

Qīnwáng = prince

Qíguài = weird

Qù = go away/leave

Shānyáng = *goat*

Shì de = Yes!

Shīfu = master, teacher

Shuō = explain, tell me

Shūshu = Uncle (polite way to address a senior)

Wǎn'ān = *goodnight*

Wū = Shaman

Wugu = diet of five grains

Xiangqi = *chess*

Xiǎojiě = miss, young woman

Xiǎo gūniáng = *little girl*

Xièxiè = thank you

Xiōngdì = brothers, brotherly

Yín = silver coin

Youtiao = Chinese donut

Acknowledgements

It may sound weird—even a little nutty—but I want to start by thanking Shén Mì and Hú Dié, my own characters. I owe them a lot.

Let me explain.

For the past year I have been in a creative funk. I'm used to publishing at least a couple books per year, this year all I published was a re-release of a previous book of mine in a beautiful new cover and inside format. Nothing else. The book I was writing—a prequel to House of Blood and Whispers—stalled, and I went for weeks without writing a word. For a writer that's one of the worst feelings in the world.

Then one day I saw a pre-made cover by the amazingly talented graphic artist, Adrijana Cernic (thank you, thank you), and something sparked. I bought it right away, and my butterfly fairy and her prince began to develop in my mind. My writer's block was gone as these two characters and all their sidekicks took over. My writing mojo was back and it felt as if I was breathing again.

So, yeah, I have to thank them. I am now almost finished with the prequel I mentioned before, and my mind is percolating with new ideas.

I must also thank my local critique group who always encouraged me with their helpful feedback, and my fabulous beta readers, especially Lisa who is always ready to read my stories. My co-teacher—and fantasy-reader extraordinaire—Christine who inspired me with book talk and was there every time I needed to bounce off an idea.

To my friend, Jessica, goes a huge thank you for being so ferociously feminist and for reminding me often that females are fighters.

My parents for always encouraging me to follow my dreams, and my sister for being my best supporter and friend.

My fabulous editor, McKinley, who made me feel like a star while keeping me from making huge mistakes (idioms and prepositions are my nemesis). And the whole staff at Hot Tree Editing who are always professional but make you feel like family.

Becky from Hot Tree Publishing who believed in my stories. Thank you.

And of course you, lovely readers. You make all the sweat and tears worthwhile. Thank you from the bottom of my heart.

Keep reading and keep dreaming.

Also by

If you liked **The Prince and the Butterfly** you might want to check out Natalina Reis's other books.

Romantic Comedy:
We Will Always Have the Closet
Loved You Always
Blind Magic
Her Real Man (novella)
Fictional-ish
Dating the Intern

Dystopian Romance:
Heart's Prey

MM Paranormal Romance/Romantasy:
Lavender Fields
Infinite Blue

Of Magic & Scales (4-book series)

Foxy Tails

Sleeping Love

F/M Paranormal Romance/Romantasy:

Dark Feathers

Kiss of the Swan

The Jewel Chronicles (trilogy)

House of Blood and Whispers

Queen of Hearts (novella)

About the author

Natalina wrote her first romance in collaboration with her best friend at the age of 13. Since then she has ventured into other genres, but romance is first and foremost in almost everything she writes. She has published romances that defy the boundaries of her genre. She enjoys writing all kinds of rebels and outcasts into her stories and she always roots for the underdog.

After earning a degree in tourism and foreign languages, she worked as a tourist guide in her native Portugal for a short time before moving to the United States. She lived in three continents and a few islands, and her knack for languages and linguistics led her to a master's degree in education. She lives in Virginia where she has taught English as a Second Language to elementary school children for more years than she cares to admit.

Natalina doesn't believe you can have too many books or too much coffee. Art and dance make her happy and she is pretty sure she could survive on lobster and bananas alone. When she is not writing or stressing over lesson plans, she shares her life with her husband and two adult sons.

To keep up to date with Natalina's news and books, follow her on the Web:

Facebook: @authornatalinareis

Website/Blog: natalinareis.com

GR: https://bit.ly/GRReis

BookBub: natalina-reis

Instagram: @reisnatalina

FB Group: Rebels and Outcasts

Pinterest: lisboeta62

TikTok : @natalinareisauthor

Enter
the magical world of
International bestselling author
NATALINA REIS

Writing romance for the rebels, the outcasts,
and the lovers unafraid to run against the grain